LETALIS

Rishika Porandla

LETALIS

RISHIKA PORANDLA

ISBN 9798843923075 (paperback)
ISBN 9798844394546 (hardcover)

Cover design by: Sia Arya

for my family. thank you for the boundless,

relentless support that is dynamic enough

to propel the earth's shift from polaris to vega.

for the women of physics and literature,

you curate a world of your own.

Author's Note

"I'm so indecisive with this book.
I just want to change everything"

is the last text I sent.

It feels largely awkward to write a preface when I have nothing prolific to say, but it also feels necessary. The truth lies in the sheer *quantity* of the words I have, rather than the quality, and this fact is incredibly prevalent in my mind this morning. Perhaps it's the all-nighter, or the three consecutive cups of coffee, or the fact that *A Brief History of Time* is beside me and that novel always finds a way to elicit a strange thought.

I began *Letalis* when I was 14 and at the forefront of my high school career, which is a pretentious way of saying something completely inaccurate. I had read a total of two classics and thought myself to be the greatest young mind in the history of American literature since the last teenage author published something. I completed the first draft of *Letalis* when I was 15 and found myself maintaining dreadful, continuous eye contact with a docx. file that contained 120,039 words.

Only 77,996 of those words are still here. To be honest, that value is generous in itself, considering how between May 29, 2022 and July 15, 2022, I rewrote the entire novel. Let's say about 10% of my original freshman year writing still is on these pages. Only 10% of my younger self's entire life, pride, and joy made it to print, while the rest is preserved only by my mind.

Here in August 2022, I am hoping that this manuscript open in another tab will no longer be a figment of my imagination by tomorrow morning. It's been turbulent, to say the least. I have never simultaneously disliked and worshiped a piece of writing as thoroughly as I have with *Letalis*, and it's shameful to admit the amount of sleep and sanity I lost for Ceres Relasin and her convoluted, tragically fractured story.

Ceres is the culmination of the most eccentric and unbearably mundane of my thoughts. I don't know if she is the same person now that she was when I first wrote her name on paper, but I love her regardless. I adore her obliviousness to the intricacies of outer space and how she doesn't know that her name is my favorite dwarf planet. I am fascinated by her inability to tell right from wrong, or her sheer ignorance of the fact that there is even a difference. I am in awe of her ability to tell this story, and even more in awe of myself for writing it.

Forgive the thoughts of a 14-year-old that are sprinkled in this novel. I hope for the following 255 pages, particle physics and cosmological principles enable you to remain suspended in space-time (for at least as long as Ceres is).

— Rish

PROLOGUE

*I*t is when the Queen feels turbulent anger, her blood pulsing feverishly under her temples and external cries muffling against her eardrums, that she knows death is imminent.

She doesn't ponder the concept often. Death has never concerned her; it never had to. Her hands are privileged. They have never pressed back against a blade inches from her skin. Her painted eyes have never widened in fear or latched shut in defeat. Her spine has never become comfortable with collapse—nor shall she ever let it.

But now, she imagines a terrible execution from *his* perspective, and her previously resolute mind stutters.

Do not show restraint, the Queen orders herself, pressing the words against her teeth harder by the second. The thought feels bitter, but familiar, against her tongue. She doesn't care for the action of showing mercy; she thought she proved that fact when she ripped out the voice of the Queen who preceded her. Death was buried in the crevices of her nails for weeks. She knows that. The man on the floor knows that. So, why is her sword unmoving?

The Queen allows her mind to spiral past the bounds of morality, illustrating the scene she is creating with a twisted intent contained within it. What she is capable of, what she is moments away from committing, is a tragic sin. Her silhouette, startling against the white crystal and polished marble surroundings, harbors the unrestrained feelings of impulsivity and fury—traits that she should've frankly exchanged for her crown.

But there she stands, dominant and foreboding above her fallen lover, her golden weapon adeptly wielded between her fingers and poised at the man's throat. The Queen nurtures her soul in a womb of terror, and the upturn of her lips proves she relishes in the fact.

Her fingers itch to tear the blade into the folds of his throat, but flickers of uncertainty flood her joints, freezing them in this single frame of time. One is not to look too closely but stand to her side and it's all visible. The small indentation between her eyebrows, the lurching of her throat when she swallows, and the undeniable weakness of what should be ice.

"Vega," the man on the floor sputters, slick palms slipping as the struggle to lift himself onto his elbows persists. A wince contorts features already weathered by time as the Queen's sword twists against fragile skin. His head gradually lowers in response.

Anger floods the stagnant woman, and the emotion becomes increasingly apparent when she channels it into more potent energy than what should be possible from her. The mythical darkness reveals itself as a striking beam of light gliding across the sky, a vast plain absent of any hue other than a dark silver. Moments later, the rumble of thunder erupts, every entity in the land trembling in the wake of its footprint. Some villagers are awakened by the commotion, but they simply fall back into their slumbers with faint smiles on their lips; they already know their Queen expresses her emotions violently.

Vega's chin twitches, in rhythm with the bob of her throat as she swallows a harsh breath. The depth of her stomach twists with nausea as she drives the blade further into the man's dignity, or maybe that hesitancy is purely a bitter trick. Perhaps the uncertainty surfacing within her is not her own, but rather the work of her beloved Saints. A soft laugh nearly echoes past her pursed lips as she considers the possibility. It wouldn't be the first time her free will had been overrun by the only deities she holds value in.

The Astral Saints. The Queen feels warmth in those syllables, how could she not? The godly beings inhabiting those cliffs beyond her kingdom are the curators of her strength. They built the poison to her touch and the powers of hers that draw blood. They deliver her gift to her every sunrise with loving, yet malicious, hands.

It is amusing to her as of late how the only individuals she seems to tolerate are those centuries old, descended from the Olden Ages and hiding their outdated minds under a cloak of smooth skin.

The Queen's drifting consciousness is abruptly shifted back to her surroundings when a desperate voice splits the heavy silence of the palace.

"Halt!" the body below her weapon bursts out midst a terrible cough, recoiling as the point of the Queen's sword draws a drop of crimson. "As the King of Solaris, I command you to halt!"

As soon as it had faded, it is back. The solidified, vindictive aura of immorality that characterizes the Queen rests atop her shoulders, both a shield and a blade. It reveals its presence when a sudden laugh escapes the painted lips of Queen Vega, her fingers dancing over the hilt of the newly stained sword and teasing the King with their behavior.

"Please, I beg of you. Please grant me mercy," the King, Mensa Jacque, pleads with an anguished glint appearing beneath his eyelashes. "I-I was not thinking. I regret my decision. Forgive my actions, just this once."

"*Tch.* I thought you would understand by now." It's as if the Queen had never harbored an ounce of hesitation, for now her features are absorbed in the type of iniquity she *knows* her Saints would condemn. She should pause, she should turn away. Instead, she brings the bridge of her nose parallel to his, her darkened gaze fuming as her composure begins to fracture. "I do not know mercy. I do not tolerate mercy."

She spits the final word from her tongue as if it burns to hold it any longer.

"I will do anything," Mensa Jacque breathes. In a world where his limbs maintained the strength to lift his body onto its knees, he would be beseeching the Queen through clasped hands and a lowered chin. He would beg until his mind lost the definition of propriety in the flood of terror that now seeps through him.

But even the privilege of movement has been robbed from him, and the flailing nature of his gaze proves that fact. His eyes have left his Queen and now memorize the interior of his palace behind a glossed layer of tears. Mensa Jacque now understands the gravity of this moment, the nature of his last encounter with the familiar gleam of wealth that defined his rule.

And his crown. *Oh*, his crown. The golden artifact, now chipped along one fragile side, is now haunting the King mercilessly with every glint it sends in his direction. With that fractured light comes the memories that the crown contains within it, memories of the King with his Queen right by his side.

"Do I need to remind you? Those were my daughters," Vega spits against the chilled air now coating the palace interior. It doesn't quite come to her realization that the abrupt temperature change was fostered by her own mind, not by the Aerth.

In her mind, her tone is unwavering, yet it is the weakest it has ever been, caressed by the fury laced into the syllables of her words. In the pit of her stomach, she feels not but one inkling of fragility, but the King watches as harsh remembrance finds a fissure in her demeanor.

"Those were my daughters!" Something deranged snarls the corners of her mouth. The echo of her words persists through the ballroom and her clenched fists tremble with the consequence of them.

The palace servants would later mention hearing the scream and feeling an urge to bolt their doors.

King Jacque's limbs are stagnant, chained in a state of self-inflicted paralysis. The man he was when he first entered this palace pushes against the walls of his cell, yearning to spit a retort into the air, but that man has long left the King's consciousness.

It's a simple exhale that tells all. The fall of Jacque's tense chest and the motion of his shoulder blades sinking into the ground. It's a question in his mind: *Have I given up?*

It's a confirmation in the Queen's view. *He has given up.*

Her eyes travel along the trails of blood leaking from the wound and she finds a bittersweet relief in the vibrance of it. She finds the solace that creeps past her exhaustion when the whimpers from Jacque fade back into his tongue, painting an image of his demise.

"I will do to you what you did to my children. I will do worse." Vega traces a line down the curve of the King's neck, her eyebrows relaxing from the frown that previously held them together. Her fingers are poised and nimble, maneuvering the large weapon with the delicacy of a quill.

He has become her canvas, being painted into a mural of red and black tragedy. She accompanies her artwork with a symphony of her nails running across fabric, a barely audible hum from the depths of her throat, and her finger tapping to the rhythm of his breathing. Her previously downturned lips adopt the appearance of a thoughtful line as she meets the eyes of her victim.

"I will ruin you and then ruin your name. I will make it a curse to be a Jacque. I will rise in power as your body lays rotting in this very ballroom, and I will laugh at the mention of your name. I will laugh."

Queen Vega of the Kingdom of Solaris moves as the artist she is, locking her lips with those of Mensa Jacque as her weight shifts to plunge her blade into his already fragmented heart.

PART ONE

THIS IS NOT YOUR HOME

SUN DISTRICT

Vires acquirit eundo.

- VERGIL'S AENID, BOOK 4, 175

(she gathers strength as she goes.)

CHAPTER ONE

C   E   R   E   S

"*Suns,*" I breathe with exasperation as my palms struggle to grip the wooden edges of the opening barely big enough to call a window. I wrench a single arm out from being plastered against my side, which is immediately classified as a poor decision when my torso lurches forward into my bedroom. The rough texture of the jagged wood scrapes against my skin and, to my dismay, does a great deal to escalate the discomfort of my fall.

I could consider it an improvement from the previous morning when my knees landed before my mind reoriented and the yelp that left my tongue could not have been stifled in any circumstance.

But still not discreet enough, I chastise myself when my soles stumble onto the flat stone and the sound presses against my ears, encircling me with its distinct tone.

My limbs lose their movement as abruptly as the fall happened, all but my index finger. The single digit, the indicator of my brother's position in this home, taps rhythmically against the inside of my opposite wrist, to the memorized rhythm of Izar's footfalls.

My skin feels the fourteenth beat, and I allow my fingers to unclench and relish in the freedom accompanying his absence. That concerned gaze finding my torn knuckles and voice dripping with reprimanding remarks are both far from my proximity for one more blissful moment.

I wait for the newfound relief inhabiting my mind to pick out the knot in my throat, but I feel it sink lower instead, to a depth unreachable by human touch. Even when I release that feverish adrenaline from the pit of my stomach and allow the sensation to spread its warmth, something still burns against my temples, the wrist I tapped my finger against, and the skin above my heart.

I find that it's only the metrical clashing of blades and relentless glints of silver at the Thieves Gate that manage to ease this feeling. The image of dark figures dancing under dim lighting, trapping themselves in the power of warfare and drawing blood—that's what removes the weight from within me. Even as I stand in the room that should remind me of the comfort of home, my mind remains in the corridor miles away where I pressed a blade against a man's throat and watched as he surrendered. It's a place encased in such passion and devastation that it must be done under the shield of moonlight and away from bitter tongues.

Several moments pass before I tear my mind and joints from their tranced state. They shiver as the Sun casts a beam against my feet and experience a prompt return to a well-oiled routine.

Wrenching off black leather and padded fabric and pressing the clothing into a crevice underneath my cot is nearly second nature, as is slipping on a worn gown and ripping out the ribbon tying my hair. The strip of blue is quickly busied with cinching my waist, my fingers struggling with the movement as they cramp to the rhythm of my heartbeat.

Breathe.

What fills my stomach and mind is nearly nausea now.

Brushing knotted curls out of my sight frees my vision but deepens the stinging sensation emanating from my touch. Twisting the sash around my waist with my fingers and creating intricate motions in the air returns me to a brawl at the Thieves Gate but wrenches at my skin and stifles my breath with a chokehold. A simple turn of my body towards my mattress is simple in theory, but results in my hands flailing and pressing hopelessly, repeatedly against my body—everywhere it burns.

When did I lower to my knees?

My palms encase my forehead, deepening their pressure with every pulse from my heart. Slivers of glass rip at the inside of my throat, and I cough the pain out, but swallow it again just as easily. The throbbing spreads to a single shoulder blade and cinches my veins, forcing me to release a strained gasp from whatever abyss lies in my interior.

He heard that. Suns*, Izar heard that.*

The pain is coating and seeping into my left wrist when his presence envelops me. I can nearly see his figure. I can almost sense his clutch seizing my forearm, wrenching at the roots of my hair, reaching into the opening of my skull, and tearing out my mind with bloodied fingers.

"Ceres!"

"Ceres!" Izar's fingers snap against my ear with the harsh sound of a man in fear, and suddenly, I'm not collapsing. I'm not ripping pain off my skin. I'm not anything.

I'm breathing and on my feet, in the midst of pulling the sleeves of my gown around my shoulders. My fingers are not holding my temples as I remember but rather rest on my elbows, cupping the protruding bones as if the action will push them deeper into my body. My teeth clench around a tongue itching to scream and release the pressure winding around me and my eyes want to travel anywhere except to Izar, but I'm trapped.

My vision remains contained within his and monologues of pleading and screaming transfer in the tunnel our two gazes create, even as I stumble backward and feel every blade that has ever pierced me, all over again.

Izar says much to me in those fragile moments of silence. He batters into my skull the same inquiries I have heard from him since my first episode. He forces a tragic realization into me—the fact that he is the only individual that will be beside me when one of my visions escalates beyond my control, as he has just proven.

Will you tell me, finally? I can nearly hear him ask—no, implore.

"I-I shall go to the market." My statement fractures whatever understanding the two of us had managed to establish in those passing seconds. For an instant, it was *there*. His presence was felt as distinctly as I ought to feel it, and I recognized the eyes I was reflected within—ones that are the same shape as mine but hold thoughts exceedingly different.

Izar's spine releases its hold on his posture and his slouched frame returns, mimicking the image of the child I grew up with, rather than the guardian who replaced our fallen parents. His stare, which was concerned and questioning only seconds prior, is now distant in its entirety, and I can't even be surprised by the sharp switch in demeanor—not when it happens so often.

I'm incessantly searching for someone to blame when I consider the turbulent relationship he and I have built since our parents were removed from our gazes. I always struggle to place a source, but Izar seems to be resolute in his, radiating that same need for vengeance but having it point toward me.

Ceres, damn it, where have you been?

Suns, *do you hear yourself? I never left; I have always been here.*

Like hell you have. Tell me what is happening to you, please—

I have. *Do you see the tears on my face? I have told you* everything, *you know* everything, *so why do you not believe me?*

Just tell me, truthfully, what happens in your mind! Tell me why you scream and tell me what you see in your visions. Suns, *who have you become?*

You. I have become you. I give you just as much as you give me, and lately, your contribution seems to be exclusively overwhelming, unwarranted paranoia.

What more am I expected to do when you're going down this path with no reservations? You used to live and smile, and now you're crafted by despair. You're ruining us.

I never ruined us, Izar. You did that yourself the moment you stopped seeing me as a sister and as a mental patient instead.

Our souls coexist in a tragic pattern we can't seem to escape; perhaps it's *their* fault. The two of us never experienced that treasured parental bond, our mother and father eloping and dissolving into existence when Izar was barely a teenager and I was an infant in his arms. I was never given an opportunity to memorize the warmth of their presence, learn the caress of their fingers, or capture the scent of their hair.

The person I do have, Izar, stands before me and yet won't offer me the courtesy of his attention. His thoughts appear to be invading his mind and the abrupt flick of his eyes toward me is quickly washed away by his growing exasperation. Two trembling fingers pinch the bridge of his nose as I lose sight of his face, my eyes now facing a hardened back and a closed demeanor.

My left-hand rises, then falls, then rises once more. I give him the lightest touch against the base of his neck.

Understand me, I say in a vague, concealed tone. *I'm here, you're here. Help me, don't hurt me.*

Izar's unmistakable hiss interrupts the silence, causing our simultaneous movement away from each other, his out of fear and mine fueled by shock. He's moving quickly, reorienting his figure so I see his gaped mouth and heaving chest.

"What did you do?" he says so softly that the words are mere whispers in my ear. Izar's shoulders roll backward, a masculine attempt to reestablish the dominance he feels is necessary to assert, but his expression tells all.

He's afraid—petrified. His palm presses against the nape of his neck, where I laid my fingers, and I watch as what should have been the traditional Sun District act of alliance is turned into something of terror.

My confusion envelops me and my feet push forward, needing the closing of the tense space between me and Izar, but before I can get much closer, he shoves my presence away. It's a savage push against my torso that hurts, not just physically but mentally. His fingers dug deeper into my skin than was necessary. The motion harbored unwarranted aggressiveness; it blossomed into strange, corporeal pain—inflicted by my *brother*.

"That hurt—what you did. It burned."

"*You* hurt me, Izar. I—You have never hurt me. *Suns*, what the hell is wrong with you?" I all but spit those bitter words onto his feet, puncturing him deeper than I should, but it feels so justifiable within this moment. It's difficult to discern the line between what he has done to my mind and what he has done to my skin, but I chose the latter, as insignificant as it feels.

I have endured more bodily injuries than I am willing to recount, scars willing to corroborate. Nothing Izar could do would successfully draw blood that I have not already seen, and yet, this is the one action I can blame him for amidst dozens. Tangling the threads of anger and betrayal within me into one pulsing knot and pressing it between us feels so much easier than addressing the true issue that ignites the corners of my mind.

"What is wrong with *you*, Ceres?" Izar's eyes have turned wild and look less like mine with each sliver of his sanity lost to dread. Or perhaps my eyes hold a gleam just as violent and I'm too consumed in my criticism of his character to recognize it.

Well—according to him.

Izar's fingers rip at the fists I've pulled mine into and he expectantly waits as he stares at my unknotted hands. The seconds pass, forming minutes, and I cannot bring myself to leave, instead being overwhelmed with something resembling curiosity.

"Ceres, I am not bluffing. Listen to me." His touch finds something new, clutching my chin, not unkindly—the way I would redirect the attention of a child. "Your touch *burned*. When you touched my neck, *it hurt*."

I am silent; he is desperate for me to hear him. The pain I had wanted to press into his throat only moments ago, wishing to choke and devastate him with the grief he himself created, has left my hands.

"*It burned.*"

———————

I go to the market, as I said I would. I left that home behind me and though I will return, I can already sense the dependence I shared with Izar dissolving, being replaced with a fast-developing distance.

Existing with Izar has never reached the tension it had just minutes prior. It was the worst form of pressure that was stifling both our throats, fogging both our minds, and leaving the air between us so precarious that one action executed too soon would break both our hearts.

He uttered those words again, and *again*, and once more. To another, it might have seemed like he was emphasizing the sensation, proving its existence to me, but I stood before him and saw only a man tragically lost in his own contempt. I understand his mind—it was once mine—but every joint that holds me standing protests his declaration.

Whether my doubt is from a dedication to logic and practicality or driven by a subconscious mistrust of Izar remains the question circling my thoughts—accompanied by a distinct fear of his truthfulness.

But now, that experience is gradually fading into my memories, substituted with the morning chill that has now enveloped my figure and wafts between the strands of my hair. It's shielded today, the Sun, and that state of the sky deepens the negativity of my circumstances.

I tilt my chin up to air void of fallen rays; it's a terrible feeling to recognize that the Sun's warmth is not there to coat your tired skin. In a home named after the safety and relief of a universal constant, it's difficult to find security when the sky fails to comfort me with its consistency.

It's a familiar routine, however, to weave through the arms and belongings of the villagers flooding the main square, all either preceding from or heading toward the same place I am. It's rare that my eyes ever stray from their forward position, but upon stumbling over the outstretched foot of a child, my gaze dips, and I notice a chalked illustration below me. Swirling, faded streaks circle together to form what is absent from my view today—the Sun.

Sun District doesn't have a true culture—that's what we tell all our visitors, whether they're kingdom-raised or hailing from the neighboring district and being built of the same misfortunes that we are. We hold the Sun in our highest regard and press it into our souls to make us one with the entity, but that deference is minimal when compared to the power the kingdoms have accumulated through their centuries of reign.

Once again, their names reveal themselves in my mind, displayed in my vision just as clearly as they were when I was memorizing them under the watchful gaze of a schoolteacher.

Recite them.

Europa, Soleil, Galene, Kepler, Lyra.

Again.

Europa, Soleil, Galene, Kepler, Lyra.

What order did you say their holy names in?

In order of worldly importance.

You are dishonoring Galene and Lyra. From any outside perspective, you are neglecting their influence and scope in the favor of Europa's beauty.

Europa's beauty is superficial. They are the performers of a cosmetic agenda—all of them. There is nothing lovely about that kingdom's presence—and that makes them the most intriguing of them all. The most prevalent.

You cannot think like this outside of these walls. You will always be subordinate in their Aerthen world and you must understand that. We must say their names correctly. Do you understand?

I know. You don't have to tell me.

Yes, I do. You pretend to understand, but frankly, you do not—and that frightens me. One day your rash mind and soul will overwhelm whatever self-control your actions maintain, and that will be the moment you die. You want something more than to be a territory of something with more power, and you cannot have that.

I never returned to that classroom after she whispered those words against the fragility of my young ears.

It's unpleasant to recognize that the town that defines my character has little to hold up with pride, not when the Astral Saints dissipated into existence and took Sun District's prosperity with them—and whatever capital our banks were furiously clutching onto.

Maneuvering past a clique of giggling young ones, I duck into the canopy of the District Market and immediately sense the comfort that accompanies the aromas and sounds of this setting. Perhaps there is another universal constant in this life—*this.*

CHAPTER TWO

E R I S

"Good morning," I mumble to curious passersby as they hover before my stand, my voice having lost its enthusiasm hours ago. Even though I have been doing this for years and I endure more insults than I do compliments regarding my work, I still grasp onto shreds of hope as I watch people debate whether to visit me.

This particular morning, I haven't been able to secure one customer. It might be due to how preoccupied my fellow villagers have been recently, being plagued with some unwarranted doomsday outlook—or perhaps I have finally been deemed as a fraud.

I smooth back my ink-colored hair with fingers that itch to be occupied with work far more productive. As a disheartened sigh rises in my throat, I give myself yet another opportunity to ponder if this job is worth the little it gives me, and the much it rips from me.

My answer is always the same: a simple *no*. That declaration should theoretically end this mundane internal conflict, but this stand remains in the center of the market no matter what conclusion my mind draws. Even vandalized and held together by only tightly coiled ropes, my booth stands half-sturdy, and I do as well—even if my mind is beginning to reel and I feel its foundation trembling with my every exhale.

I mindlessly run the digits of my right hand over the skin that granted me this ability and I regret the action within seconds. What I feel when I remember what put me in this position is a bitter sensation, but one that I am forced to welcome at times. The children that leaned on a leg of my chair many years ago, now teenagers who refuse to offer me a kind glance, often used to imply that I'm self-destructive. It was pounded into my mind by not only them that I'm consumed with reliving my sins and breathing in that agony repeatedly until I can find a release from this pain.

As nihilistic as I recognize that I am, the depth of my being is not very populated. All I am is what I did—what I can do, and perhaps I just need to remind myself of that fact.

It fails to surprise me any longer how quickly I can revert to that instant of my life and visualize it more vividly each time. I may have seen so many iterations of that day that the current one is no longer truthful, but the pain feels the same.

"I am not a witch, please—believe me."

My voice was raw and shredded as it dissipated into the air between me and my foster mother. Mirroring the pain in my tone, my face was streaked with tears that burned against my already salty cheeks.

My mother was stumbling backward, swallowing her winces as she collided into furniture and antiques in her retreat away from my figure. Even as her uncovered soles tread over shattered glass, what should've been a reaction of affliction and discomfort was masked—no, overwhelmed by her shock.

She may have been feet away from me, but it was as if her disgust was a hair's breadth from my pupils. I could feel the gravity of it—of her—as if she spit onto my skin and allowed her saliva to burn me with its fury.

"Please... Please, forgive me. I-I do not know what happened. I couldn't control myself." I stuttered as I spoke, searching for a veil of confidence that could have eased the heaving of my chest and evaporated the self-resentment growing in my mind, but my touch could find nothing.

"You are not Eris. What have you done with Eris?"

"I'm here! Mum, I'm still here. Please believe me." I felt numb. In my subconscious, I was tearing every ounce of my love for this family from my body and laying it at my mother's feet, as *if to say*, Look at how much you mean to me! Look at all this— this is the true me.

"Y-You killed... You killed Leo..." She was sobbing, digging into her frail frame with one blood-soaked sleeve, and having the other rest above the heart of a young boy—now void of its beating, but once overflowing with enough life to fill two souls.

"You murderer!" My mother quivered furiously, every limb of her body trembling to a new rhythm as if this trauma rewrote her heartbeat and replaced it with one forever plagued with the ache of this scene.

Driven by the affliction in my mother's voice, my consciousness fractured even further in my palms, disappearing and taking my dignity with it. The correct—the human—action to do would have been to take Leo in my arms, apologize to him feverishly, and kiss the blood off his forehead.

Nothing compelled me to do that instead of what I found easiest: leaving.

"I shall go. I will leave you at peace. You must never have to see me again," I remember saying, but I can hardly recall the thoughts behind those words, having been overstimulated by the image that was created that night.

I remember his eyes so vividly, how they were paralyzed in their open, void-like position, accompanied by steady streams of blood from his torn waterline. I remember the gaping of his mouth—the mouth that once ricocheted laughter through his torso before it died in the position of a silent scream that he did not have the privilege of releasing.

The skin of my left wrist burned so strikingly that I was convinced I had set myself on fire and willingly allowed flames to swallow my limbs. I had held those searing limbs to my eyes, blocking the sight of Leo and my mother as I followed the signature of the pain up my arms and across my shoulder blades. Its path stopped at my temples, where the sensation emanated from a single pulse under the taut skin of my mind—the culprit of Leo's death.

I call myself a mind whisperer, a vague and utterly innocent term that shields the public from the true corruptness of my actions. My name is almost a tribute to Leo, who used to giggle incessantly when I spoke softly into his ear, the act of endearment triggering his ticklish instincts. He often used to bat me away and in between breathy laughs would say, "You're like a... like a mind whisperer."

The name does nothing to ease my conscience. It hardly does anything to provide justice to Leo either. In some twisted manner, it's almost reminding me of who I used to be with Leo and how I have tragically fallen from that pedestal—but the title intrigues my customers with its obscurity and allusion to the unknown, so what else can I do?

I find myself wishing that what my mind is capable of is nothing short of magic—something lovely and kind and stereotyped with wonder and shiny imagery. I cannot dismiss the fact that there must be some form of magic within me to allow my fingers to wield such complexity, but it's easier to believe that I've fallen under a terrible curse. At least with this mentality, I can believe that what I must do to survive is fueled by something larger than me instead of something ingrained within me.

It all begins with the human touch, a simple nudge of my skin against theirs, and within that minimal movement of my hands, my mind has traveled acres and begins to press against the fabric of my customer's mind. I can influence—no, force—them to open that gate for me. Those with stronger intellects, those who had the glaze and protection torn off their brains and heart years ago, sense my unfamiliarity. They resist it and some even find the strength to pull their hands an inch towards them.

But they fail to recognize that this action pulls my hands as well.

In some cases, it's easiest to dissolve those barriers and reveal whatever sin festers in their souls, but what I've learned is that I am not always correct in my instincts. I see someone's mind only as they themselves see it. I cannot retreat into their subconsciousness, at least not without tearing myself apart in the process.

But I have to do it. I am coerced into the action by the thought of them rising from their seat before me and realizing that I have done nothing for them, that I have not been able to find the pain within them and now can be deemed as even larger of a fraud. All because of one hesitancy.

So, I find a path inside. Some crevices exist so small that I must sever my knees and my arms to fit through them, leaving me limping, crawling, breathing my way to false salvation.

I no longer have to concentrate past this point. My soul holds the burden for me, no matter how poorly. It navigates through memories and weaves through powerful emotions—tragic and intense in their full capacity. My fingers dance through a well-recited choreography, convulsing, extending; joints seizing in sharp movements.

The rhythmic thumping of my heart will have deafened my ears and obscured my vision, but none of those senses are necessary. I must simply braid our two souls together, freeing the threads of their mind from convoluted knots in fear of losing my sanity within the depths of their existence and spending years searching for an exit.

It's a constant push and pull, the cadence of the movements becoming comforting at a certain point. My peace is never uninterrupted, however. Wrenching out the wavelengths of anxiety, sadness, and stress with cramping fingers and weaving in notions of fulfillment rips eons out of my life.

Disposing of that procured energy is agonizing and meticulous and never becomes subconsciously mechanical, no matter how many times I swallow it, choke on it, and nearly vomit it from my throat. The clusters of emotion I bring into myself are talented in their purpose; they know how to plague me and settle in my temples, my brain, my veins, my blood, and every limb I have.

They are felt everywhere, no sliver of my body free from the tragedy of another's hurt, and yet, the exchange between me and my client seems tranquil from an outside perspective. To an onlooker, my services are nothing more than a calm, pensive state of being between two souls.

I wish I could batter into their skulls the words—the scream—communicating that they are hurting me. I yearn to wrench out knotted clumps of my hair, cleave my skull in two, and open it up to them. Hold my mutilated skin to their eyes and show them through laughter what they have done to me, how little of me still exists.

But I only allow my hands to fall from theirs while spreading a wide smile across my bleeding lips. I bid them a good day and watch their figure jostle into the market crowd, relieved of their worries while I suffer with the sentiments I stole from their mind.

I'd greet the next person with that same expression of distorted happiness, the weight of the last one's grief spreading across my chest and cinching my heart.

CHAPTER THREE

"**W**hat is the price?" *Mensa Jacque inquires in a low, brooding voice, eyes latched onto the boy before him as he avoids passing his gaze over his two sleeping daughters. The two of them are lost within slumbers in their respective baskets, seemingly untroubled, though their minds are captured in turmoil.*

As is their father's.

"Fifteen hundred coins," the young man responds, his tone firm and radiating its presence through the corridor. He stands over the Solarian King, even when his height puts him several inches lower. He boasts an air of dominance even while in the company of a noble. It doesn't concern him, however, for Mensa Jacque is not his royalty. "I do not understand your methods, Mensa—"

"It is not your job to understand my methods." Jacque's voice attempts to match the same venom of the trader but to a lower degree of success. Nevertheless, he escalates the tension binding the two of them together and the boy's dissatisfaction grows. "I have my reasons."

"You are doing something unjust. And to your daughters, of all people. The Queen will not like this. She will bring agony upon you."

"I know the consequences," Mensa Jacque breathes in resignation, retreating away momentarily to peer out the glass opening of the chamber and onto his sleeping kingdom. Silver moonlight encases the small houses and landscape below, as the two small children not three feet away stir under the gleam of its rays. "I also know the good I am doing for Solaris by carrying out this act."

"They are different, Mensa. That does not mean they are dangerous," the trader pleads in a last futile attempt to steer the King away from this decision that would no doubt wreak havoc on his marriage and kingdom.

"Vega is different. That is the sole reason she is dangerous," Jacque has now grown agitated, his nostrils flaring as his fingers follow a haphazard pattern of clenching, unclenching, and convulsing with fury. He tosses the sack of coins onto polished moonstone, which makes the unmistakable sound of gold clinking as it glides toward its new owner. "You may take the girls and leave."

The trader refuses to shift his position straight away, surveying the King with disdain, and following that contempt with a soft shake of his head.

The boy is intelligent and harbors a kind, moral heart, but even ethics hold no power against Aerth's royalty, much less the royalty of the lost kingdom.

He is gentle as he lifts the two baskets into his arms, careful not to disrupt the children's sleep and he accompanies their bodies with the bulging pouch of misdeeds and deceit.

One child is barely larger than a newborn, and the other is not much older, both too young to be the dust the Solarian King is trying to sweep away. Mensa Jacque always told himself he must be resolute when confronting his wife, Vega, and decisively endure all the misfortune that she creates.

But even someone that has lived as little as the trader knows this is not being resolute, this is being cowardly.

He hesitantly moves towards the chamber's exit, but as his small fingers wrap around the polished doorknob, he speaks the words that will haunt Mensa Jacque until his grim death on the floor of the palace ballroom.

"You are making a bad choice, Mensa. Ceres and Eris Relasin will live on far longer than you, as will their mother."

CHAPTER FOUR

A   N   T   A   R   E   S

*M*y eyes are resting but open in slits, and my vision is a blurred mirage of gold and black from the dim lamplight and charcoal walls of The Thieves Gate. I busy myself with the repeated motion of tossing my sharpest bowie knife into the air and nimbly catching the worn handle each time, despite my eyelids taping shut in exhaustion.

It's not physical fatigue that seeps through my bones, but something more cerebral. My body feels the most alert in months, but my mind finds itself shutting down the instant I'm not actively shaking its shoulders, screaming, asking it to hold out for just one more fight.

If I said I was tired, I would get no sympathy from Castor. If I said I did not wish to fight, I would have to watch Castor arrange the most difficult, most straining brawl to descend me into. It is all to exploit the hold he has over me, to utilize the information he stores in that small mind of his.

Because that's what Castor asks for. Just one more fight and I'm released from this debt I will inevitably spend the remainder of my life fulfilling. I say it like that because I know I have little time left, as cynical as that may sound. It's something you learn after being characterized by this life for a collection of years. Too many vengeful souls pounding against the glass of your mind and pouring demands into your ears gradually kills you.

Especially when those demands are fueled by unconditional power.

The only thanks I give to this setting is that the sound suffocating me from all sides is close enough to white noise for me to ignore, those distractions all fading when I zero in on *her*. Not a woman, not a girl, but something just as sharp and enchanting.

I call her *Periculo,* my knife. The name translates to "dangerous" according to the Latin index we referred to when we acquired the foreign blade.

Knives are not treasured as valuable weapons under Castor's roof, a fact that sours my tongue. It's accompanied by minimal disappointment though. Anyone with skill has ceded their campaign to make this facility means something, and those who still fight are either terribly dense, or stubborn, beautiful creatures.

These men are not talented, or intelligent, as I have observed. It's as if Castor's agenda is fueled by this one desire to create more of him—and to build a disorganized, spite-driven army of large men that will protect Sun District from all its big, frightening enemies.

The Thieves Gate understands that their large fists and heedless tendencies are pathetic, laughable even when standing before a military indestructible under armor and fortified by minds fond of triumph, not blood.

Victory in the absence of agony is a fascinating concept, but one that is far from my reach. Especially when the weapon I consider to be my second spine has become permanently stained red.

Occisor is my only sword, one of the last two weapons that I have not bartered for spare coin. If I had known what Sun District does to people and their livelihoods, I would have brought more with me from Solaris, but alas I cannot change that now. Not when Solaris exemplifies the most grievous of my memories and the most frightful of my screams. *Occisor* is the only entity from that kingdom that I'm able to hold to my heart and escape the burn of, and nothing is more valuable to me than that fact.

Solaris may have smothered the life from my parents' bodies, it may have collapsed my father to the floor of our cottage, and it may have extracted too great an amount of blood from his weak frame to survive, but it gave me *Occisor*.

Sometimes, like at this juncture, where *Occisor* digs into my ribcage in a manner that should hurt but provides me unparalleled ease, is when I understand these men just for a moment. It's when I hold *Periculo* with fingers far more adept than most military men can, with the sword from my childhood acting as my posture, that I feel the thrill of the fight. Castor and his lackeys feel it too, except the feeling is less pure and more tainted; it's purely fueled by the virile life they choose to live.

My evidence arrives sooner than I thought.

"Ay! Boy!" There's nothing beautiful about Castor's voice, nothing resembling the delicateness of a flower. "What the hell d'you think you're doing here, Arinel?"

Castor is large with limbs that are more wasted flesh than muscle, which is not the expected appearance of a man who considers himself to be at the peak of his athletic physique.

"This is the Hole, not some pretty boy hangout." The man is looking to instigate a fight. I can almost sense the pulsing energy from his chest, the need to see some true action instead of petty brawls with little physical consequence.

"No one knows that better than me. I did name this place after all," I counter with a sluggish movement of my shoulders. It's all intentional, calculated. I'm not void of energy in the slightest; it's just best to nudge Castor in the direction where he believes I am.

There's something deeply off about the man but even he has the l to common sense to recognize that forcing a tired man

39

against a secure one doesn't make for entertainment, it makes for a monotonous fight.

"Arinel, you're on awfully thin ice here. I can get you jailed faster than you can blink."

There it is, the inevitable reminder of the supposed influence Castor has over me. It's almost become his signature line, a finger pointing towards the future I would have if Castor revealed my status, the genuine reason for my arrival in Sun District, and the imminent deadline I have been forcing farther from my mind.

He saw the letter the one afternoon I had allowed my guard to fall. I was unpacking before Castor, searching for the package of coins that would provide for the monthly due I pay him for the residence, and in my flustered state, I had let a certain letter unfurl into his consciousness.

He read it all, every word, before I could identify my mistake and tear the parchment from his grasp and into as many pieces as I could. By that moment Castor knew everything, things not even the Solarian townsfolk had heard. He had learned the flourishing nature of Queen Vega's handwriting, the sweeping ink that formed my name at the top of the paper, and most notable of all— her one request of me, a soldier designated to her Fire Council army.

Castor is an individual who didn't care much for the kingdoms surrounding his outpost in Sun District. Nothing much mattered to him other than himself—which conveniently worked for him since no hesitation or confusion accompanied his reading of that wretched letter. He simply took the words for what they were and recognized the terrible dilemma I was in as a young man under the watchful gaze of a vicious queen.

I was expected to deliver the two daughters of Solaris to the Queen, her children that had disappeared as children from the confinements of her palace under the consent of the late King Jacque. It took my Queen over a decade to locate those girls, delayed by the need to keep Solaris a hidden kingdom away from the magic-desiring population of Aerth, but at the same time fueled by vengeance and a concealed love for her blood.

Once a trader had brought news of suspected witches within Sun District, Queen Vega was intrigued, and due to her inability to leave her kingdom for both the stability of the land and fear of outing Solaris as a kingdom, I as her most capable soldier was given the inconceivable task. The responsibility of her daughters, the Relasin sisters, was so easily placed into my hands, and so I was thrust into foreign territory and made to search relentlessly for brown-skinned, light-haired women with inklings of magic emanating from their fingers.

It's practically unfeasible given that the territory of Sun District consists of thousands of villagers matching this exact appearance profile.

And Castor recognized that fact nearly as soon as I did, leading to an advantage immensely skewed in his direction. He holds the knowledge of who I was, the origin of my blood, and the Queen that would slit my throat herself if I did not fulfill her wishes—and that knowledge in and of itself is as deadly as what the Queen is capable of.

Word travels fast in Sun District, word travels fast within Aerth. The moment my story becomes public knowledge is when a Sun District trader would allow it to slip to the Queen that I'm not maintaining my anonymity, nor Solaris', and anything past that I do not think I would be alive to witness.

Spreading what he knows is exactly what Castor would do upon being aggravated. Everything regarding him is predictable and derivative, and I wish he was told that every now and then. It's not much of an insult, it doesn't reveal gaps in his character or cause a big reality check, but it would notify him that he's not quite as exemplary as he believes himself to be.

So, the line appears in my thoughts seconds before Castor pulls it out of his throat.

Who wishes to challenge Arinel?

"Who wishes to challenge Arinel?"

Someone speaks up after a silence that expresses everything those men fail to communicate. They may refer to me as lanky, naive, and foreign, but not even those who stand the tallest can see themselves achieving glory after witnessing me wield *Occisor* and *Periculo*.

"Put him against the other kid! She's hot-headed and violent, it would make for true bloodshed." His voice echoes toward Castor and the thought elicits a grin from his twisted lips. It's a single firm dip of his chin that solidifies the decision—I would be fighting the *Praedo* tonight.

One thing brings us together and that is the unspoken agreement to never speak, never fight, and never put ourselves in the position where a friendship could form.

There is a sharp divide, our mutual animosity having surfaced months ago amidst a heated argument of mine with Castor which the *Praedo* stumbled into. I was close to Castor's face, one angering thought away from striking his head with mine and sending him to the floor.

I was never good at being in control of my emotions, especially not rage.

I recall hearing a female voice over my shoulder. I failed to turn. I was irritated—furious—upon hearing the threat Castor had just sent in my direction, a vile declaration of what he considered me to be.

"You're a miserable orphan, Arinel, who has nothing. I refuse to allow you—you, an 18-year-old fetus consumed in his own self-pity and political affairs—to take my power here. I know what little you have left, and I know how minuscule your existence will become when the Queen finds that you're not in Sun District to fulfill her kingdom's duties, but rather to address your pathetic desires."

And she was there, stagnant behind me, during the full monologue.

The *Praedo* attempted to leave, recognizing that this interaction was not meant for her, or even one to witness. Her escape was nearly successful until Castor sensed the flash of black fabric and quickly trapped her exit.

My shoulders were still heavy under the staggering weight of what Castor vocalized, some of it more accurate than I was willing to accept, but the transfer of Castor's focus so swiftly drew my concern.

Nothing intrigued me about the woman yet, she was half doused in the shadows of the chamber with nothing visible to me except a vague silhouette of her frame. Castor, however, was fully visible, as if some external force gave him a spotlight at this moment and forced the audience's eyes on him.

"Praedo, I thought we spoke about this," Castor murmured almost lovingly, but that tone with the repulsive nature of his character alerted every facet of my paranoia.

"It wasn't important anyway—I'll go, alright?" She had a soft, hoarse voice that at first listen, wasn't very pleasing to hear. I rescinded that statement, however, the moment her words continued and burned into my ears, enclosing me in a ring of intrigue. *"Castor, release me."*

It was inconspicuous—what he was doing—and I had to shift to my left to even register the movement. He had his right ankle looped around the inside of her left knee, holding her in place. She was agile and very intelligent; I wouldn't doubt that she knew exactly how to slip from that grasp, and could do so easily, but she harbored the same reservations that I would in that exchange.

Fight Castor in any way, and he'd use you in whichever way as a puppet in his demonstrations. You'd be the bad apple that his eyes find when it comes time to teach The Thieves Gate a tyrannical lesson. This girl was too perceptive to dismiss the fact that in an establishment with far too many hot-headed men, she as a woman was in a poor circumstance.

Intervening was the only course of action in my mind, and I lost all previous thoughts about my personal issues with Castor when this newfound confusion and concern revealed itself. I hadn't but taken two steps when a flash of silver interrupted my vision and stilled my feet, coming from *her*.

Her hand was positioned with her knuckles against her back, fingers toying with the belt of her trousers—or so I believe before I caught that intentional glint passing in my direction. It was all so clear then, what she was attempting to communicate.

Stop moving. I'm warning you, she expressed without a movement of her lips, without a single bodily gesture. Just the language of weaponry.

It's incredible, frankly. How quickly that interaction occurred when she didn't know my face and I did not know hers, when I hadn't learned the language of her existence and she hadn't learned mine.

It's even difficult to communicate in a fight when faces are breathing in the same pockets of air and every thought of yours is laid out at your feet for your opponent to see and gawk at. But then, I knew that the shift of her right foot to the side was her telling me to move and that the slight lowering of her chin was a warning directed at Castor.

I would tell myself weeks later that this was the first instance I found myself enraptured in something, fascinated by a human, since my life spiraled towards Sun District.

But I didn't know that then just yet.

Castor uttered some disjointed words as if he didn't truly know what he was saying. Something along the lines of, "Where does Izar think you are right now?"

He was halfway through a bitter chuckle when the *Praedo's* left leg tightened around Castor's lock on her, cinching his foot in her knee in a position where I knew the joint is going to dislocate. Her movements were the closest replica of water I had seen, the way her body glided the two of them around so she was beside the exit, all while maintaining that grasp of his limb and gradually tightening her hold.

Castor's features were contorting. He was always one for pain, always the first volunteer to batter his knuckles and knees against cement, always searching for that adrenaline rush he so desperately desires. But I could tell that he's never been subjected to this type of discomfort before, not when it's so oddly placed and beautifully executed.

I barely registered how she did it. It was the lifting of her left knee so that Castor's right leg was bent so unnaturally that I had to wonder how it had not broken yet. Then, I grasped that I had misjudged—it *was* fractured.

She tore the bone somewhere in between the movement to the door and the action of her knee, and it brought Castor to the cement, forcing him to surrender all his weight onto that one joint.

"Leave!" Castor bellowed from deep in his chest, growling out the word with his clenched teeth, stifling the yell he surely needed to release. Harsh lines formed in the folds of his face as he grimaced, digging a fist into the ground as if to divert the pain from his foot, but what the *Praedo* did was unmistakably overwhelming.

And she wasn't fazed, at least not visibly. Her feet had retreated slightly, but her unblinking gaze had felt Castor long before and was now wavering over my body.

I saw her features then, and I wish I could have told myself at that moment to not stare for as long as I did. The lines forming her cheekbones, the haunting set of her eyebrows, and the strikingly soft lines of her eyes and hair—those images would stay imprinted across the backs of my eyelids for far too long.

There were slight hollows in her cheeks, yes, but it felt like they were meant to be there. So strangely carved that someone could place their thumbs in those spaces and hold her face forever, right in the position that she was looking at me.

Accompanied with a bruised, bronze tone to her skin and light hair streaked with red chalk, she truly was a sight.

As I was surveying her with wonder, she was matching that observation with a similar intensity, but I believe hers was partially an inquiry.

45

She didn't have to speak it for me to register what was circling her mind, coating it in a sheen of disgust.

You're here on behalf of a kingdom? You're kingdom-born?

I wanted to tell her that it's not what she believes it to be. *I'm not like them and I'm trying to leave,* I wanted to inform her, but I had questions of my own that I desired explanations for as well. They were bewildering inquiries as to why—how—she managed to inflict that pain on Castor, so abruptly and with such ease and surety.

She would not answer. I could tell from the shifting of her weight towards the opening of the chamber, which led back to the collisions of fists and exchange of harsh words—trivial when compared to the tightness of the air around us at that time.

I believe that was the moment we established our distance, even without uttering a syllable. She was far too fascinating, and yet much too secretive for me to ever feel safe in her presence. I exemplified the kingdoms in her eyes, and thus would be regarded with a dull contempt.

I should have merely asked for her name instead of filling my thoughts with the alias *Praedo* for the following weeks. Instead, her presence dissolved, and I returned to my previous position: contained in a room with Castor with unfaltering hostility directed at each other.

CHAPTER FIVE

E   R   I   S

I live in a flat atop the District bakery. Of course, the bakery closed its door decades before I established my presence there, for why would anything of delight have a prolonged stay in this town?

There are still faded pieces of parchment plastered onto the cracked window of the structure. The least disheartening of them are advertisements for businesses that never rose out of the pit that Sun District tucked them into, while others force me to look away when my glance finds the words.

HAVE YOU SEEN ME? CYNTH HANNER, 9 YEARS OF AGE, BROWN SKIN, BROWN EYES, LAST SEEN IN THE DISTRICT MARKET.

I don't believe the poor child was ever returned to his parents. Several children in Sun District are so easily robbed of what should be their right to happiness, their right to live and love and exist without fear of the political motives of the kingdoms—or the accidents of people like me.

The well-worn bell recites its tune above my head as the heavy door closes behind me. Sometimes when I enter this home,

I stand with my limbs frozen and fantasize that the dust spiraling into my nostrils is the scent of vanilla and the rubble collecting atop panels of wood are fallen sacks of sugar. I see the bakery trembling, not from the weakness of the establishment, but rather due to the overwhelming voices and movement occurring within these walls instead of haunting, broken silence.

I blink the reverie from my eyes when the fatigue of the day eventually settles into me. I did not have as successful of a market day as I had wished, which meant a smaller dinner than I would have liked. With that pit inching up the edges of my stomach, I find my way to the flats on the ascending floor, rickety steps supporting my feet for all they can.

This was a perfectly occupiable space to live in when Sun District boasted a liveliness that has since faded. Sometimes I believe that my arrival at this home was the beginning of its demise because as fate would have it, misfortune follows me. I required a destination after I left Leo and my mother incidentally that night itself found the bakery and flats, obsolete but vaguely familiar and intact enough to live in.

My movements don't move faster than a lethargic trudge when I reach the second floor and the overwhelming aura of dust and bleach plugs my nose with its strength. There's an expression of disgust on my face when I ram my body weight on the second door to my left, the only room in this small apartment that felt stable enough to exist in.

A grunt escapes my gritted teeth when the door remains held in place and all I have to show for it is a developing bruise on my shoulder blade. I do the action once more and this time the joints give in, and I'm thrown into my bedroom.

It's small. There's hardly enough space to move freely, the piles of discarded antiquities and furniture spreading themselves across the wood being too ingrained in the culture of this home for me to move them ever. Sometimes I believe that the reason I am reluctant to part with these items is because they're reminders of a life that is happier than mine. The objects and frankly trash are all the remnants of the family that occupied this floor decades ago, hints of their life left in the teddy bear tucked against the wall, the pile of men's clothing folded atop a table.

Maybe these stolen fragments help trick my mind into believing that I lived as beautifully as they did.

When my satchel falls beside my feet, dust escapes from the fissures in the wooden floor, polluting the air around me even more with its stifling nature. My steps are heavy as I ready the cot, lower myself to its level, and then fold my body into its modest comfort.

Nothing in me feels ready to, but I grudgingly begin the treatment that is necessary for me to put my mind through as soon as the Sun sets. It's the only way I know to prevent a second Leo from meeting my eyes—

—He was nothing more than an innocent child who had reached for me, arms held wide to bare his heart to mine.

The feeling of having small, fragile arms encase your torso and give you that incomparable warmth of innocence and youth is beautiful. It is something I would have wished to capture in a scent bottle and hold with me long after Leo was no longer a child, but I never memorized it well enough. I effectively robbed myself of more chances to experience it.

Simple market days do not mean much. I was weary and holding more unease within me than I should've been able to handle, and I was correct in that notion—there was nothing about it that I was able to handle.

That terrible despair was rising through every expanse my body made up: my throat, the length of my arms and legs, the ends of my hair. What I was experiencing in those few instances was the climax of every emotion that I had ever torn out of another, all enveloping me in a way that was so tragically painful.

I can only describe it as a persistent flame beginning at the root of each of my veins and gradually ripping out to the air from the inside of my skin, giving no care to the wounds it created and scattered across my body. I knew I was reaching my limit with *how much pain I could hold, especially when that energy was dark and foreign, but this—*this*—proved to me just how far gone I had allowed myself to descend.*

He shouldn't have come closer to me. I shouldn't have allowed him to.

I remember our bodies and spines giving out at the same instant, almost synchronized in our descent to the floor. With what little vigor I could wrench from the depths of my mind, I was attempting to stop it, to rescind all that energy and force it back into myself. I would press it against my skin; I would swallow it whole and do any unimaginable act to prevent any more of it from reaching Leo.

But, by that point, my power was affecting Leo more than even I.

I told myself to not watch, but a sight like that—you can't dismiss it. You hold your palm against your screaming lips and glue your eyes to the black threads of energy pouring into your victim through the sockets of his eyes, the openings of his nostrils.

You puncture your nails into the skin of your thigh as if to say, 'Here, here! There's room for you again, you just have to come back. Please! Please, just come back and hurt me and no one else.'

That darkness would never come back to me, I had passed it on and continued the cycle like a true element of the Aerth. Nature was laughing at me. I could hear it snickering behind its shield of green beauty.

Shame someone had to take the fall for you, *it taunted.* My Sun *taunted.*

My body convulses in repeated spurts of movement as I twist out the last slivers of dark energy from my mind, fingers grasping at my temples with a pressure that elicits nothing short of a scream. The moment I allow my hands to unclench, those threads of energy empty into the bowls I create with my skin, feeling so much lighter in this position than they have ever been within my skull.

Right now, where I wield the power and tower above the very thing that killed Leo, is when I feel content. That relief fails to stay with me long, however, soon to be replaced by a frigid emptiness once the soft breeze from the night lifts the energy from my touch and wafts it out of the window to my right. It's bittersweet, watching magic so lovely leaving you, but knowing that in a matter of time, it will rest in the crevices of your consciousness once again.

This is an improper way to dispose of the darkness, I recognize that, but my allowance of its re-emergence into society is the only way to maintain that stability nature yearns for. The energy will find its way to a new host and prosper in their mind until that individual grows sick of it and finds their way to me, hopeful that my rumored gifts are true.

It's a curse, I think as my gaze lingers at the spot I saw the threads linger before they became one with the night sky.

Curses eventually kill you, don't they?

CHAPTER SIX

C E R E S

---

*I*zar maintains a large portion of my thoughts as I traverse the familiar path to the Thieves Gate, forgoing the usual burlap cloth gown and instead wearing a simple shirt and trousers. It's not his face that burns into the apex of my mind, but rather the words expressing his disgust—the fear—of what I supposedly did to him hours ago.

It has become difficult to dispel his presence from today, so at some point, I believe I simply accepted it and have begun to tolerate his insistent prying at the corners of my sanity. Though, I still could not find the patience to speak to him during my brief visit to our home to exchange my clothing, which makes me fear whether our relationship will ever revert to some semblance of normal again.

My pace is slow but driven as I reach for the establishment that could ease the tension stifling my breathing and choking my lungs. The Thieves' Gate is the epitome of disorder, but somewhere under all that testosterone and forced bravado, there's a true culture of precision and dedication, and that's what I adore so deeply.

The building is a ways past the outskirts of the city center, meaning very few townsfolk really know about the complex or the activities that occur within its walls and a treasured shield of privacy is there to be enjoyed. After all, anything straying from the mundane existence of Sun District is generally condemned by the public.

The Thieves Gate greets me with the same wave of stale, heavy air and the tickling of dust in my nostrils, elements of the atmosphere that I disliked previously but have begun to enjoy. Ignoring the fight brewing to my right side, I swerve bodies to duck into the training room, a sector of the building that stays abandoned for the sole reason of grown men being too vain to admit that they could use some practice.

Immediately upon resting my back on a brick wall bordering a fighting platform, I sense the presence of *Letalis* once more against my thigh. I don't have to grasp onto her to feel the energy tying me and my weapon together, my *chosen* weapon. Here at The Thieves Gate, it's rare for one to choose a blade for any reason other than practicality and efficiency, but when I first entered the weapons depository as a teenager who trusted the word of mouth far too much, I found myself disregarding the beautiful, venomous swords that could cause the most destruction. Instead, it was *Letalis'* simple structure and unembellished front that was the magnet to my heart, drawing my body closer to the weapon and compelling my fingers to close around the worn handle.

Since then, *Letalis* has proven herself to be stealthier and more fatal than her counterparts, even those larger and sharper, which has made her most deserving of her spot in my hand. She truly is *letalis*—lethal.

I should be itching to fight with her in a series of long, sweeping movements, but my focus strays when I notice a presence at the entrance of the corridor, one that doesn't feel prevalent enough to turn my head towards but still piques my interest. It's a boy, maybe a young man by the sound of how his weight falls, the scraping of distressed shoe soles against the concrete, and the faint waft of a cologne that most likely is sold within the market.

It's simple to deduce that he is looking at me—no, staring at me.

The boy's fixed look feels heavy against the side of my scalp, and a certain annoyance builds in my stomach, especially when I hear an intentional clearing of his throat that probably was louder than was necessary. My eyes shift to watch him through my peripheral vision, and something immediately breaks the unbothered facade I had built.

He's familiar, and I know distinctly from where too. But I allow my mind to ignore the events of that night as I observe facets of him that I could not before.

He is not native to Sun District, or anywhere close to here for that matter. I can only assume that he is a transfer from a more northern kingdom, by the paler color of his skin and the strange hue of his hair. His hair. The color is very light, too pale to be yellow but too warm to be white, nearly the exact shade as mine. The platinum-colored locks that have always set me apart from the majority of those in Sun District—he happens to share.

I notice his eyes too, and I can't find the incentive to tear my attention away. They look as though they were carved from glass, with silver hues and sharp glints embedded into his irises. They're a beautiful sight, something that feels so rare but so familiar at the same time.

He's in front of me and I fight the urge to speak to him, to ask him what makes his hair and eyes so full of light and what the sword strapped to his back is called. He came to me first, after all. Some petty instinct within me wishes for him to initiate our first conversation and save me from any discomfort.

Thankfully, he recognizes my message and blurts out such a convoluted sentence that I have to stretch my hearing to even begin to decipher.

"...What?" I ask, doused in confusion midst being entranced by the whirling pools of his irises.

"Uh—" Is he scared? Or flustered? Something about his composure has fallen, revealing a vulnerable young man that most likely has no idea what he's doing or saying. "I—Alright, so Castor is expecting a fight between the two of us."

A slight shake of my head stops whatever words he is about to utter next.

"No," I say simply. I do not subscribe to Castor's strange and ineffective matchups, much less do I believe that a fight between me and the man before me would do anything productive.

As much as I dislike admitting it, I've observed his work and I've seen how battle is not merely a hobby but an occupation and an art form for him. He's been formally trained, everyone at this facility can see that, and it's exactly why I am mistrustful of him—why would a kingdom-hailing man reside in Sun District and lower himself to our level *willingly*?

"I'm telling you—Castor is going to be on my ass about this if I don't oblige." He says, backtracking his previously hesitant tone for something more rushed. It's then that I realize there is an ulterior motive to his words and there might be a reason he is pushing to have this fight take place.

Driven by hesitancy and intrigue, I silently surrender. I turn so I'm facing more of the man's body as a sign of newfound willingness. It puzzles me why I gave in so easily, but I suppose some part of me finds a thrill in getting the opportunity to fight someone who is most likely more skilled than me; finding a sparring partner who can challenge you to a high level is just so few and far between.

"What's your name?" I eventually ask, realizing that it's impolite to conduct a conversation for this long and stare unrelentingly at someone without knowing what to refer to them by.

"Antares." His name is beautiful and strange, of an origin I do not recognize, which further confirms his inexplicable past. "Yours? Besides *Praedo*, of course."

"Ceres."

The first thing I ever learned about Antares came from that moment when I saw every emotion he felt spelled out upon his features. He made no effort to stifle that transparency, or any attempt to do so was easily eclipsed by the gravity of how much he could feel—all at once.

He looks frightened but simultaneously wistful as if the two reactions were fighting for dominance in his mind. Something about my name, or the way I said it, brought a concealed memory to daylight.

"There's someone with that name back home," Antares breathes, shaking his head softly to dispel the thought. He clearly regrets the words from how his eyes flit to find another magnet for his focus.

"Which kingdom?" I ask under my breath, the question resurfacing in my mind as it has countless times before. I knew Antares would dodge the inquiry, but I suppose I simply needed the gratification of seeing him do it.

"Weapons?" Antares' voice is a sharp interruption and I grudgingly accept it, reaching to pull *Letalis* from her sheath against my leg. Antares' eyes follow my movement and once he witnesses the dance *Letalis* performs between my fingers, he knows it's a chosen blade.

"It's not very often you see a weapon and fighter pair like that," he murmurs, his attention plastered on *Letalis* and how she appears to move with my mind, not my touch.

"Yes," I respond with a quieter tone, slightly entranced in my own blade for a moment. It's an instant later when my thoughts retrace their trajectory and I allow *Letalis* to slip back into her sheath. "Is hand-to-hand an option?"

Antares' face is painted with surprise, and I'm sure part of mine is too but I'm more skilled at disguising it. I don't quite understand why I relinquished what could have been my greatest strength in this fight, but I feel an overwhelming urge to exercise the adrenaline of a true test of skill, independent of those bladed advantages.

Antares' chin dips in a nod once he overcomes his stupor and a hidden knife drops from his hand and collides with the stone flooring. An involuntary raise of my eyebrows occurs and Antares chuckles from deep in his throat.

"Didn't see that, *Praedo*, did you?"

My eyebrows raise higher, slight amusement apparent in the crinkling of the corners of my eyes, but that indication disappears far before Antares can detect it. I gesture for him to lift himself onto the fighting platform behind me, and he does so in one motion with incredible ease, a sort of athleticism that turns my previous security into reluctance. I don't enjoy losing.

His hand is outstretched for me to join him, and before I can effectively deny the request, my arm seems to move on its own accord to take his grasp.

Suns, *he is strong.*

Situating myself on the new floor below me, I allow my body to take a firm stance. "Fair match?" I address Antares without exactly looking at him.

"Fair match."

My heels are light against the ground as I begin my initial circling of his body, a practice that he replicates to instinctively search for a weakness, a fault that could help either of us overpower the other. I narrow my eyes when I watch his skilled movements, every motion swift and deliberate, and I swallow when I realize I am struggling to find an imperfection in him.

I feel frustration flooding me, but I swallow it back down just as easily and focus on his unprotected torso, an area that unfortunately wouldn't reap me the largest benefit to attack but would disarm him for a moment. Being the *Praedo*, I strike first, low on the ground as I aim a powerful hit to his stomach. My chest reels backward when Antares dodges my fist and immediately uses his momentum to direct a punch to my body.

With the slight warning I was given, I'm able to turn the move back onto him by wrenching his outstretched arm and sliding it effortlessly behind his back until he feels his shoulder blades between his fingers. With any other opponent, I would have expected a cry of alarm or pain, but Antares only grunts with distaste and spins his gaze so he can grin at me.

"Stealing my signature move, are you *Praedo*?" He says half-mockingly, a smile licking at the corners of his lips.

His words are a simple, but effective, distraction. During the half-second I spent listening to him, Antares managed to kick his feet backward at my kneecaps, causing a sudden loss of my footing, and a not very graceful tumble to my shins. I bite back a word of anger and roll my body backward before I even truly land on the ground. My feet are quickly stabilized and propelling my torso towards Antares in one prompt motion that takes Antares a moment to even decipher.

For one extremely satisfying instant, Antares boasts an expression of utter confusion and I exploit that hesitation when my weight lands on Antares' shoulders. It's an abrupt collision that he fails to foresee, which means I achieved what I wanted: a fall onto his back with my body driving the movement.

I frown when I see I have not flustered him, but rather have elicited some thought from his mind. Antares merely runs his tongue over his upper teeth and bores his gaze into my eyes, observing, calculating, questioning.

A flicker of pain darts over his expression as he speaks his next word, two fingers quickly massaging his temple before disregarding the motion like it never occurred at all.

"Solaris." His tone is experimental, but his eyebrows are quirked upwards as if he's expecting a certain response from me. A response to a word that isn't familiar to me.

At least, not *very* familiar.

It's a combination of syllables and letters that I'm sure I have heard before, maybe I have even said it in the past, but I forget the meaning and why it would be relevant to Antares.

As expected, Antares turns our bodies over on the padded fighting mat so he reclaims the advantage and my limbs are pinned in a manner that is not at all comfortable.

"You'll have to say more than that for me to know what you are speaking about," I hiss as the plane of my forearm pushes back against Antares' collarbone. I do not know who rose first, or whether the actions were simultaneous, but again we have returned to our initial circling stance, this time with a larger amount of space between us.

The unfamiliar feeling of apprehension flows through my veins, a sentiment that is not at all comfortable within my body. Again, Antares acts upon my betraying uncertainty, and brings the edge of his foot forward in a hard collision with the inside of my kneecap, resulting in the unexpected crumbling of my right leg.

I do allow myself to descend, but during the motion I latch onto his dangling arm and shift my weight at an angle, bringing Antares down with me. His feet leave the ground and his body contorts in a flip onto the mat, ending with a jarring hit of his back against the surface.

Antares displays that unrelenting stamina and persistence once more and lifts himself somewhere between the closing and opening of my eyelids in a blink. The man manages to pin my body in the corner of the ring, his hands clutching the ropes on either side of me and illustrating a scene that I would not be able to break out of unless I overpower Antares tremendously.

"Your name is Ceres," Antares gasps out between hasty breaths. His breathing has become as haphazard as mine. "There's not many young women with the name Ceres, especially not one 17 years of age and living in *Sun District*, of all places."

"How do you know my age?" I spit at him, trying to escape the encasing nature of his arms, but not putting much effort into it. I want—*need*—to unravel this man's mysteries and perhaps it is here in this fighting ring where his words will reveal themselves.

A laugh escapes Antares' lips and his hands immediately release from their clench on the bordering ropes and travel to his temples. I notice the white tips of his fingers from the pressure he's applying and I feel an urge to bring his arms down.

Antares turns away from me, but the shaking of his head is still visible as he begins a pace to the end of the platform. When a step away from leaving it, something changes in his thoughts and his body promptly swivels to return us to the same position we were trapped in before.

"So, it *is* you." His voice is slick with wonder and his eyes stay wide as he surveys me.

I scoff, confusion enveloping my features. "You are acting so strange. Could I get an explanation of what it is I am? What *Solaris* is?"

This position is compromising. I tear myself away from that corner of the platform and plant a calculated shove against Antares' shoulder that possesses enough vigor to spin him slightly. In return, he attempts to launch at my torso, which I block with a frustrated swerve of my arms.

The impact of our skin colliding sends a wave of pressure through my body, feeling his breathing fluctuating just as rapidly as mine. It's an unplanned movement, but I opt for lowering to the mat and abruptly aiming a powerful kick at his shin. I regret it almost immediately when I realize I'm no longer in control of my feet. A turbulent wave of discomfort trembles through my legs as Antares adeptly catches hold of my ankle and, with incredible agility, flips me over—with one arm.

Perhaps I'm angry now, the embarrassing landing flat on my back and my skull elicited something irritable within me. It's almost second nature to lose my last inhibition and simply tear Antares' frame to the ground, and it's simple this time. He's guarded himself perfectly, but no one expects several concurrent hits to differing joints. So, upon a deliberate overtaking of his balance through his kneecaps and a staggering blow to his torso, coupled with a lock around his neck that distracts his focus from remaining upright, Antares tumbles to the ground.

"Answer my questions, you're making me paranoid—" I press, dispelling the thought of my obvious victory as a strange dread rises in my chest. I usually don't care for sensations of fear, but something feels strange about this instance, especially since I feel a strange familiarity with this boy and with the word he repeatedly mentions.

"—I'm from Solaris, it's the kingdom I have been so... so cryptic about." Antares stumbles along his words, but the trembling of his fingers as he addresses me proves the gravity of his words—or perhaps the disruption of his mind. He presses a knuckle against his temple for a moment, as if to ward off intruding thoughts, and then continues. "As are you, Ceres. You... *Gods*, you are so incredibly important, and you don't even know. You don't know who you—and your sister—even are, do you?"

The words spill from his body and into my ears, but my hearing seems to reject them. My senses are plagued with immense disorientation and it's like I'm attempting to comprehend Antares' sentences but find myself getting more lost with each syllable.

"You're the daughter. You *are* Solaris."

CHAPTER SEVEN

A   N   T   A   R   E   S

*M*y voice scrapes the sides of my throat as I release yet another sharp scream, the sound almost silent to the ears that have closed off to me hours ago. One of my hands is gripping the blood-stained handle of Occisor, *the sword that was given to me by my father only minutes ago, and the other clenches tightly onto the skin of his arm.*

I am young, but I know that a slight pulsing within the inside of one's wrist is a sign of life, and as my fingers curl around my father's chilled wrist, I can't find that sign. I search for it—I hold my ear to the skin and squeeze my eyelids shut midst fallen tears, but I still cannot detect that heartbeat.

It was the steady rhythm of the stories that were read to me before I fell asleep and the feeling that would ground me when I was overwhelmed with frustration and my father would bring my face against his chest.

It's gone—he's gone—and the kingdom doesn't even care. Two burly soldiers attempt to lift my body from the wooden flooring with calloused palms on my torso and shoulders, but their touch simply sends another flurry of rage through me. I kick backward at the men's legs with as much force I'm able to exert and I fumble for my mother's body, yearning for the familiarity of her hand encasing mine.

It's an unexplainable relief that surges into my mind when I see her gaze open and wide, yet unmoving. I crawl towards her, half-smiling as I thank the Saints for her living breath, but that reassurance quickly dissipates when I sense that her chest is not rising and falling. Neither are her eyes anything but glossed-over and stagnant.

"Mumma...? Mumma!" My voice finds its ability to scream once more. "Mum, I know you see me! Say something!"

"She's dead, boy," a gruff voice barks from over my shoulder, laying a gentler hand on my arm as if that would make him seem any less foreign.

"No—no, she can't be," I repeat over and over in a pained susurration that can't seem to fully escape my throat. I can see her dead before me, but my naivety refuses to accept the fact, instead consumed in childish hope. She used to take my face in her palms and tell me of all we would do together with my father in the future and how happy we would be once we managed to escape the unhinged grasp of Solaris. She couldn't have lied—my mother doesn't lie.

"Kid, they're dead—both of them. Happens to the best of us," the man offers in return, attempting some form of sympathy but the delivery turns his tone into something of amusement. From the corner of my lowered eyes, I sense a big sweeping motion of his arm, a signal for the men and women who paused behind him to step forward and collect the bodies plastered to the floor.

"We have been told to bring you to the Order of the Grim," speaks a woman with a soft, yet haunting tone. Her touch takes over for the man, but the lighter pressure against my skin does nothing for my spiraling mind.

Feet away from me, they lift my father onto a stretcher and I truly witness how much life his limbs have lost, now utterly limp and hanging from his sides as he lays horizontally. I'm not sure *when the scream faded from my chest, but now I'm silent, sobbing into the shoulder of the woman behind me as she runs a light touch up and down my spine.*

"You're free now," she whispers into my ear, and that's when I understand that this woman, in addition to the other adults now filling the crevices of the room, was never on my family's side. They're with the Queen.

———

"What is your name, child?"

I resentfully raise my chin, furious tears brimming across my waterline and my gaze holding a rare but vivid depiction of my heartbreak. Realizing that I'm standing before those loyal to the Queen provokes me, but something you learn early on in this kingdom is that showing your vengefulness publicly provides you with nothing but additional pain.

"Antares Arinel," I respond, my voice fragmented and barely discernible. I attempt to lengthen my spine and seem presentable to the Grim, but the pain of what had occurred only hours earlier, releases a sharp jab of agony and I can only slump further into myself.

"Antares Arinel." A male figure rises from the shadows bathing the edges of the chamber and his hood is brought down from his head, revealing a shaven skull and sharp bone structure that frightens me. "What has brought you to the Order of the Grim?"

It's difficult to say at this moment, even though I had trained my mind on the journey to the Order to establish the phrase in my mind. The Order of the Grim rarely provides a favorable outcome to an individual who cowers before the truth.

"My parents have passed," I nearly spit from my tongue, needing to force the words into the air before me.

A hush sweeps through the expansive room, and barely audible murmurs begin to circulate me, carving chasms in the already falling composure I had instilled in myself.

With one sweeping step conducted by them all, the Grim reveal themselves in a gradually closing ring around me, beginning the practice that meets all lost souls, the test of one's true place in Solarian society when all other direction has been lost.

It's difficult to discern when observing their figures because of how starkly different they look from their ancestors, but The Grim are the children of the Astral Saints. Like their superiors, they maintain the ability to exercise their given power, the gift of foretelling. The Grim are haunted creatures, constantly battling the endless fates, the endless lives one human can live, and being subjected to the burden of choosing that direction for them. It's viewed as a gift in their eyes, but a fear in the perspective of the Solarians, those who are powerless under the influence of the Grim.

Once a teenager has completed their education in Solaris, they would stand in front of the Grim to receive their fate and be given the path in life that would theoretically guide them to prosperity, though the expected outcome is not consistently reached. The Grim are troubled souls that are fond of misinterpreting what their gift allows them to see for the favor of elevating Solaris as a kingdom. It's not uncommon for a terrible fate to be decided for a Solarian simply for the benefit of the kingdom, with no regard given to the family and living nature of that human.

As my parents became a pawn in Solaris' tragic games, I don't expect myself to be anything but.

"Antares Arinel," the voices drone, various tones blending into one. They've begun their work.

I expect myself to lose my balance and sink into myself as the Grim takes authority over my mind and begins to dissect it, and all this occurs, but the most prevalent sensation is the feeling of complete disorder in my mind and body. There is no longer a ground pressing into the soles of my feet or a dome stretching above my head. I instead am falling, tumbling through air and memories and pain in a spiral towards the deepest parts of myself. My sense of stability is long gone and is stretched further away from me with every new word uttered by the Grim.

"Family," they hiss through my skull and I'm promptly enveloped in the depiction of my own vision. My gaze erupts into colors and seeping light accompanied with soft laughter echoing within my eardrums, that of my mother's. Behind my eyelids, I see everything I have treasured so deeply over the past few years. Those vulnerable moments douse me with nostalgic memories of perching on my father's shoulders while watching vibrant warrior dances and entwining my hand with my mother's during the night.

"Occisor." I stumble into the moment where Papa had laid the gleaming sword in my hands, light rays reflecting off the metal so harshly that my vision is white for several moments. My mind yearns for the blade, the only piece of my father I have left, but the recollection vanishes faster than it came, replaced with a glimpse of when the soldiers had torn Occisor from my hands. I watch my features crumble in despair, a phenomenon that is reflected in my face as I re-experience the anguish.

"Blood and ruin." Flashes of gore and wreckage coat my vision and surround me with their horrific image. I see appalling open wounds that someone as young as me should never have to witness, and then mutilated joints and skin replaced the image, sending a stronger surge of nausea through me.

I want nothing more than to tear myself away from the evocation and return to the isolation of the Grims' chamber. Why were they showing me this—the sight that I fear the most?

Thankfully, it's not long before the Grim relinquishes their grasp on my mind and my feet sense rigid stone underneath me once more. My body is stagnant in the same position I remember, as I did not move during my reverie, and that thought is terrifying to repeat in my mind. It's alarming to recognize that you have such little control over your own body and consciousness that you were transported to an interdimensional state of mind with nothing at all occurring to your body.

The Grim are conversing in their own silent, secluded manner, the only visible communication between them being slight head nods and inaudible hisses. All the cloaked souls manage to still their movement and speech at the same instant, and then resume it immediately, all with the same agenda in mind.

"Antares Arinel, this is your fate," the voices pulse in unison against the rhythm of my heartbeat, but I do not have a chance to hold my palm to the left side of my chest and still the beating as my father always did, for Occisor launches itself into my hand.

My eyes fill with bewilderment at the sight of the only possession I wish to see and draw comfort from, and disbelief as well. The Grim do not provide gifts or condolence, they give you ultimatums—so how exactly does Occisor fall into the situation?

"We see war in your future," a man justifies, his fingers convulsing with a minor degree of energy as his telekinetic strength lifts Occisor from my grip and sends it spiraling around my frame, almost taunting me with its freedom and beauty.

"Fighting."

"Destruction, ruin, and the acquisition of justice."

My lips part, overburdened by the strange claim of the Grim, that I am destined for war, as a mere child. I know nothing of weaponry, much less kingdom politics, so how must I defend this territory with little loyalty to it and the position I would be placed in?

"What does that mean for me?" I call into the whispers of the Grim, desperately needing a response that isn't shielded by the animosity of the figures.

Their woven voices begin to speak again as one entity as their ominous decision is driven into my mind, eliciting a burning fear.

"Antares Arinel, you are bound by duty to the Solarian Kingdom and your Queen Vega of the Kingdom of Solaris to serve *in her name within the palace army—an honorable position that requires the utmost respect and dedication."*

My willingness to respect and be dedicated to the Queen was ripped from my body the moment Vega authorized and conducted the murder of my parents.

———

Ceres' expression is incredibly guarded, frigid with the harsh set of her eyebrows and the chewing of the inside of her cheek. It's what I've noticed the past hour while fighting her, speaking to her, watching her. She's nearly unreadable and it aggravates me but simultaneously holds intrigue.

At this moment, however, after I told her the story of my childhood to convince her mind into believing me, I realize that I used poor judgment in the act. Ceres doesn't appeal to emotion and sympathy like so many others do. Instead, it's reasoning and practicality that breaks her mold.

"You're a great storyteller," she offers after scrutinizing my words. She says it with an easy shrug of her shoulders, a simple movement that notifies me that this task would be difficult if I continue progressing in the manner at which I am.

"Look at me, Ceres," I pressure her, forcing my voice to penetrate the blockades around her mind. "Why is our hair the same color? It's so blonde, it's white. What kingdom do we originate from, you tell me!"

Ceres' pursued lips indicate her silence, but I watch as her eyes run over my hair, then my skin, and finally my eyes. She's noticing characteristics that are out of place, and I can tell her mind is sweeping through the multitude of notes in her glossary of the kingdoms to find an explanation.

"Our hair matches that of the Europas, but we don't have their green eyes or their ebony skin. Sure, your skin is darker, but that's from your *mother*."

She's opening her mind to my thoughts and I can almost watch her unravel, starting with the pull of her lower lip into her mouth and the raising of her chin so she knows I have her attention.

"What about your parents, *Praedo*? You don't have any, do you?" I would wince at the harshness that emanated from my later words, but Ceres shows no emotional reaction, only a simple nod. "Why do you think that is? You were left with a fabricated tale of how your parents eloped when you were young and now you live with your sibling. Ah—what was it…. your brother, Izar?"

Ceres' eyes flicker with alarm, squinting slightly before wiping the expression clear off her features. It's incredible how she does that, restarts her mind and face so easily—I wouldn't be surprised if she inherited the quality from the Queen.

"Have you noticed how much older than you he is—your brother? 15 years. You tell me if your parents would've had the time to leave a 15-year age gap between their children. They didn't. Your parents, Queen Vega and King Jacque did have two children, but your brother is not one of them."

"How do you know all this?" Ceres murmurs, cast in stupefaction as her gaze shifts to her hands. A miniature feud persists between her fingers as she wrenches at the joints incessantly, perhaps subconsciously.

"I'm here under the jurisdiction of Queen Vega, the ruler of the Kingdom of Solaris, our home—"

"You keep referring to it as *my* home," Ceres counters, her tone sharp and insistent, completely having lost its mellow nature. "Sure, I believe Solaris exists. Your childhood anecdote seemed truthful enough. I don't believe someone could simply come up with something like that and I really doubt that anyone would lie about being an orphan. But still—this all feels too alien for me to subscribe to."

"You're plenty alien as it is," I bite back in response, turning the inches of atmosphere between our faces into a space of tension. I have to stifle the dizziness that envelopes my mind when Ceres says *Solaris* without warning. *I should learn to control this instability.* "Why do you think you're such an agile fighter? Yes, you train diligently and have grown into an incredible warrior, but how did you adopt the practice so quickly? When did you begin at The Thieves Gate, a year ago?"

I can sense Ceres brewing with counterarguments, most likely revving up to say that I'm invalidating her talent and reducing it to an innate quality, so I intervene before she can voice that thought.

"You're brilliant, you are. But there's a sort of magic inside you that propels you to fight as well as you do, and you curate it every day. That's the beautiful energy that you hold and that Solaris molded into you," I speak to her from the depths of my heart, devoting every word, every ounce of sympathy within me to imagine myself in her position and determining what it is I would need to hear in that case. "There's darkness as well, a gift that originates in your mother—the Queen. Have you... have you been able to cause strange incidents, either through your mind or your touch?"

Ceres' stubborn, stubborn self is nearly shaking her head before I finish my words, but then suddenly stills midst the movement, a memory revealing itself.

Her head tilts slightly and the gnawing on her lip deepens. "Well, I suppose something... strange did occur this morning."

Relief spirals within me; I had finally found something within her to appeal to. I gesture for her to elaborate and a soft exhale leaves her mouth.

"I had my hand on my brother—or the man you say isn't my brother at all—and he abruptly... recoiled." Her eyebrows diverge and I sense flurries of pain in the action. "He said my touch hurt—burned."

My mind revisits the monologue the Queen had told me weeks ago where she expressed a vague description of her gift, the power of the Aerth. She had influence over the four elements of life and prosperity, sometimes in lovely ways like soft rain and luminescent sunlight, but other times more disastrous. Flooding, the cinching of air in one's throat, dust storms. The woman was capable of much more than possibly even the Astral Saints.

Ceres' gift inherited from her mother was described as budding when she was sent away from Solaris by her father. He had touched her and felt a stinging sensation travel through his arm, and then he had held her sister and had been instantly overcome with a subliminal dread.

The explanation fits.

I repeat my thoughts to Ceres, my gaze stilling on her hands when it finds a chance to. I find it incredible how much magic these women in the Solarian royal family hold. The amount of power they hold within themselves, both as nobility and as associates of the Astral Saints is staggering—and some like Ceres don't even realize it.

As I reiterate the reason for Ceres' presence in Sun District, a cowardly action by her father that ultimately resulted in his death by the Queen's hand, a sharp pang disrupts my head and I sigh at the continued nature of its presence. My mind should have adjusted to this new reality by now.

"I know a part of you still fails to believe it, so let me prove it to you," I plead, hesitantly encasing her fingers with mine and keeping my touch faint to allow her to wrench herself away. She doesn't, so I strengthen my grasp. "Come with me back to Solaris, even just for a day's stay. This is your one chance; you will not be able to reach the kingdom on your own because some intricacies require my presence. I need to prove to the Queen that you exist, and you need to prove to yourself that you belong in a world larger than whatever you have in Sun District. There, you're *important* and *powerful*, isn't that what we all want?"

"This is absurd," she murmurs against the edge of her shoulder. Ceres has turned her head away from mine and proceeds to squeeze her eyelids shut. Her lips move in the gentle formations of words and I watch her incredulously as she ponders my proposal.

I comprehend then that it's not her trust in me that is leading her to consider the idea, it's the prospect of escaping Sun District and finding something worthwhile that contains none of the hardships of this life—as improbable as that may seem.

She repeats that phrase multiple times, her mumbling becoming fainter with every reiteration. Somewhere along the way, she squeezes my fingers back.

CHAPTER EIGHT

C   E   R   E   S

---

*B*y the time I had separated myself from Antares, the Sun had fallen far past our view and Sun District was now plagued by darkness. Though I was navigating the path back to my townhome, the remainder of Sun District was heading north for the annual Astral Festival which was making its way through the Aerthen plain. For this single night, the villagers within our town divert their energy from their own adversity and devote themselves to building an extravagant setup in the Silamine Desert: the destination of the Astral procession. The entire event is an attempt by the Astral Saints to stimulate interregional interaction and a ceasefire of hostility between the districts and kingdoms—but the effort has failed every year since its beginning.

I wonder now why Solaris has never come to the festival when they have the most glory and power to showcase. It's strange to consider why they have kept themselves concealed for centuries upon centuries, hiding their treasures and souls from our blind eyes.

Even still, I don't ponder the thought for long because I recognize that delving deep into the intricacies of Solaris will force me into a rabbit hole of questioning that I won't be able to suppress. It would also revive Antares' face and words in my mind, and that would most definitely be an unwelcome distraction.

Recognizing the truth about the man I had just met, and possibly the truth about myself as well, was jarring, to say the least. I consider myself to safeguard my emotions and inner thoughts, providing them little exposure to a world beyond my mind, but I could tell that I faltered on several occasions during Antares' explanation. The man did make strong arguments, expressing a compelling enough case that made me consider taking him up on his offer and suddenly leaving behind this life for the more fulfilled one he was promising.

The closer I get to Izar and the cottage we own, the more I begin to undo that newfound faith and allow my cynical nature to overwhelm me. It is, however, a possibility that Izar will agree with Antares' claims that he is not my true brother, that the person that should be in his place is a 20-year-old woman—my sister.

If I had been put in this position a year earlier, when I was a naive young girl who could not handle more than two simultaneous inconveniences, I know I would have broken down under my own fear and disconcert. Now, I still feel those sensations pressing against the edges of my mind, but they're duller aches, developing alongside my maturity.

I catch sight of Izar's black mess of hair before I see the rest of him—a slouched figure sitting atop the steps to our door. His gaze is fixed on a tear in the sleeve of his shirt and a single finger runs along the ripped fabric. He's waiting for me.

My feet are soon interrupting his downward cast vision and he acknowledges my presence with a furrow of his eyebrows and the locking of his jaw. Even if he isn't my true blood, there's still something between the two of us that maintains a connection, and I can feel it as our gazes lock and he surveys me, most likely biting back an inquiry as to where I was the entirety of the day.

I take a seat beside him and watch as the strengthening moonlight bathes my knees with a sheen of white rays, a stark contrast to the sunlight I adore. It's frowned upon to think of the moon as a deity anywhere near the beauty of our Sun, but no individual within Sun District can deny its influence.

Neither can I deny the gravity of what Antares communicated to me, all those words resting against the tip of my tongue and praying to be said again, except with my candor launching them.

"Who are you, really?" I ask Izar, turning my chin towards him and observing the faltering of his previously serene expression, quickly overtaken by something resembling panic.

"I don't know what it is you mean, Ceres," Izar returns in a low tone, dropping his gaze from mine. "I'm Izar."

"You are. But are you my brother?"

Izar rolls his shoulders backward and brings his fingers to his under eyes as if to say, *Damn you, Ceres. Damn you for bringing up this subject before I'm ready to speak about it.*

"Just tell me, please," I urge, wrenching Izar's hand towards me and wrapping my fingers around his. I squeeze once, half-terrified that what occurred that morning under my touch would resurface again. "I know most of the truth already, I believe. I know of—of Solaris and the Queen. My mother, correct?"

I don't exactly believe the final words I speak, but the lurching of Izar's throat became the final push I needed to succumb to the fantasy of Antares' tale. What escalates in my veins is nothing short of terror, but I keep it bottled as best as I can—Izar would not contribute anything if he knew how close I am to becoming unhinged.

"I was a trader." Izar surrenders to the ever-tightening grip of my palm against his. "I began at the age of 9, shuffling goods, mostly metals and oil, between the kingdoms and districts. I was one of the few traders at the time who was exposed to the Solarian Kingdom, so I was entrusted with all transactions within that realm, including the wishes of King Jacque."

Antares mentioned that name, and the inkling within my mind is confirmed by the continuation of Izar's voice.

"Your father. The man was weak, a coward. He was scared of you and your sister for what you two children were capable of doing, even as innocent as you were. Disobeying the wishes of your mother, Queen Vega, he put the two Daughters of Solaris in my hands."

Izar isn't exactly addressing me, which would irritate me on any other occasion of this magnitude, but I understand his hesitancy. He feels shame for not acting with more honor and keeping my sister and me within the safety of Solaris. He feels like a bastard for following the orders of his King, instead of his rightful and distinguished Queen. He may have been hardly a teenager when given this task, but he feels regret for it all the same.

"I was expected to kill you both. He told me to drown you in the Lira River and promised me a cessation of my activities in Solaris in return. He said he would no longer call on me and I would be free from the dark magic pursuing the individuals of that kingdom. I took his deal but didn't fulfill my part of it."

"You came to the most obsolete of them all, Sun District," I offer, edging his speech forward even through the disgust repelling through my body—not directed at him but at my father. I never had a paternal figure in my life, Izar not exactly embodying one, so I have nothing to compare my father's immoral behavior to—but even still, I can sense the immense wrong in it.

"Yes." Izar breaths, his shoulder bumping mine softly before he leaves it there, in contact with mine. Heat presses at the juncture connecting and for a moment I can find no resentment for Izar in my body, I only see him as a savior.

"I raised you as my own and surrendered your sister to another family. I was young and didn't know much, but even then, I understood that the two of you being raised together may reap far more harm than good."

"Where is she now?" I finally utter the largest question in my thoughts, the one that has been haunting me the strongest since Antares first referenced it. The idea of my brother being exchanged for a sister is strange, but a concept that I somehow am beginning to welcome, especially knowing that she shares the same eccentricity that I do.

He chuckles, almost by accident based on how he draws the sound back into him so quickly.

"Have you heard the rumor that there's a witch in town?"

I had heard the gossip regarding the suspected witch. When one spends enough time within the market and The Thieves Gate, anything that shouldn't be common knowledge easily becomes just that—especially when that information concerns something... eccentric.

Izar told me what he believed, the fervent opinion that she— Eris—consisted of everything I should stay away from, not because of some unwarranted bias but because of the tragic act she had committed years earlier. Izar painted the story as if she was a murderer who callously channeled the life out of her foster brother's body, but something about that tale doesn't sound right.

If her power is anything like what is beginning to emerge from within me, she must have a limited amount of control over the energy she emits—at least she must have back when she was hardly a teenager. She's spoken about with terrible words, but even the least compassionate facet of my character yearns to give her the benefit of the doubt, especially because I find myself in a similar position as her: lost, feared, and developing a gift that reaches farther than me.

I had urged Izar to accompany me to the address he provided me with, a larger shack close to the market where Eris used to live. He gave me very little clarification on what her current position was, providing me with very clear signs that he wanted nothing less than to be in her proximity, which felt both irritating and understandable. Izar never was one for pushing his limits of comfort, and now being detached from my forced blood relation to him, I'm able to recognize and accept these faults in his behavior.

I said something similar to a goodbye when I left Izar on those steps, in that same position. This night feels precarious, like each word and action I conduct determines vital aspects of my future, and I'm beginning to believe that that notion is true. Nothing felt more right than leaving my home, knowing that there would be very little chance that I would see it again, nor would I see the man that lives within it.

Solaris is guiding me, is what I tell myself as I catch my thoughts bidding farewell to the Sun District I have memorized, breathed in, basked in. What my future entails I have little idea, but now given this greater purpose, no matter how mythical and strange it may seem, resonates with something in the depth of my soul. This feeling seems more tangible than anything else I have encountered.

Two sharp knocks against the door of my destination are all I manage before I bring my fist back to my side. The night seems too still and serene for me to damage even further. Two heartbeats pass before the latch keeping the wooden slab stagnant slides out of place and a single skeptical eye of an elderly woman becomes visible to me.

"...Yes?" Her grave tone almost reaches out and scratches me across my face, that's how much pain she holds in her voice.

"Hello," I quickly respond before my mind discards the predetermined lines of speech I created during my trek to this home. "I'm looking for someone, you may know her. She lives in this home, actually—or, she used to."

Though only half of the woman's face is in my line of sight, even that portion shows me the fall of her previously dubious features into an expression of contempt. Scorn curls the corners of her lips and she releases her hold on the slightly ajar door, or rather puts her strength into closing it. She accomplishes the movement successfully without me trying to slide my foot into the crevice between the door and its frame. I do not wish to elicit more devastating memories to that poor woman's mind, and clearly, Eris does not live in this household any longer.

A turbulent exhale separates my lips as I turn slowly, facing the night-shadowed expanse of land once more. A sense of dismay settles over me as I run a hand through the tangles of hair that escaped my braid and knot my fingers into it. It becomes clear in my mind that the previously brilliant idea to search for Eris in a deserted town was clearly not the easiest course of action.

Or *perhaps* it's most ideal. Eris, known as the woman who killed Leo Delve, would only be able to peacefully visit his grave during a night when she wouldn't be seen and outed.

My palm slams against the door of the woman's home once more, except my motions are more urgent this time, demanding the attention from her that I previously lost.

"I don't want to speak to you," her disgruntled voice echoes through the barrier between us and attempts to communicate a definite ending to our conversation.

"Please, I—I wish to pay my respects to Leo." I stumble upon my words in the rash manner in which they fall from my lips, and I hope that the sincerity is still present.

She goes silent, and I hear her fingers fidgeting with the lock separating us. I gnaw the inside of my cheek as I wait for her to overcome her hesitancy and offer me a response, one that I most likely would not use to pay respects to her son—but rather to speak to the woman who she abhors.

"A little ways back from this home," the woman murmurs so softly that my ear nearly has to touch the doorframe for me to discern the words. "That's where he lies."

"Thank you," I blurt, most likely louder than I should've considering the alarmed yelp the woman emits. "I hope—Uh, have a good night."

I scrunch my nose in a condemning action directed towards myself. I have never been adept at conducting consolatory behavior or speech, so the act of saying a comforting word to the woman when I have no idea of the gravity of her loss feels... foreign.

I circle the home, keeping two fingers on the wooden walls to maintain my direction in the darkness, and upon finding the south-facing side, I notice the area the woman was referring to. It's a single elevated gravestone surrounded by much more flowers and gestures of love than most in Sun District are lucky to have.

Accompanying the raised platform is what I was expecting to see, a single figure leaning her dark head of hair on the curve of the memorial and holding a dried bouquet of flowers in the crook of her elbow.

Even stranger, she seems to surround herself with a haze of glowing light, one that's only noticeable when you contrast it directly with the murk of her background. It seems to emanate from her fingers, all of which are pressed tightly into the skin of her forearms and carve themselves deeper with every passing moment.

I almost feel the urge to laugh—how could one look at this girl and ever believe Sun District created her?

CHAPTER NINE

E R I S

I don't say much to Leo this time. I've found that the more times you speak to someone who is unable to respond, the shorter your once endless monologue of words becomes.

Instead, I allowed the curve of my neck to mold into the slope of Leo's gravestone, imagining for a moment that it's truly his shoulder and I'm leaning on him like how he once leaned on me. He would be tall now, if he were alive, with dark, ruthlessly tangled locks and the large ears he was beginning to develop.

The reverie upholds itself for a moment, just until I sense an energy different from mine entering my surroundings, and immediately every shield I own covers me. The inklings that my fingertips feel are strange, detecting a field of darkness that is different from mine, but maintains the same vigor—or possibly stronger.

"I'm sorry, I didn't mean to frighten you," a female voice says softly as slender fingers pull a cloak down from her eclipsed head, revealing a young woman—beautiful and strangely nostalgic.

I clear my throat, offering the girl a hesitant shake of my head. I even manage the courage to gesture for her to take a seat—both acts that I would never dream of directing towards any other stranger. There's something about this one though that makes her nothing like a newcomer, but instead like an old friend—or rather, enemy.

Maybe it's her appearance. The haphazard locks spiral from her scalp and boast a golden-white hue that nearly matches the color I had for the majority of my life—at least until I took black dye and swept it through my hair. Having light hair in Sun District just gave the townsfolk another anomaly of mine to analyze and exploit. Perhaps this girl just lives a sheltered enough life to where it's not an issue.

I've always taken particular joy in observing an individual's features—it's simply all you can do when you need a grounding element in the process of robbing someone of their pain. For this woman, I'm absorbed in something that feels completely different: her aura.

Her atmosphere feels like shadows and oil seeping through my fingers, she looks like an agile creature whose mind is eons beyond ours—something about the air she wafts towards me contains an element that's already within me.

It should comfort me how familiar she looks and feels, but instead, I feel increasingly cautious as she nears me. She holds some kind of energy that is beginning to encircle mine, challenge it, and it feels like a threat.

"I—uh, have we met before?" I question, returning to my survey of Leo. The gravestone is slightly chipped on one curve.

"No." She settles into the grass mere feet away from me, her fingers immediately attracted to the strands of green and wrenching at them. "But I know what you're feeling right now, I feel it too."

"Do you?" I edge her on, curious as to what infectious thoughts roam her mind and if they truly mimic mine. I wouldn't be surprised if they did, to be truthful. As an individual whose job is to predict and absorb the human mind, I can tell that hers and mine have been interwoven since before this encounter—far before.

"You feel like you've known me for years, since birth." The girl speaks her mind—or, rather *my* mind, considering how accurate her words are. "And you also sense something in me, don't you?"

Her words are my unfortunate last straw before I cannot swallow down the urge any longer. I must determine what it is within her that radiates that power, and how I can quell its desire to encroach on me.

"Could you give me your hand?" I ask her absentmindedly, my mind consumed with the energy she is emitting, all of it pouring directly into my skull and plaguing me with its imprint.

She's hardly fazed by my inquiry, which allows me to realize that she either has heard about my services or she feels this connection as strongly as I do and interprets it as a reason for trust instead of skepticism.

Upon placing my palm against hers, I realize that she is no mundane Sun District human, instead containing more magic within her than possibly even I. Perplexity envelopes me and distinctly appears on my features as I entwine our fingers together, experimenting with the touch to see how much of her consciousness I can discover without even having to employ my power.

She maintains strict barriers over her thoughts and inner emotions, but her soul is so distinctly in the crevice between our hands, baring its insides to me with no hesitancy, as I imagine mine is as well. The sensation goes beyond just merely exploring her mind, it consists of greeting a kind of power that mimics mine. The only difference remains that her energy harbors a certain sin that I don't hold.

I would expect to welcome the unifying notion that follows this realization, but I instead experience something like intimidation and disgust. Even without certain confirmation, I know this girl has a power of her own, and that fact feels terrifying and invalidating. One is not supposed to feel this powerless before someone who is younger in age and experience, but I cannot prevent the feeling.

"I don't know what I can do, exactly," the girl clarifies, answering the inquiry I was nearly about to voice. "I burned someone the other day—with my mere touch. And I feel... inklings of the energy constantly, like—"

"—Like it's haunting you." I finish her sentence with my words and her reaction is a bewildered movement that barely resembles a nod. That's the most intriguing thing about her, how little she feels and shows in her actions.

Humans are emotional creatures, and I'm sure she allows those feelings to be released somewhere within her, but that conduit is clearly not her demeanor. That placid expression has a permanent home upon her features, even as vehement sentiments attempt to tear down that blockade, which is a feat in itself.

"What's your name?" I ask, partially afraid to hear her response. With every new piece of information I receive from her, the more I find myself descending into the unlikely bond between our souls, giving into it even when my mind doesn't consent to that surrender.

"Ceres."

"I'm—"

"I know who you are." Ceres' tone is firm, having lost its former amiable nature somewhere along the transition of her saying her name and me responding to it. "I know much about you actually."

She's beside me but this prompt reversal to a distant manner makes her feel as foreign as she truly is.

"You're not a stranger, are you?" My voice is wavering as I inquire yet another one of the pulsing thoughts in my mind that itch to leave my tongue. *Is there a reason we have the same hair color? Do you feel as disoriented and out of place in Sun District as I do?*

"You're my sister, aren't you?" she counters so quickly that I barely catch the syllables before they dissipate into the space before Leo's grave. Silence envelops us as Ceres and I uphold a steady mutual gaze, mine holding shock and hers almost demanding a response.

She rises quickly, brushing grass-stained palms against her trousers before she gestures into the expanse.

"Come. Let's catch the Astral Festival before the procession continues. I'll explain what I know." Her offer is almost inviting, but it's clear an ulterior motive lies in her agenda. It's distinct that nothing Ceres ever does is purely moral—not even that facade of congeniality at the beginning of our interaction.

She doesn't hold a hand out to me, she simply watches with a tranquil gaze as I conduct a less graceful rise to my feet, silently accepting her request.

The Astral Festival erupts in my vision with an array of color, aroma, and the fusion of various dialects into one incessant hum pressing against my ears, all while my mind flares with that single word.

Solaris. Solaris. Solaris. Solaris.

Ceres seems to be more open to the festival than I would assume her to be, taking the time to streak chalk onto her skin and keeping an ear pointed toward the direction of the Eillyian choir. I assume at that moment that this is her form of saying goodbye to the district that fed and raised her, no matter how poorly of a job it did.

When Ceres voiced her mind to me, pouring out the tumultuous details and intricacies of an ancient kingdom named Solaris, a land she claims she and I belong to, I found no notion of absurdity in my mind. When I carry a gift that labels my character as that of a vengeful witch, it's difficult for me to doubt the mystical elements of our world, considering that I am one

85

myself. For me to question her words would be the same as me doubting the undeniable emotional link between the two of us, the replicated features on our skin that hail from our mutual mother, or the terribly potent feeling of *belonging* that accompanies the name *Solaris*.

Ceres isn't a rash individual. I don't believe she is even capable of acting on something without turning over the decision multiple times in her mind, but this? This is a true demonstration of her impulsivity, but I still find it difficult to blame her.

Yes, she is tearing both of us away from the place we have learned to call home, partially for the sake of saving the life and reputation of a young man she denies an affinity for—but it's a justified decision. What may seem to be a myth to outsiders has become an actuality for Ceres in a matter of days, for me in a matter of minutes. When both of us hear the kingdom's pulsing heartbeat in our eardrums and relish in how the ripples of blood in our veins match the rhythm of Solaris' Lira River, it's simple to surrender our futures so easily.

The choice becomes increasingly uncomplicated when considering how little of a grasp Sun District truly has on our souls. Both of our families have faded into existence, with Ceres seeming to hold very little emotional care for the man she lives with, Izar. I couldn't imagine living like her—maintaining everyone at an arm's length and never revealing a smile, not unless it gave her something in return.

I had told her to say goodbye to Izar when she mentioned him for the final time, urging her to offer some courtesy to the man who acted as the father she was robbed of. Ceres shifted her gaze to me in that instant and something inside me broke and trembled. Embracing her frigid exterior had become the new standard, but her eyes held a fit of undeniable anger that I felt myself cowering under. She said some words after that with a bitter tinge to her speech, but all I could remember was the violence that flickered across her features at that moment.

If I didn't know any better, I would think she had thoughts of killing me.

But rather, she seems to be following another agenda, especially when her movements act like she is enjoying the Astral Festival in all its glory, but her flailing gaze says something quite different.

I follow the pattern of her eyes for a moment, watching as they shift aimlessly over the waving banners of various kingdoms and vibrant hues of the foreigners as they mingle through the labyrinth of tents and people. It's not often that we see such a diverse collection of cultures in one setting, with the Moons engaging in passionate interactions with delegates from Lyra, and Keplers indulging in spices and sweets that they're restricted from in their own home. In terms of appearances, it's almost as if we do not all originate from the same Aerth with Moon District boasting white and black clothing and towering over the remainder of the population and the Galeneans showcasing their leather, skin-tight outfits and frigid sets of eyes. The Europas often seem more welcoming with their fingers wound through their waist-length hair and long capes announcing their presence, a deviation from the feverish state of the Keplers, dressed in blood-red robes with beads of sweat visible on their starkly pale skin.

I always adored the Soleilas. They radiate all notions of warmth and amity with curls of dark hair and permanently etched smiles, though the intrigue of the Europas always manages to shift my attention. I observe as Ceres' gaze fixes on their delegation, eyes hovering over the aura of elegance they cast into the festival with their white dresses and tunics accompanied with golden paint streaked across their foreheads

The kingdoms are beautiful, that is beyond a doubt, but there are fissures in their facade if one looks closely enough. Those inconsistencies lie in the bones of the Keplers seeming unreasonably noticeable, the silent movement of the Europas past the Soleilas without the slightest acknowledgment of the other, the tendency of the Galene delegation to keep one palm indefinitely placed over a certain pocket of their trousers, within which is most certainly a weapon.

As my gaze becomes transfixed in the lives of the kingdoms I could never, until now, be one with, Ceres' direction seems to wander, reaching towards a certain individual.

It's a moment before my vision can reorient itself from the disorienting nature of the Astral Festival and focus on the young man who is now shoulder to shoulder with Ceres, but when I register the locks curling above his eyebrows I know who he is.

"Look at you, Ceres," he congratulates with a dry laugh, half gesturing towards me in the process. "You did my work for me."

She doesn't acknowledge Antares, which I find amusing. She instead wrenches the arms of both of us and pulls our bodies with her into the canopy of a recently unattended tent. The swiftness of the movement shocks me, everything about her shocks me, but I keep my inquiry stifled in the pit of my throat as Ceres addresses Antares with an urgent undertone to her voice.

"I—Well, I've been considering this," she begins, her lips fumbling on words that are surprisingly resolute. "And I have realized that it's not a—a physical trek we're completing, correct?"

Her eyebrows are raised at Antares as her mouth pauses in its monologue to receive confirmation. Halfway into Antares' nod, a fulfilled smile brightens her cheeks and she adopts an expression of gratification, clearly having something clicking into place within her intricate mind.

She whispers the next words, holding a finger to her temple in a sort of naive joy that has never been associated with her before. "It's a psychological journey."

CHAPTER TEN

C E R E S

I began to unravel the issue somewhere along the trek from Leo's grave to the desert where the Astral Festival had paused in its journey. Though I diverted my attention to speaking to Eris for those few minutes, I promptly reversed back to the inquiries that I had been turning over in my mind.

Antares had offered me hints of the truth, no matter how unintentionally. He expressed being in Solaris one morning and by nightfall he was within Sun District, searching for a place to sleep. That fact struck me as strange, considering no kingdom or other entity is within a day's journey to Sun District, especially when one is traveling by foot.

Antares later unraveled his mystery even further by rubbing his temples far too often when one would mention Solaris, or by seeming disoriented at strange times. He even went as far as to suggest that Solaris wasn't something I could find on my own— not without his explicit help.

I'm not exactly sure of how the journey occurs, but I'm confident that it takes place within your subconsciousness, possibly borrowing Solaris' magic to fuel the transition. The conclusion becomes more resolute in my mind as I ponder it further, considering the lost nature of the expansive kingdom and how exactly it had managed to maintain that isolation for such a prolonged time.

Perhaps the land lies in a secluded, undiscovered portion of Aerth, or perhaps it doesn't tangibly exist at all.

"It's not that we don't exist," Antares interjects my thoughts with his own, or rather his facts. "We do—did. Solaris was a corporeal entity for centuries, staying hidden on the accord of its own magic. However, when Queen Vega had children, power was deposited into the heart of Solaris instead of remaining within Vega. It was a death and assumed shift of the crown that occurred too soon and too unnaturally.

"The kingdom was failing; it was clear with the newfound imbalance of magic. When the ruler holds less power than the land, tragic phenomena occur, and Vega was forced to address them. She... she altered the existence of the kingdom—the land was no longer usable, and it was her mistake." Antares winces often as he communicates this tale to us, a knuckle indefinitely rubbing his right temple, and I realize that there's a truth to my prior analysis of him. He *is* a complex individual with a mind that extends beyond him, and it's because he's forced to exist in two realities simultaneously.

Antares continues his words after a short pause, beginning to direct his attention solely towards Eris who seems overwhelmed with bewilderment. "Her powers were associated with the Aerth and its abilities, so she transferred whatever energy she could access from the land and channeled it into our minds, the souls of the Solarian public. The Queen required a safe haven for Solaris and her people while the land was plaguing us all with its potency, and that sanctuary became our minds."

Eris interrupts with a wavering tone. "So, you can just... travel there? Whenever you wish to?" She's extremely frightened, and that's the moment I learn just how fragile she can sometimes be—not as a result of her own weaknesses but because her mind has endured trauma in a way that tears parts of her down with its presence.

"Not exactly." Antares tilts his head, furrowing his eyebrows at the vibrant canopy above him as he fights to grasp the correct verbiage. "It's almost a science, traveling like this. We have to be trained in the discipline in Solaris. It's a safety measure and a prison cell. Villagers don't have the freedom to escape like I do without undergoing extensive education, and if they attempt it—well, the results haven't been great."

"How do you do it?" I ask with slight impatience drifting into my voice. Eris may need additional clarification, but every moment we waste circling the topic endlessly, the more violent the pit of energy in my chest grows. It's trembling to be released—but not here. It searches for the comfort of Solaris, and so do I.

"Sit." Antares gestures toward the cots strewn about the grass below us, and I realize that we're standing within a fortune teller's tent. It's obvious based on the haphazardly stacked piles of cards and the strange scents wafting through the expanse, and it's almost amusing to me that three individuals destined for a land of pure power are finding their way there in an area of false, fabricated magic.

Eris sits on the cushion closest to Antares, taking his hand to help her lower, while I rest on the other side of her. I'm close enough to my sister to sense the anxiety almost radiating from her as she folds her hands under her thighs. She's distraught and unraveling further by the second—how will she survive what Antares is conveying as the most turbulent journey we will experience?

"The transition may be easier for the two of you," Antares begins, sealing his eyelids shut and revoking the amicable demeanor he upheld just seconds before. The man seems to almost curve into himself, distorting his spine so his forehead rests against his folded knees and entangling his torso in a cage created by his arms.

"Replicate my position," Antares whispers, and I do not need another reminder before I tuck my legs under my thighs and lean my torso low, just as Antares had done. Any other version of myself on any other day would regard my current blind obedience with contempt, but I can't help but deliver Antares piles of my trust—especially with this matter.

Eris takes longer, being delayed by her own paranoia, but soon we are how Solaris wishes for us to be, condensing our bodies into lines and sinking into ourselves.

"I'm going to have to warn you of a few… circumstances." Antares' voice is muffled as he speaks into the cloth of his trousers, but the words still burn into my ears. "It's incredibly simple to become lost in your own mind as you follow this process. I know you both have experienced insurmountable trauma and thus have… overwhelming thoughts—so there's much to be distracted by within your minds. You may allow yourself to be led astray, and if that occurs, there's nothing I can do to help you."

I'm nodding softly, expectantly waiting for Antares to proceed past his formalities and plunge the three of us toward the world that my soul believes itself to be a part of, but Eris harbors a completely opposite reaction. I hear the rustling of the fabric of her dress as she presumably lifts her head and addresses Antares.

"What do you mean *lost in our own minds*?"

"Your body will still be here, in this exact position—just as the Solarian's bodies are littered across the native Solarian land. However, your soul will be caught in an endless spiral of emptiness, and your consciousness will fail to tether you to either land. The matter of your mind will neither reach Solaris nor find its way safely back to Sun District—you simply will not exist at all."

Antares speaks his words with a frightening sense of confidence, but the substance of his dialogue is nothing that surprises me. Once determining the method of arriving at Solaris, I had run across all the possibilities of conclusions to my story, and this seems to be by far the best. I have little to lose, and neither does Eris.

"Ceres, Eris." Antares addresses us both and a chill coats my arms when I register the purpose in his voice—which conveys the gravity of our situation far too vividly. "I need you both to imagine a ruby, the size of something you could hold between your fingers."

I mindlessly bow down to his instructions, visualizing that stone against the black expanse of my closed eyelids. It's strange, but I don't question it.

"That stone is the heart of Solaris. It lies in the land which we once called ours and provides the kingdom with a path back to reality. They call it the Jewel of Darkness. We lie within it, our true souls caged in its depths. I hold with me the fragment of the stone that binds me to the corporeal Solaris, but also connects my mind to the fabricated Solaris—as do the both of you." The instant Antares mentions the supposed part of the stone that he claims we have, I feel it against my skin.

Sharp, jagged, and pulsing with power.

My mind lags in thought, flustered by the ability of Antares to place this shard in my palm without notifying me of its presence—and I realize that it occurred when I grasped his hand to wrench him into the tent. The red shard of something so powerful had become invisible as it was pressed into my flesh and my thoughts so violently turned elsewhere.

I can hear Eris' soft gasp as she recognizes this fact too—her exchange most likely occurring when she took Antares' hand to sit atop her pillow.

"Feel the fragment beating against your palm, replicating Solaris' heartbeat. Feel it puncture your skin and draw droplets of blood the same color it is. Recognize that this stone you have a piece of has a piece of you as well, *Daughters of Solaris*."

Even before that final syllable leaves Antares' lips, I succumb to the pressure of the stone, tilting my torso toward the hand that holds it and trembling as the energy of Solaris begins to emanate from the entity and flood my frame. As alive as the rest of my body feels, my mind becomes overwhelmed with a haze that chains me in place. My thoughts no longer encircle my skull, in fact—they're not present at all. In a nearly magnificent reverie of bewilderment and resignation, my consciousness begins to slip from reality—from Sun District.

Moments earlier, I could discern Eris' presence to the left of me. I could hear the shifting of her legs against the fabric of the cushion, the shallow rhythm of her breathing—but now, she's dissipated. Antares' voice is the single grounding factor of this experience, and even that sound is beginning to fade from my mind as he continues to speak.

"Channel that energy—what you are feeling—into something larger than you. Delve into that pit in your stomach that always feels Solaris, wants to return to Solaris—and embrace it. Allow that desire to collect in your heart, seep through the veins of your arm, and congregate in the shard of the stone that is yours." Antares' voice is trembling to the metronome of my heart's palpitations, which most likely means that it is I who is distorting the rhythm of his tone.

His words do more than just press against my ears; they incite the exact hopeless longing for Solaris that he described and that sensation follows the same path he specified. My body no longer feels compressed, but rather elongated in empty space and following a predetermined path towards… *something*.

I attempt to search for Antares, my arms spinning my figure in nauseating circles, but my mind works against my body. It instead leads me deeper into what feels like a conduit of electricity. It's not painful, but I don't exactly know what the intensity can be described as. It's all-consuming in its utter chaos, yet if I focus greatly enough—I feel peace lifting the illness in my mind.

My stomach is voracious in its hunger, aiding in the leaning of my body so the shard of the ruby is shifting from being embedded in my hand to imprinting itself into the skin above my heart. The flesh is stretched thinner than it should be, just as my mind seems far more aimless than it should be.

A haunting susurration begins to tear at the hands I've now placed over my eardrums, inflicting its turbulence on a portion of my soul that I have never bared like this before. I feel exposed, terrified, and possessed by a force that is strengthening the desire within me and selfishly multiplying its energy as I crumble under its weight.

The dark matter I hold in that small pocket of my soul initiates its unraveling, encircling me with its tight cords of restraint as I lift my mouth up to an endless sky. I search for the breath that will calm the unrest brewing within me, but I'm gasping the wrong type of air. I'm inhaling what only deepens this terrible craving for destruction and any grounding element I would have previously curled around has been sucked into a different reality, leaving me alone to bear the force of my demolition.

It's nearly unbearable—what shakes my skull and scoops life from my body. Hands, claws, or branches puncture every square inch of me visible to them, but my blood never falls. Instead, it pools inside of me. I choke on its magnitude, gagging against the wave of crimson that threatens to drown me from the inside, and lucidity becomes an abstract concept in my mind.

I need this to stop. I've lost my way. I need to stop.

I have relinquished control over my own movements long ago, so I know that my hand being led to the sheath against my thigh is not my own work—it is that of Solaris. I know that the curling of my fingers around *Letalis'* handle is not under my mind's jurisdiction, it is Solaris guiding me towards her with a vicious sort of intuition.

It is Solaris that plunges the dagger into the flesh of my stomach, splitting the skin with unnerving ease and releasing that dam of blood with it.

PART TWO

HOME IS NOT A HAVEN

THE KINGDOM OF SOLARIS

Vae, puto deus fio.

(ah, I think I am becoming a god.)

CHAPTER ELEVEN

E R I S

"**W**hen you're nearly vomiting within your own mind with your vision taped shut and palms slick with the blood your fingernails drew, it's difficult to recognize that you're no longer where you used to be.

There's no heavy Sun District heat wrenching at my skin; there's no cushioning under my knees, but those facts take far too long for me to comprehend. In fact, the first string of misguided words that I manage to weave sounds something like, "*Why are we still in Sun District?*"

To that inquiry, I receive an amused chuckle that most likely was released quietly but seems to barrel through my mind with a tremendous volume. It disrupts the inner contents of my body with its strange clarity. In fact, everything I can sense without my vision feels far too lucid for a human to be experiencing.

Though my eyelids are resting, the hints of gold flaring through the spaces of my eyelashes give the effect that I'm bathing in a haze of light. My ears, corrupted only moments earlier by the tension of the journey, are now blessed by the rhythm of chiming bells and distant laughter. *Who is laughing?*

It feels like spring—a season that Sun District rarely was gifted with but arrived often enough for us to memorize its presence. The scents of exotic flowers envelope me, along with a soft chill that surrounds my body—*chill*? Sun District hasn't had a cold breeze for years.

Ceres? Antares? Where are we?

Gradually, elements of my setting that I should have registered immediately begin to shuffle into my consciousness. First, it's my position that I comprehend. I lay, unmoving on a floor of polished wood, head tilted up to breathe in air so clear and rich that it inserts strength into my bones. Then, it's the fact that I have unknowingly drawn my eyelids backward, revealing an array of blurred light and color above me. The growing focus of my vision is slow, but effective in enhancing the structure of a large, intricate mural across the dome-shaped ceiling I'm under.

Pulling at the bundles of my eyelashes that have become sewn together, I wrench my eyes fully open to appease the curiosity brewing in my thoughts. The mural is not simply a painting, it's an experience—a story—depicting six slender figures, all donning hooded robes the color of blood and curving their bodies around the slopes of mountains. Though some lay horizontally, others with their feet raised higher than their heads, they each maintain a clutch on a single candle with an inscription adorning it. The soft creases of their throats are visible as they bow their heads over their flames, making their faces stark against the shadows of their bodies.

The Astral Saints.

"Get up," Antares nearly hisses in my ear, drawing my now unclouded attention to his face. There's something different about him, and it draws a gasp from my throat.

The white locks of his hair are glowing—radiating a light that almost blinds me—and his cheeks are flushed, mimicking the hue of his lips. I thought Antares seemed like an eternally ill individual when I met him, irreversible darkness painting his under eyes, but the current sight of him cannot be attributed to anything short of *life*.

He's still speaking with an urgent tone, grasping my shoulders and wrenching them off the floor between his desperate inhales.

"They can't find us here. We must go *immediately* to the Queen—"

I wish Antares could understand that he is speaking to a woman who only has a quarter of her mind functioning, not to mention my state of being distracted by the scent, the texture, the utter *magic* of this atmosphere.

Why isn't Ceres speaking? I wonder with a slight distaste in my head, squinting my vision to raise it up from the ground and toward the direction of a stifled groan. I'm fairly confident that it's her so I brush Antares' hands off my arms and shift my weight, a dull ache presenting itself during the movement.

"Ceres, are we in Solaris?" I murmur through the fog that besets me. Reaching for her shoulder, I shake the joint softly, waiting for her to sweep her incandescent locks away from her eyes—but she doesn't. She lies stagnant, her limbs contorted and hands considerably lighter than the rest of her skin, trembling under the pressure they exert on a dagger.

A dagger that is buried deep in her torso.

Then, I see the pool of crimson blanketing her body, previously obscured by my notion that she's wearing a cloak of red. The clarity I have been struggling to maintain is now rushing into my mind in its entirety, upending innate elements of myself with its rash nature.

And I scream, even despite Antares' timely lunge to press a hand against my mouth.

It's not a moment later when I realize my terrible mistake.

"Invaders!" a low, foreign voice bellows from a ways behind us, interrupting Antares' attempt to rush us into a shadowed area of the large chamber. He even had his arm around Ceres' bloodied waist, caught in the motion of heaving her onto his shoulder.

Antares curses violently from my side and promptly releases his hold on both of us to direct his energy toward our visitors.

I follow his fuming gaze to glimpse the figures of a group of a dozen men, all clad in golden armor and a multitude of sheaths that all hold the glint of metal. They speak and proceed in our direction in a manner that seems collectively executed and I'm entranced by the sight. When I watch the movement of their limbs in a sharp, simultaneous choreography, all I can think is, *this is Solaris.*

"No!" Antares counters the dominance of the guards with his own as he shields mine and Ceres' bodies. "I bring the daughters."

"The Daughters of Alia do not exist," the frontmost guard says after a perplexed exchange of glances between him and his men.

His tone has adopted something more casual upon addressing Antares, clearly induced by some prior memory, but he and his companions harbor nothing but ignorance towards Ceres and me. Of course, they haven't seen her unconscious body yet—not with Antares shielding it from view and holding me in place to do the same, despite my incessant squirming.

"What the hell are you doing?" I question with urgency, wrenching my arm away from Antares' grip and stumbling back to my knees before Ceres, the Solarians only paces behind me.

"Eris," Antares pleads, caught in a battle between addressing me, running his gaze over Ceres, and attentively observing the guards that are inching closer despite their confusion. "Ceres is not dying, I promise you. I assume she got lost during the trip to Solaris, and the Saints chose to direct her in exchange for a blood sacrifice."

I shake my head with uncertainty, not comprehending how the loss of *this much* of an individual's being is not something to be concerned about, not to mention Antares' casual reference to the Saints which I cannot even begin to unpack. Antares' words continue, untangling the mystery between us and I begin to see how the blood encircling Ceres is not remaining still. It's instead seeping into nonexistent fissures in the marble beneath her, dissipating faster than it arrives.

Once Antares catches the first register of my understanding, he shifts his attention back to the guards, raising his hands in a show of peace. Why he is expected to prove his allegiance to people who clearly know of him, people who share the same white hair and glinting eyes as him, I do not know.

"The Daughters of Alia do not exist," Another man repeats the same phrase but harbors more venom in his rendition. His silver eyes comprehend Ceres' unconsciousness, my distraught figure, and Antares' raging expression painfully slowly. "Who are these girls? Arinel, did you truly take your girlfriends on a field trip out of Solaris, all for your own pleasure?"

A flicker of amusement presents itself in his final sentence as he gestures for the men surrounding him to march forward. They all begin to flank Ceres and me and give minimal warning before I'm wrenched to my feet. In Ceres' case, it's more like her being pulled into a bridal hold with the dagger still embedded within her.

I almost want to tear words from my throat and throw them at the guard holding her, wanting him to toss the weapon so her wound can heal, but he acts like the circumstance is commonplace. I suppose in Solaris, anything concerning violent energy is intrinsically part of the kingdom—even me.

"She's drained; at least bring her to a Healer," Antares pleads, succumbing to the guard that holds his wrists behind his back as his thrashing attempts to break free begin to cease.

Faltering for a moment, the guard considers the state of Ceres and the fact that, *yes*, the Saints are absorbing her blood, but the amount being lost is worth bringing to attention. With a huff in Antares' direction, the man undoes his initial steps and heads toward a smaller hallway leading outwards from the chamber.

With Ceres' presence leaving the setting, it feels as though a weight has shifted from the center of my chest to somewhere in the air above me. The tension of my initial animosity towards her bleeds into the overwhelming need to see her safe and taken care of, resulting in a contradictory state of my mind—a sensation that I'm glad has passed.

With a jolt, the men holding Antares and me force us forward. I blink strands of my fine hair out of my eyes as my troubled gaze finds Antares'. He doesn't seem quite as flustered anymore, surrendering to the energy that encroaches on us both—a mutually welcomed feeling of being wanted, *needed*. Solaris feels incredibly foreign and almost fictitious even as I stand within it, but I cannot deny the warmth and clarity that it injects into my veins.

The men march us out of the large chamber, all following the same stringent, rapid rhythm that forces Antares and me to replicate something similar, all in the favor of not stumbling to the ground. My rising curiosity aids with the swiveling of my head as I observe the entirety of the room we are beginning to exit, appreciating what was invisible to me earlier during my shock.

The interior resembles a spacious lounge, wealth evident in every entity lining the curved walls. Paintings rest on those very surfaces, their colors and artistic excellence glowing and almost bursting past their frames with an authenticity that Sun District chalk drawings cannot rival. The moment my eyes travel upward and find that beguiling mural of the Saints, I know that even if I fail to have a purpose in this kingdom, I will never be forced to relinquish my connection to this culture that I can now call mine.

While I remain consumed in my surroundings, Antares simply looks past the beauty and addresses the man holding him.

"I am Antares Arinel, a soldier of Queen Vega," he says, attempting to turn so he can garner some level of respect in the interaction he is in, but the iron grip on his wrists prevents him from doing so.

The man looks down at Antares upon hearing his words, allowing a flicker of recognition to sweep through his small eyes before he resumes his frigid demeanor. His head shakes firmly and adopts a facade that acts like Antares had never spoken at all. He says nothing.

"I know you," Antares persists, attempting to draw a word from the man. "You were an instructor at the academy."

As Antares remains entrapped in his battle for recognition, I grow bored of his conversation and shift my attention to the new setting that is appearing around me. We proceed down an expansive hallway, just as lavish as the chamber we left and bordered on all sides by portraits of the earlier royalty I've never known.

I try to tell myself that this is all concocted by my mind, by that stone fragment that I now carry in the depths of my sleeve. However, this version of Solaris contains more life and prosperity than anything I've experienced with a sound mind, making it the truest entity I know.

I sense that Antares' initially bothersome questioning has developed into something of an annoyance, and the guard pushing him forward feels it more than anyone.

"Shut it." With a displeased, sharp tone, he cuts off Antares vocalizing his newest thought.

Antares doesn't speak again, to my relief.

Antares and I are all but tossed into a small room, the roughness of our release contrasting with the velvet furnishing and rose-scented air of the interior. Confusion besets me and I turn to Antares—who has already found a comfortable position atop a royal blue loveseat. Upon one mutual glance, he registers my disbelief regarding how the two of us have been treated by these men who call themselves the protectors of this kingdom.

"They don't know who we are," Antares mumbles, shifting his gaze from my standing figure to the ceiling of the room, imprinted with yet another complex depiction. "At least, they don't know who *you* are. I was a soldier here, in Fire Council, before my departure—so they recognize me. I suppose you could justify their behavior as necessary precautions, but it's hardly been three months since I left."

Upon Antares' mention of time, my mouth falters in its movement and a question develops on my tongue—which he quickly predicts.

"Yes, time passes the same way here and in Sun District." Antares chuckles, pulling a fraying end of his sleeve between his fingers and twisting the fabric absentmindedly. "Nearly everything is connected to the conscious world. The weather here matches that of the true Solarian land, our clothes are the same as what we left Sun District in, and you still have the same mind, memories, and soul. You're just harbored within an object now."

Ceres had explained to me Antares' role in Solaris, his surrender to the Order of the Grim, his position as a royal soldier, and his promise to the Queen—my mother—to procure her daughters from the assumed sanctuary we had grown up in. I know nearly everything about Antares that is to be known, Ceres having spared very little to the imagination in her desperate attempt to transfer her knowledge of Solaris to me—and yet, this man remains an enigma of sorts.

How is an eighteen-year-old trusted with the task of delivering the royal daughters and held to such high regard amongst royalty—at least before he left?

What is the story behind the sword flattened to his back, the one that glints with a reflection of light every time he turns?

Why do his appearance and dialect live within Solaris, and yet the corners of his lips curve downwards in distaste while being here?

I'm older than the man by at least three years but beside him, I feel strangely young and artless in my existence. He lives almost poetically, presenting all his thoughts upon his face and nearly flaunting their presence to people like me who fail to bear complex emotion without crumbling under its weight. The trauma that rattles my mind during the night most likely is equivalent to

108

what he holds in the depths of himself, and yet I feel that he has exploited that darkness for his own growth while I have succumbed to mine.

Antares' transparency is largely evident at this moment, having discarded the frustrated, talkative demeanor he displayed earlier and instead conceding to what seems like uneasiness. Out of the corner of my eye, his fingers aimlessly weave themselves together, pulling at each other relentlessly.

I recognize that this could be my opportunity to prove that I am not simply a woman who falters upon every inconvenience but rather someone that holds a remarkable skill within her—as corrupt as it is. Thinking primarily out of a need for redemption instead of my usual practicality, I shift into a seat beside Antares and allow my shoulder to brush his.

Invigorated by that brief contact, I practice what I have memorized—stretching my soul to his and entangling the two entities. My mind follows the predetermined path that I have learned to perfect, wrenching knots of anxious energy from the hollows of Antares' interior and swallowing them promptly, allowing those thoughts very little exposure to the Solarian atmosphere.

Conducting the exercise affects me differently in Solaris than it did in Sun District. The fingers that quivered only days earlier, now rest comfortably in the act—though a burning ache still sears my skull and threatens to expand larger as I continue. I still must press my tongue into the edges of my teeth to stifle a grunt of pain but when I turn to Antares, this all feels nearly worth the trouble.

His eyes have widened to their full capacity and sway between my face and where our shoulders brushed, conveying his blossoming shock in the action. I had delivered Antares a mitigated offering of what I can truly accomplish, and his reaction proves my power—my influence. A part of me cherishes that validation with open arms.

"You did that?" Antares questions, following the furrowing of his eyebrows. I know that he comprehends the various contradictions in his inquiry, beginning with the fact that he has learned much about the gift I possess from both my mother and Ceres, and ending with him witnessing my work, so I only respond with a simple nod.

"That's an incredible talent," Antares breathes, shaking his head in disbelief as he begins to draw into himself and examine the thoughts I have just conjured in his mind.

"It is," an unfeeling female tone says into the expanse, the voice radiating from the ajar entrance to the room. I feel almost apprehensive to turn my gaze, for the voice resembles Ceres' so closely that I feel compelled to believe that it is her.

Like mother, like daughter, I suppose.

CHAPTER TWELVE

C E R E S

"*D*on't hit me this time," a female voice mutters, cautiousness evident in her tone and the delicacy with which she lifts the cloth of my shirt. *Lifts* isn't the right word, actually. It's more like she peels it away, considering the inability of the blood coating my torso to dry, remaining in its damp, adherent state.

I've trained my pain tolerance to be higher than most, but I can't help the sting that bursts from the wound when it meets the air. I hiss and tear my eyes open, attempting to adjust my vision to my surroundings—even though the moment I retained my consciousness, I knew where I was.

It would have been difficult for me to have not recognized this setting the second I was thrown into it, not when I've been breathing and absorbing bits of this kingdom my entire life. The sheer realization of understanding that I was within Solaris, that every coat of tension that I've worn in Sun District had been lifted, was enough for me to disregard the blade plunged through my stomach. I was bleeding, pouring handfuls of myself out onto the floor as I was carried to this cot, but none of that bore anything of consequence to me—not when this newfound consolation was rocking me to sleep.

But now that I've tasted this air and memorized the scent of it, I've been given an opportunity to truly feel what I did to myself to arrive here—or what the Saints coerced me to do, according to the Healer at my side.

Her fingers place soft touches on the skin of my stomach while winding a long bandage around my waist. She's so delicate with her movements that I hardly register her presence, instead being focused on the sight of *Letalis* glinting from her lap, having been removed from my body moments earlier while I drifted under a sedation spell. I feel an urge to take the dagger and protect it within my sheath—her home—but I know the instant I exert myself, the very adamant Healer will protest.

"That's better," she says, referring to my now tightly encased torso.

Still reeling from a deeply rooted cramp in my stomach, I sink into the mattress below me and relish in its softness—a dramatic shift from the threadbare cot I slept on in Sun District. My vision fails to stay focused on the plants hanging from the ceiling of the room—as the Healer advised me to do—but instead flicks around my surroundings: the vials of rosemary and mint, the pillows strewn about the wooden paneling, the young woman observing me attentively as I avoid her eye contact.

"I'm Sidra," she offers in an attempt to ease open the barricaded demeanor I am presenting to her.

"Ceres," I mumble in response, courtesy of the rough lining coating the inside of my throat. I would assume that my vocal cords have worn themselves out from hours of screaming, but I can't imagine where it would be that I strained my voice—other than that endless canal of emptiness that brought me to Solaris. I internally laugh as I realize that my time in this kingdom has begun to amount to me attributing every inconvenience of mine to that terrible journey from Sun District.

"That's a beautiful name. Do you know what it means?" Sidra's lips curve into a smile containing such genuine warmth that I want to pocket the sight, as much as I resent her for the unburdened aura she exudes.

I scour my memory for the origin of my name, knowing that I was informed of it sometime in the past. "A Roman goddess, I believe. A deity from the Olden Ages."

Sidra nods softly, and the ease at which she conducts the action makes me realize that her asking me for my knowledge was merely a formality. She knows a lot more than I gave her credit for.

"My knowledge of Ceres more concerns the planet—dwarf—that was named after the Roman goddess," Sidra begins, and her sentences incite curiosity in me. Within Sun District, we had little familiarity with astronomy and the night sky, being barred from accessing the magic or technology that would permit us to look deeper into the black abyss beyond us. Judging from my impression of Solaris, in addition to the enchantments that seem to be taking place within this healing room, there is more than enough energy available to direct towards what is beyond Aerth.

"As a Healer, I contain a form of magic within me—a pulsing energy that connects me to Aerth, and every entity beyond it." Sidra waves a hand in the direction of a collection of parchment and novels stacked in the corner of the room, all emitting dust and the scent of ancient literature. "It is similar to what the Queen is gifted with, but to a lesser degree. I'm a Healer, meaning I draw my powers from the universe that existed during the Olden Ages—the nature that has fallen extinct but still lives on within witchcraft."

Her casual mention of witchcraft nearly frightens me, my Sun District roots prevailing, and the shields around my emotions that I had slowly begun to relinquish revert to their original position promptly. Sidra notices my reaction with a piercing attentiveness to her stare and a flash of panic crosses her features, though it is quickly covered by one of her smiles.

"I work with all that is good in the world: light, minerals, the interstellar and natural world. I harness this energy and focus it on my patient and their festering wounds, and I complete my job in that manner. In fact," I follow Sidra's hovering gaze to the now concealed puncture in my skin and I absentmindedly pull down the remainder of my shirt so that the bandage is nearly covered, "it helped you."

"Why are you telling me this?" My tone can be interpreted as rude, especially when considering the turn of my body away from Sidra and my refusal to make eye contact any longer. My animosity towards communicating with an individual without hostility confounds me as well, but I allow this tendency to flourish anyway—it being the only grounding connection to the persona I'm clinging onto.

"Because Antares informed me of what you and your sister can do—the similarities of your abilities with that of your mother's. I know of the true reason your father sent the both of you away." Sidra's voice is hardly a whisper, edging on the corners of my mind with a dull blade. I notice how fixated her eyes are on me as she speaks, a quality that most would consider polite, but I regard with suspicion. It's almost as if she refuses to let me out of her sight. "You need to know that this magic that you have doesn't make you an abomination. Aerth worships the Saints, and we are their descendants. That must count for something."

As unwilling as I am to accept Sidra's words, I must recognize the truth behind them and the relief they bring to my mind. I've seen Eris suffer the wrath of a world terrified of her and I've existed as the victim of Izar's relentless shaming, and here is a woman who has the gift of magic as well—but thrives with it. It's nearly comforting.

"Thank you," I whisper. "I-I appreciate it."

Sidra notices the strained quality of my voice and abruptly turns to find a pale liquid on the bedside table. She holds it out to me with an expectant raise of her eyebrows and I find myself surprisingly inclined to trust her. "Here. Drink this."

My fingers timidly grasp the vial and lift it to lips that are cracked beyond belief, gently tipping the potion onto my tongue. Like all things regarding magic, the effect is seemingly instantaneous and rushes an alleviating coolness down my throat, delivering a relief that I never want to pull away from. That's the addicting consequence of my relationship with magic, I've learned. The more exposure I have to the compulsion of our abilities, the larger my affinity for them grows.

When the waves of medicinal bliss begin to ease, I place the vial back onto the table and feel Sidra's gaze following the movement. The air between the two of us turns silent, suspended in between the realms of awkwardness and comfort, but I enjoy the serenity for a moment. I could never find a quiet time in Sun District. I couldn't find much of anything in Sun District, and suddenly being deposited in a place where I assume I'm royalty somehow doesn't do much to change the fact that I still have nothing.

The Healer to my side works for the Queen, this kingdom belongs to the Queen, hell—even *Antares* is chained in an eternal servitude for the Queen. I suppose I'm in debt to her as well for calling me back.

Upon the mention of his name in my thoughts, my interest piques. "Where's Antares?" I question, feeling a sense of instability after having spent the entirety of the previous day with him, learning from him, and depending on him for my safety.

"He's speaking to the Queen. The servants say it sounds tense," Sidra replies, hiding a soft laugh under her breath as she moves from my side to wipe her hands with a washcloth.

"Oh," I breathe, considering the thought of the two of them being caught in a conversation—no, argument. I nearly wince out of empathy for Antares. I don't know how he can conduct a civilized conversation with my mother when she essentially killed his family and robbed him of his freedom.

She *is* my family, which should stimulate a desire to meet her, but the longer I lay within her proximity, the more I discern that my attraction towards Solaris concerns the power and mythical energy that lies in this world, not her.

Sidra has left my side and now attends to the items strewn about the small room, which I now realize doubles as her living quarters and workspace. *Oh*, I think as I look down at the cot I've been bleeding into for the past hour. *Is this where she sleeps?*

Sidra pays little regard to her bloodstained mattress, however, either indicating that she truly does not care about where she sleeps, or she changes out the furniture between every visitor of hers. Whichever it is, it highlights the fact that in such an opulent palace, the servants, Healers, and soldiers live in circumstances not much more elevated than what one could find in Sun District.

With those unsettling thoughts still floating in my temples, I watch Sidra's actions as she jostles around containers, uncorks them, and spills the liquids into each other. It seems like a disorderly practice, but when I pass my gaze over her once more, I see that there's more of a science to her than one would assume.

Sidra's movements are accompanied by a rushed string of words mumbled under her breath—some kind of spell or incantation. Upon her swallowing those sentences back into her throat, the liquids in her hands begin to swirl and upend themselves within their vials, completely independent of her touch.

"Your story is intriguing," Sidra voices, interrupting my analysis of her behavior and forcing me to return my attention back to our conversation. "I mean, I always knew there was a chance that Queen Vega had children. People started assuming after Mensa Jacque disappeared from our sight and the Queen's forbidden pregnancies seemed to be both suddenly terminated with no formal announcement of a child."

"Does the public truly know that little?" I ask with what I assume is genuine shock, but I notice that my delivery contains a little more amusement than I intended. Sidra doesn't seem offended, however. She hardly even perceives the bite to my words, and I find that this quality is something I am beginning to enjoy about her.

"I live in this palace and I can hardly put the pieces together." Sidra pushes strands of her light locks away from her forehead with a heavy breath before sending me an exasperated look. "But, Antares had kept me updated before he left Solaris—the two of us grew up close so I expected him to. I remember the day the Queen had informed him of his strange task of collecting you both from Sun District. The man had stumbled into this room certain that he was going to die in the process. I'm not joking—the poor soul was considering writing a will solely for the possession of his sword."

The corners of my eyes crinkle as my unalloyed laughter erupts into the room, clearly shocking Sidra with its legitimacy. She hesitantly shares a glance with me before allowing her youthful giggles to accompany my amusement, and for this instant in time, we both hold the same mirth within us. Hers fades faster than mine does, though.

Upon remembering that I too have a weapon like Antares', Sidra's eyes move to *Letalis*, who has gravitated from the bedside table to my right hand. The metal is clenched between my red-tinted fingers as my thumb lovingly traces the inscription of her name, as I have done countless times before. If fingerprints could be embedded within objects, this dagger would hold all of mine.

"Is that what you... fight with?" Sidra inquires with reluctance distorting the traditionally high-set state of her eyebrows. She's confused, which greets me with surprise. Yet another finding—the people of Solaris have little exposure to warfare. I couldn't expect much differently, I suppose, not when Solaris exists in a blissful, elementary facet of our minds that discards all notions of ruin.

"Yes." I wield *Letalis* between my thumb and index finger and spin the blade with ease, retracing a familiar routine that I would progress through before I started practicing with her. "Her name is *Letalis*—I assume she's the one who got me here."

"What do you mean?"

I sigh, lifting my chin from its position of being plastered to my chest and allowing my hair to pillow my head as I lean backward. "*Letalis* has defined my existence since I can remember. I never had much in Sun District; I wasn't living in the most... supportive environment. And still, I had this weapon that thought in unison with my mind and mirrored my movements as if it was another body part of mine. It gave me a true passion— fighting—which later became a release for me."

Sidra's silence speaks volumes. Though she sits a ways away from me and my eye line falls above her figure, she has never seemed closer or more cautious of my vulnerability. I have to dig my fingers into the sheets underneath me, pressing the pristine, white fabric into my nails to calm the protests of my pounding heart that condemn such an honest dialogue. I've never said this much to anyone.

"And then later," I find myself continuing, "as I was attempting to find my way to Solaris, I got lost. I was suspended in a world I did not wish to be in, and it was *Letalis* that redirected my mind—or motivated another power to aid me."

"It's always been *Letalis*, hasn't it?" Sidra brushes her palms against a dress streaked with dust and stands so there's no separation of space parting our gazes. "Not a person, nor a family, but your weapon." She doesn't speak in a matter-of-fact manner, as her words may suggest, but rather is slow and calculating with her tone. She's trying to figure something out about me, and I hope my interpretation of her good intentions is correct.

I contemplate her words for a moment, repeating them in my mind until I cannot deny their truth any longer. She's right— Letalis is the closest thing I have to anything resembling love, and I'm glad that it's her in my heart rather than anyone else.

The bite I have over my lip becomes increasingly tense as I gravitate toward what the doorman beside me is gesturing to—a doorless opening to a room embellished with velvet and golden accents.

It had been several hours since Sidra and I conversed in her quarters, my eyes eventually giving out on me and falling closed, only to be awakened by a servant informing me of the Queen's request for my presence in the drawing room. Sidra had put up an argument, referring to the fresh wound that was painting my stomach, but my curiosity about my mother motivated her into conceding the debate.

I'm now regretting not agreeing with Sidra, because yes, my injury douses my torso in flames with every movement of mine, but the intimidation of standing mere feet away from my mother may be more displeasing.

As I peer into the drawing room, I see that it's not one woman within those walls, but two. The first is donning black hair and a short frame—Eris—and to her side is a taller figure whose crown nearly allows her head to touch the sloped ceiling. Her figure is enveloped in rich robes of fabric that I've never been exposed to in Sun District, the kind that glints and emits a soft glow when the Sun casts its rays on it. Bundles of white hair cascade from her scalp in perfectly arranged waves, contrasting with the dark skin of her only partially visible face. Her posture is immaculate, her crown seems to be an essential part of her frame, and the upturned tilt of her narrow chin makes it so that all before her are forced into the position of her subject.

The Queen is lovely—and disturbingly dominant.

Eris angles her head upon hearing my voice and her expression wipes away to blankness once her gaze finds mine. I would've expected her to smile or show a sign that she's glad to see a familiar face, but her survey of me is nothing warmer than a pursing of her lips that attracts the attention of the Queen. In a slow, terribly dramatic movement, Vega follows Eris' gaze to my figure, and her lips part slightly.

"I'll be taking my leave, mother," Eris says with sudden haste, splitting the silence into fragments as she attempts to excuse herself from what seems to be a tense exchange of words. Before she can take more than a step, however, Vega's words freeze her limbs in place.

"I did not give you the permission to do so."

Her voice is cold and absent of emotion or purpose, rather acting like a vessel that merely transports words from her mental dictionary. Some aspects of her speech remind me of my own— the depth of her tone, the pronunciation of her 'o's'.

Apprehension overwhelms Eris' features as she throws a cowering glance over her shoulder at the Queen, evidently regretting her rash getaway. It's several moments before Vega continues speaking, this time finding my gaze and holding it as she reprimands Eris.

"Leave, Eris. The moment you relinquish your ability to think for yourself is the moment I will be ashamed to call you my daughter." Vega's tone is definite as she sends her daughter away. Upon Eris hurriedly brushing past me, I can sense the panic disrupting her breathing and the glaze developing over her eyes. I feel sympathy for a moment, but that emotion quickly shifts to pity as I watch my sister get torn down so easily by just a handful of harsh words—that are all true.

With Eris' presence dissipating behind me, it is just my mother within the room. She's not quite facing me but the tilt of her shoulders in my direction seems to be enough of an invite. I gradually proceed towards her, unknowing of how one acts before royalty and frankly not caring enough to concern myself with the struggle.

I pause at her side, recognizing that though my eyes are planted on her, she remains fixated on something above me. I would turn to see what it is that enraptures her attention if this was any other person, but I predict that my mother is enough like me for me to know that she feels too vulnerable with eye contact.

"I'm Ceres," I mention, my voice dripping with a faux tone of informality.

"I know who you are." She manages to acknowledge my presence with a faint nod of her head as her fingers reach out for a lock of my hair—an action that feels uncharacteristic but intriguing in my eyes. Vega's slender fingers lightly press strands of mine against her own skin and I stand with a strange reassurance as she observes the color, the same white-gold hue as her locks. She lacked that similarity with Eris' dyed hair— perhaps that's why I almost suspect a smile curving on my mother's lips, but the expression vanishes before I can confirm its arrival.

"Do you have anything to say to me?" I inquire after Vega's silence stretches beyond pure thought. "You did call me here to speak to me, even considering my injury—"

"Like hell it's an injury," my mother counters with ease, even allowing a scoff to accompany her words as she shakes her head. "Don't kid yourself or me. You've experienced far worse than to consider this anything more than an inconvenience."

I'm taken aback by her blatant choice of words, conveying a message that is in fact true—but she shouldn't be able to know that it is true. I frown as I survey my mother and notice the eyes that are now trained on mine, having discarded their earlier reservations once I uttered my first word.

"I didn't want to speak to you as much as I wanted to see you," the Queen concedes, gradually finding her way back to the direction I am attempting to steer this conversation towards— even as I itch to be anywhere but in her presence. The woman has not displayed her hostility forthright to me, so I fear my discomfort has nothing to do with my negative perception of her—but rather the fact that she reminds me so much of myself. Her height, her appearance, her voice, the bite behind her words, the way her features fall into an impenetrable mask. Anyone could sense the likeness.

"Well, you see me now." Exasperation inches into my sentence, revealing my growing irritation at my mother's ability to dodge the unanswered questions that are clearly suspended between us. "Suns, you know a competent mother would offer me an explanation? Maybe she'd throw in an apology for discarding her daughters for 16 years—and don't offer the excuse that you didn't know where Eris and I were. I have learned enough from Antares to know that there's nothing that avoids your attention in this kingdom."

I recognize that my unabashed disrespect is not concealed in the slightest with the exigency that fills the spaces between my words, and yet my mother seems unphased, still upholding that expression of restraint. Her painted lips do not quiver, her eyebrows are firmly set without so much as a quirk, and her eyes remain as narrow slits that just barely display her silver irises.

"I could say that I searched tirelessly for the past 16 years; I could say that I drained the last droplets of the effort I could give and devoted those years to you and your sister—but I didn't." The honesty that I demand from those I meet is not convenient for me at this moment. In fact, it edges on the border of hurtful. "I was manipulated by the thoughts of some in this kingdom. I subscribed to the freedom of a family-less rule for 15 years, but that relief began with fade with time. I felt you, constantly. Some nights I could hear your footsteps on the Aerth, and then those of your sister. Yours were lighter; it told me that you were agile. I knew you took that painful environment Mensa subjected you to and channeled it into the anger that fuels your fight, and I was proud of you for it."

It's perplexing how much she knows even considering her absence and admitting that fact initiates the dissolving of a barrier in my mind, the one that shields the innate respect I have for my mother.

"I knew where you were for a year before I decided to act on my desire to find you. It was easier for me to avoid the prospect of a family—even while I yearned for the version of Solaris that would hold your dark magic. I did not think I would be able to trust myself with a kingdom if I was plagued with the love and distraction that children bring." Vega speaks with a shadowed undertone of shame, but the resolute nature of her voice overwhelms that indication. She speaks like a mother without regrets, and instead of condemning her for it, I understand.

My mother has nothing ethical within her. She holds no moral compass that guides her towards love and loyalty and experiences no compulsion to kiss her daughters goodnight and bid her kingdom a good morning. She's unconditionally a fighter and eternally values her soul and the influence she exerts above the fleeting gratification of compassion. I can't despise her for it; I can't look at her with distaste—not when I consider her situation and realize that I would have done nothing differently.

I carry no virtue that she does not have; I hold nothing within myself that can characterize my heart as honorable, and I've recognized that over the past few days—just as my mother had 16 years ago.

At this moment, I understand the gravity of having a mother and I believe myself to be experiencing the sensation in its entirety. Vega may be a villain in Antares' eyes and a threat in my mind, but my heart aches to bond with her, with the empty cavity where her soul should be.

CHAPTER THIRTEEN

A N T A R E S

*M*y heart speeds its rhythm when I'm here and cherishes the life the kingdom presses into it, and then watches in silence as it drains that vitality just as easily. The intimate surroundings of the palace and town resurface fond memories in my mind, but the aftertaste of their presence is connected to the grim experiences that occurred here. Every room and hallway that I stumble past in this bittersweet reverie attaches me to a piece of the life I had here in Solaris before I left. Nine years were spent within these palace walls, during which a younger version of me struggled to find some sort of redemption or satisfaction that would overwhelm the urge to avenge my parents' deaths—and I never found that closure.

As I stood before my Queen with Eris at my side only hours earlier, I enveloped myself with this desire and allowed my vulnerable expression to convey it all to her. She's powerful and exudes a talent for leadership that many say is unparalleled in the entirety of Aerth, and yet my fingers sought *Occisor's* blade. I wanted nothing more than to rob her body of its heartbeats with as little hesitation as she harbored when she ordered my parents' deaths.

My desperate inquiry as to why she did it left my tongue as well, spiraling out of my mouth after years of stifling it down in the favor of not meeting a fate similar to my parents. *What callous reasoning could she have had to condemn two innocent Solarians, to condemn a young boy to such a fate?*

"You are lucky you are not the same breed as them, Arinel. Otherwise, your circumstances may have been much different," she had said simply, her words too vague for me to digest and a silent warning present in her eyes.

She turned her attention to her oldest daughter at that moment, regarding her with a similar demeanor that offered Eris none of the benefits that blood relation should bring.

As I've always done during my moments of unrest, I now choose to proceed to the soldier's quarters—an establishment nurturing all the same violent inclinations as the Thieves Gate but exercising them with far more artistic pleasure and disciplined by the Solarian commitment of protection.

It's evident that there's no true threat to Solaris—not with the abundance of magical protections that protect our territory and especially not when we're supported by minds instead of land—but the factions that had formed centuries ago still exist out of tradition. The Councils that persist amongst us soldiers are not present out of necessity but as a result of loyalty to the Olden Ages where war was more of a constant than peace. We could dismantle Solaris' army, but I believe too many of us within these walls live for its existence. Entering the building rushes the scent of sawdust and metal into our lungs, and the sensation burns as it always does, flaring its magic-fueled atmosphere into our bodies. Everything in Solaris maintains this feeling, except it is magnified ten-fold under this roof.

Red and gold flames suspended in the air below the ceiling accompany me as I move through the corridor that holds all my footprints. As I grow closer to the main arena, a collection of voices fills my ears, either interrupted by raspy laughter or pained grunts as bodies are knocked to the floor. Recognition sparks in my mind when I register the self-assured hubris radiating from the Solarian soldiers, but their names slip through my fingers as if I was separated from this setting for years instead of weeks.

During the first few moments of traversing the arena, I'm blessed with the gift of not being discovered yet and I relish in my anonymity. I would prefer it if it were always this uncomplicated between me and the rest of the Solarian soldiers, but the familiar issue consistently finds a way to reveal itself—this time in the form of Vesper Qualtin.

I feel the man's gaze far before he chooses to display his presence in that expressive, overly self-important manner of his, and being the object of his attention is always an unwelcome experience. For years the man and I have been caught in a persisting battle regarding the open position where the leader of Fire Council should stand—the only Council which still has not been able to choose a captain with a fervent enough passion to excel beyond the others. The skirmishes for leadership between me and Qualtin have consistently ended in draws or mutual forfeits—and Fire Council falls in repute each day a captain is withheld from it.

Qualtin's body behind mine is a burning reminder of what was in Solaris before I departed—a desire for a position that I assume will fill the void in my stomach that reminds me of my losses, but only throws me deeper into this pattern. Within Solaris, I no longer fight for enrichment, but rather for the purpose of hurting others to the degree where I feel stronger than I did when I watched my parents being killed.

"Antares Arinel, *quantum tempus.*" I feel Qualtin's hand firmly grip my shoulder as he spins my body and regards me with a false proclamation of friendship.

We have not seen you for a while.

"*Adsum.*"

I am here.

I know that my true sentiments will be distinctly visible across my face, courtesy of my blatant displays of emotion, so I overlook the formality of plastering a smile on my lips. Qualtin's amiable demeanor falls as soon as he recognizes my lack of one and he wastes no time releasing a rushed inquiry into my ears.

"Can you still fight?" A daring gleam presents itself within the depths of his silver eyes—eyes that I've made bleed before. He wouldn't approach the topic like this in an earlier circumstance, not when he knows that giving me a warning for an imminent brawl would only fuel me further—no, this is calculated. Perhaps Qualtin believes seven weeks away from Solaris has robbed my joints of their talent, perhaps he considers *Occisor* to be lost and discarded during my journey, or perhaps he truly does have a death wish.

A simple nod of my chin is enough for Qualtin to heave me onto the fighting platform he already stands within, attracting the attention of dozens who have lacked exposure to fights as ardent as ours generally are. The soldiers inch closer, their blades and opponents forgotten as their curiosity becomes enraptured in the unsheathing of Qualtin's sword and the reveal of *Occisor* from the inside of my shirt. I've had the weapon all along, having plastered him to my back with *Periculo* the moment Ceres notified me to meet her at the Astral Festival, and nothing makes me happier about that decision than the impending nature of this fight. As confident as I have grown to be in my abilities, I lack the prowess to defeat a fighter as astute as Qualtin without the weapon that fuels my motive for the fight.

"Fight!"

The voices surrounding us begin to yell, woven in a complex array of tones that makes me feel for a moment that *this* is Solaris. Not the princesses and their absent mother camouflaged as an authoritarian queen, not the people in the town that fall to bizarre, unexpected diseases that never existed before the Queen claimed they did, but *this*. The unavoidable inclination to fight, to watch an art form in its purest state—as destructive as its agenda might be—is the essence of what I wish Solaris would revert back to.

What is a kingdom if it doesn't resonate with the culture that the people tore their souls apart for?

Like all things regarding the terribly formulaic fabric of Solarian life, my mind is set with predictions for Qualtin's initial move. I have observed his practices enough to know that he may be intuitive in the manner with which he moves and fights—but just like every human in this chamber, he maintains his innate indicators.

The man is about to conduct that painfully obvious swipe of his sword against my shoulder blade when the movement is punctuated by the shout of a woman from the arena's entrance. Her voice is young, yet her body wears the suit of a servant, which tells me that she is yet another victim of Vega's unrelenting desire to multiply those under her control—but that's not the most surprising part of her arrival. The enigma lies in her words.

"The Queen orders that this fight is suspended indefinitely. She commands that the Councils obey her declaration of the new Fire Council captain, a binding decree that contains a lifelong commitment."

My gaze finds Qualtin's with alarm, and for a fleeting instant, the two of us share the same wave of apprehension and bewilderment regarding the Queen's sudden involvement. The Councils are the only portion of Solaris' society that she lacks jurisdiction over, at least until the rare circumstance that we become her army—but that fate has not arrived.

"The new Fire Council leader is to be Antares Arinel."

And it feels wrong—not because I have relinquished my need for the position, but because it was *her* who stole the one thing I had control over and gifted it to me as if I could not retrieve it myself.

Occisor now feels like a prop in my grip and I sense the air around me grow bitter as if the Queen herself is responding to my dissatisfaction. I hope that her Aerthen power stretches far enough to recognize the fire burning in the pit of my stomach—the very same flame that sparked nine years ago.

CHAPTER FOURTEEN

C E R E S

*M*y pupils widen with a childlike astonishment upon finding my reflection and observing the edges and folds of my gown. The red fabric curves around my torso and hips in a manner that is both suffocating and liberating at the same time—nowhere in Sun District could one find clothing that encases you in wealth and expresses your royal status to all that are in your presence.

Taurus, my tailor, doesn't believe so, however. Though I don't see what aspect of the gown still requires adjustments, I'm still subjected to the intense scrutinization of him at my feet, running thin layers of fabric over his fingers as he struggles to perfect a seam that already runs flawlessly. The atmosphere of my room is filled with his irritated grunts and my sighs of discomfort, and I want nothing more than to collapse onto the plush loveseat to my side.

Upon leaving Vega earlier this morning, I wasn't given much freedom to explore the palace, nor was I able to see familiar faces—Eris locking herself away in her room and Antares departing to the soldier's quarters almost immediately. Instead, I was expected to spend hours undergoing fittings and introductions—as if my 16 years of absence meant nothing and I

129

must promptly be descended into the royal lifestyle to keep Solaris functioning. It's not entirely unfortunate having to exist in this state of urgency and compliance—I have people to think for me, servants to clothe me, a lavish bedroom holding all the entities of wealth that I believed myself too separated from to deserve.

Taurus had skipped the cumbersome etiquette, however, instead chastising me with an irked tone the moment he arrived in my room. Within a matter of minutes, the man flushed a delicate, rosy hue into my skin and livened the hollows of my face enough for me to resemble a native of Solaris. Beyond that, golden powder is now sprinkled atop my cheekbones, eyelids, nose, and all the other crevices of my appearance that the sunlight can touch, wrapping me in a constant glow which imitates that of my mother's.

He seems to be taking great pain to ensure my appearance is up to Solaris' standards, and I fear that it is because I am not proceeding towards a mundane family dinner, but instead one concerning politics and tense questioning. Earlier, I had asked Taurus what truly occurs during these dinners, and the man only offered me a perplexed expression, insinuating that he was astounded that I spoke to him at all. The strange occurrence begged the question of how removed from royal affairs these palace workers truly are—even while they live in the proximity of the Queen.

"It's getting late, we must go." Taurus finally concedes his escalating battle with the dress and presses it flat against my legs. With a huff, he surveys the hem of the gown, observing my motions intently as I sweep the fabric against the carpeting. His gaze then traverses up to my face and his previous uncertainty is replaced by a wave of satisfaction.

"You truly are beautiful," Taurus says in his absentminded tone that I've grown used to, and he offers the crook of his arm to me in the motion of a diligent practice. My gaze is fixated on his elbow, bewildered by the action and attempting to deduce if this was a challenge, if he wished to jab me in the stomach. His exasperated expression tells otherwise.

"Am I expected to take your arm?" I ask with a gradually growing confusion settling over me, which promptly develops into vexation when Taurus releases a hearty laugh of disbelief. He doesn't quite respond to my inquiry, which forces me to simply proceed with my expectation and loop my arm through his.

Taurus still seems to be lost in thoughts of my dress as he leads me in the direction of the ground-level dining hall, a path that requires me to descend a steep flight of stairs in heels that are already bringing forth calluses. I take this opportunity to survey my surroundings while Taurus seems incredibly uninterested in where my gaze passes.

It's perplexing how different the main stairwell and royalty sectors are from the area of the palace where I spent most of my day. As grand as it is, where we first landed is designated for servants and soldiers—essentially a place where communication occurs and work is done. The royal sector is an even greater level of regal, and it begins to make sense why only royalty and select palace workers can even breathe this air.

The ceilings of the palace interior soar higher than I can fathom, and the hallways are great and expansive, downed in a pristine, white crystal that summons an ache from my temples if I stare at it for too long. The walls glimmer just as vividly as the golden dust across my face does and I catch myself getting consumed in the soft beams of light cast at my feet, a beautiful touch to the already entrancing architecture.

Upon our descent down the grand, spiraling staircase which curves to a disorienting rhythm, the opening of the dining room comes into view and I crane my neck to procure a better view of it. This room seems more isolated than the rest of the palace with a lower ceiling and walls accentuated by the lack of windows or glass, along with the display of a multitude of colors in the draped tapestries and striking flowers filling empty spaces. The dining area maintains the same allusion to wealth as the main hall with a slender glass table holding a dozen ornate plates and accompanying silverware—and the people that those items are designated for.

They all sit with an aura of elegance surrounding them, each of the guests seeming royal in their own fashion. In this environment, it feels as though every aspect of my appearance would undergo fervent inspection once they are notified of my presence, and I nearly want to retreat into the confinements of my room to allow Taurus to adjust the hem he was fixated on.

"May I present Princess Ceres," Taurus projects into the expanse, disrupting the soft hum of conversation that had developed. "Daughter of Queen Vega."

The susurration of their voices abruptly falls to a halt once they register Taurus's declaration, their gazes immediately shifting to my figure and taking in the sight of me—some with wonder and others with doubt. I feel a sweep of air against the nape of my neck as Taurus leaves with a flourishing movement, and I know that I'm left with no other option than to proceed into the dining room and showcase that this is where I am meant to be.

It's easy to find Vega's presence, her seat being positioned at the head of the table and her royalty upheld so diligently that it would be difficult to convince myself that she wasn't made for this. With her placid expression, her posture garnering the attention of her guests, and the beauty she exudes surrounding her body in a halo of enchantment, it's clear that she maintains an unnerving amount of influence over her population.

It becomes simpler for me to find my seat and release pent-up tension as I fixate my interest on my sister, instead of those who seem enraptured with my attendance. Her fingers are quivering as she shifts her gaze from our mother to me, analyzing my face with a shadowed gaze that speaks volumes. She's not elated to see me—she hasn't been since I walked into her conversation with Vega. Her animosity is evident, and it has something to do with the Queen.

I tear my scrutiny from Eris and cast my gaze across the rest of those accompanying me. Most sit with a tall and intimidating stature, like my mother, but instead of donning our deep-colored Solarian robes, they encase their bodies with white and gold fabric. Their appearance is ethereal and as far detached from Solaris as possible with their varying skin tones, raven black hair, and the harsh edges of their facial features that make me wonder if they weren't birthed traditionally, but rather chiseled from stone and polished to perfection.

Beginning to shiver under their attentive stares, my thoughts transfer to the two black-clothed individuals beside me. They both nearly sink into themselves with hunched spines contorting their torsos and scarred hands clutching silver staffs close to their bodies. In the rare moments they do choose to collectively sweep their gazes up to mine, their watchful nature seems almost intrusive. Their weathered faces observe me like they have exposure to and jurisdiction over the deepest elements of my soul.

The last collection of people, two men and one woman dressed in deep red cloaks, attract my focus on their own accord with a soft cough exiting one of their mouths. I recognize the tone before I even shift my eyes to classify him. Antares.

He's sitting diagonally from my seat and my mind reprimands me for not noticing his presence earlier, but now that I do, I'm eased by a sense of comfort knowing that *someone* here feels vaguely familiar.

Unsure of his reasons for being invited to this dinner, I take in his clothing—the element that seems to be the indicator of a Solarian's role in society—and run my gaze over a delicately embroidered fire symbol. My eyes flick to the flames on his shirt and back to him in a silent inquiry, and he only offers me a bitter shrug of his shoulders before splitting the nonverbal connection we found. Something about his demeanor seems angered and delicate, so I maintain an inkling of confusion in my mind as I concede to Vega's call for attention.

"Thank you all for joining us this evening," Vega begins, her lips curving into a smile that doesn't quite reach her eyes as she recites premeditated words. "Let us start with our introductions, for this is the first time my daughters are blessed with your presence."

My mother gestures faintly in the direction of the white-clothed individuals and their judgmental leers fall from their eyes within a blink, quickly overtaken by genteel manners. Once one woman stands, I recognize the peculiarity of her anatomy—how her limbs seem vaguely distorted and her lengthy torso contrasts with her shortened legs. As I observe her further, it becomes clear that this is no birth defect—she and her companions were created this way, or made themselves this way.

"Hello, Ceres and Eris." She communicates with such softness that she easily compels her listeners, even forcing me to lean my upper body on the edge of the table in a subconscious effort to get closer to her. "I am speaking for all of us when I say we are delighted to make your acquaintance. We are the Astral Saints."

My breath stills with her declaration and my thoughts cinch so tightly around my skull that I forget to even glance at Eris to see if she shares my shock. The Astral Saints. The divine beings painted across every free space this palace has to offer, the ones who robbed Sun District of our prosperity and ability to live in comfort, and the individuals who my family and I are descended from.

The Astral Saints, I think with a soft shake of my head. It doesn't make sense how or why they would be here. The generally accepted consensus is that the Saints have been resting for the past century and that is why they have taken no notice of their people for so many years.

"As much as you are the Queen's daughters, you are ours as well and we plan to demonstrate that fact to you during your lifetime in Solaris." My instincts flare up ceaselessly when I watch the woman's expression adopt something inexplicable—

very different from the hospitality her voice expressed. Her smile remains imprinted into her cheeks but I fear that it has lost its sincerity already and I've become a victim of a convoluted political game—something that extends beyond just Vega.

Vega signals for the Saint to take her seat once more, recognizing the underlying threat that was present in her words. "Thank you, Saints. Your presence here in Solaris is well appreciated. The Grim, will you please stand?"

My head, still spinning from the fact that the Astral Saints were dining with the Queen of Solaris, fights to transition to the second speaker with another series of words on her tongue. This time it is the cloaked women who rise with a sinister tone to their actions.

My initial confusion quickly shifts into a piercing realization that ricochets from Antares to me, causing me to look at the women in a new light. These individuals are members of the Order of the Grim; they're a sector of the descendants of the Astral Saints and were part of the force that condemned Antares to a lifetime of service for Solaris. And here they stand, directly beside Antares as he winces and attempts to ignore the harrowing atmosphere of their presence. It can't be anything less than a punishment from the Queen of Solaris, and the firm motion of her chin from the Grim to Antares proves that fact.

"We are two representatives from the Order of the Grim," one woman utters, her voice worn and exhibiting an aged drawl. I would expect her—as a soul whose role in Solaris is to break down others' minds and find their calling—to have perfected the practice and control of the human mind, but her fleeting glance at Antares and the conflicting emotions she holds within it are evident.

"We are most delighted to meet you, Ceres and Eris," the second woman finishes, offering no indication in her tone that she is, in fact, glad to make my acquaintance. The two of them hardly address me, proving that most of this dinner truly does come down to political formalities.

And with that conclusion, both women sit down and allow Antares and his companions to take the attention of their audience. As the shift concludes, a conversation begins to rise amongst the Astral Saints, proving that they are not privy to the notion of allowing a lower class to be equal in this environment.

Antares stands gracefully, accompanied by the rising woman to his left and the man across from him, all of whom are clad in the same black tunics with their designated emblems stitched across their breastbone.

"Arinel, leader of Fire Council."

"Pollyth, leader of Air Council."

"Hewst, leader of Water Council."

The introductions leave my ears as fast as they came, along with the drop of the three soldiers back into their seats as soon as their last syllable leaves their lips. I nearly ask them to elaborate, bewildered by the existence of three different fighting councils, but their polished demeanors tell me that this is all they are allowed to say. It's almost as if the only names, stories, and lives that matter at this table are the ones belonging to royalty and magical beings.

With a gesture from Vega, servers flood the expanse with trays clutched in their gloved palms, distributing Solarian cuisine throughout the lengthy table. My attention is halfway captured by the conversations brewing around me, but the scents of the strange delicacies threaten to enrapture me whole. As I watch plates being placed before me, I'm shocked by the sheer amount of food that is available to us. This meal must be equivalent to everything I ate in Sun District in the past year, and that fact makes my stomach ache.

My mind is suspended in a realm of discomfort, watching the individuals before me engage in laughter and banter over the food they greedily lift into their mouths, while I feel so utterly outcast. Eris has brought herself into an uncomfortable conversation between Vega and a Saint, and even through the initial unpleasantness of that interaction, I begin to see Eris assimilating into the environment. She replicates the actions of the Queen and the well-mannered elegance of the Saint she is speaking to, and when considering the lush fabrics that she's dressed in—she looks like nothing less than royalty.

I shouldn't interpret my emotions as anger, but I do, and I fuel it further when Eris catches my eye and taunts me with a soft smile. She even goes as far as to reach for my hand in what should be a sisterly act of affection, but instead of squeezing it with gentle pressure, she digs her nails into my skin with enough force to draw beads of blood.

I'm buried in my own vexation as I watch the tips of her fingers rip through my skin under the cloaked shield of her hand hold and I nearly laugh with the unexpectedness of it all. Gradually raising my head, I return her stare with a more vindictive intent than she can carry within herself, communicating to my sister that I have little idea of what vengeful agenda she harbors, but I am ending it.

I refer to my first encounter with my abilities in Sun District, where I allowed a handful of my magic to leave me and enter Izar through my touch on him. Experimenting with that same sensation, I crumple the barrier restraining the energy built in my stomach and allow a slow release of it through the arm I have in contact with Eris. I sit silently as I urge the threads of toxicity to exit my body through the fingers I have wrapped around Eris' joints and completing the task in a subtle nature is nearly impossible. The scalding sensation peels at the inside of my skin as I maneuver my abilities with a control that they shouldn't be subjected to.

Antares, engrossed in his plate of food and taxing thoughts that seem to be creating a furrow between his eyebrows, notices the skewed rhythm of my breathing and he's quick to drop his utensils and attempt to speak to me.

"Ceres… Ceres?" I register Antares' hushed tone, but I'm consumed in the whimpers that I'm beginning to elicit from Eris as I unfurl my abilities with minimal regard for caution. Those

137

hardly audible sounds of pain she emits easily develop into muffled screams that press against her other palm, attracting the attention of the Saints who are close enough to hear her.

Hardly anyone has made the connection yet between Eris' evident discomfort and my bloody palm against her, with the exception of Antares who is already circling the table and Vega who watches me with an undemonstrative expression.

I recognize that now is the time to stop—now is the time to cease my channeling of the unstable anger within me and release Eris' hand before I inflict a consequence she can no longer hide— but the practice is addicting. As I release harbored physical pain—the agony of sinking *Letalis* into myself, the burning sensation that would multiply without bounds during my Sun District visions—I recognize that this is my path out. Making Eris, or any human, the source of my relief is how I rid myself of this internal ache and purge myself of these persistent emotions.

Antares clearly feels differently, considering the rough, impatient manner with which he tears my touch away from Eris and grasps my shoulder. His grip pulls me out of my seat—with an ease that could only come from years of developing his strength—and he utters a simple excuse to Vega over my shoulder.

"I was told to bring Ceres back to the Healer, Sidra, before nightfall." Antares' movement out of the dining hall is initiated even before he receives a dubious nod from the Queen—as if he knew another moment in that room for me would incite my moral downfall.

Ushering me out of the proximity of the guests, Antares brings me to a secluded corridor of the palace, not far off from the staircase I had descended from. After a rushed survey of the environment behind him, his hands fall on my shoulders, as if to shake me out of my trance.

"Ceres, what the hell were you doing in there?" Antares' tone is distressed but a reprimanding element exists within his words that makes me feel like I'm being chastised. "Why did you need to do that?"

I half-heartedly hold my hand up to Antares' eyes, displaying the nail marks and dried blood Eris' touch left on me while simultaneously attempting to blink away the now stagnant waves of energy. In a meticulously slow process, I wring my mind of the threads of darkness and deposit them back in the repository they're meant to stay in, away from accidental exposure to the outside world.

"She did that? Why?" Antares asks, bringing my hand closer to him and watching intently as fresh beads of blood continue to emerge from the fractures in my flesh.

Another lethargic movement leaves me, this one being a one-shouldered shrug. It's the extent of what I can manage, especially considering the drained state of my mind after the effort I had just made.

Antares regards me for a moment, his line of sight traveling from my hands to the incline of my head as I struggle to keep it upright, and then to the tight clench my teeth have on my lower lip. He, unlike most others who have seen me this way, understands the gravity of what my abilities can do to me—not just others—and the ease and unknowingness with which I can slip it out of me.

It's pathetic to admit and contains no indication of my strength, but in situations like what occurred with Eris moments earlier, it is easier to triple my pain and redirect it than continue harboring it.

"I want to take you somewhere—one of my favorite places in this palace," Antares says after an extended silence that escalates the tension within me. "And hopefully one of yours too."

I don't give a true response as I allow Antares to weave me through the labyrinth-like corridors of the palace—except, they're the hallways I have never seen before. We head in the direction of what I assume is the workers' complex, considering how comfortable Antares seems, and I notice that we're entering an area different from what I've encountered in the past.

Instead of being adorned with magnificent paintings and displays of wealth, my surroundings are now starkly pale and unaccented—and this theme stretches through every new space we enter. Amid my confusion, I send Antares a perplexed glance, to which he responds with a sigh.

"Only half of this palace was ever refurbished by the Queen when she assumed power," Antares begins, gesturing toward all the elements of our surroundings that lack the touch of affluence. "These halls, these rooms—they're the only remaining facets of the Solaris that existed before Vega, and I feel as though it gives her satisfaction knowing that her touch beautifies. She must relish in the comparison between her area of the palace and the bland remainder that represents the kingdom before she molded it under her influence."

I pause in step when Antares stills before two wooden doors, worn with age and use. His eyes run over the patterns of the bark in a nostalgic manner before wrenching the doorknobs and allowing me to enter first.

Abruptly, my body inhales a chilled air that nearly freezes the sweat against my forehead. Under my feet, I can feel a soft surface that moves as I shift my weight—snow. I experiment with the substance for a moment as I allow my eyesight to adjust to the blinding lightness of the environment, rolling bundles of snowflakes with the toe of my shoe and casting my footprints on the malleable surface.

The observations of my eyesight prove to be even more lovely. The small room Antares has led me to is blanketed in a hazy snowfall, flakes falling straight through the ceiling and coming to rest on the carpeted floor and softened furniture. I can't prevent a laugh from exiting my throat when I watch the snow dissipate into my clothes and my skin, leaving a soft sting in its wake. This setting seems like something out of a child's imagination with the whiteness of the snow contrasting with the

140

dulled vibrance of the furniture strewn about—almost like something I would've dreamt up in my youth.

"*How?* How is this possible?" *Suns,* snow has never been more truthful than a myth to me. Sun District would not be capable of producing the slightest snowfall, and frankly, considering its humidity and warm climate, Solaris should not be either.

"Queen Vega," Antares offers in response, and that mere name is enough for me to finish the remainder of his answer in my mind. Solaris' weather is only what it is because Vega makes it that way. If she could control the atmosphere of an entity endlessly larger than her, there's no reason for her to resist exercising the same skill, only this time in the confinement of an enclosed space.

"Do you think she did this for herself?" My curiosity shines in my inquiries, showcasing my desire to understand Antares' interpretation of my mother, even while I'm gradually developing my own.

Antares' eyebrows furrow and I can sense that he's considering what he knows of Vega. In the meantime, I crouch to the floor and take bundles of snow in my palms, pressuring the flakes into a small snowball by the time Antares finds his words.

"I think Vega does everything for herself, but not necessarily to *appease* herself. I've always assumed that she leaves portions of her magic strewn about the kingdom to attract attention and influence, rather than appeal to the happiness of the public or herself. The fundamental flaw of her character is that—"

"She values beauty over substance."

"I was going to say power over love."

My words die in my throat when Antares says the phrase whose meaning has been circling me relentlessly, and whose belief I now know I share with my mother. A defensive urge rises in me when I hear Antares refer to the condition as a weakness, rather than an advantage.

"I believe power gives you more freedom than subscribing to love ever will," I begin, recognizing the controversy to my words and the appalled nature of Antares' face. His image of me most likely erodes with every additional word I speak, but I'm beginning to care less the longer I watch the order of this kingdom. So many individuals in this territory think the same way I do, including my mother, and it's comforting to know that even if Antares looks at me with distaste, my values are shared.

"Care to explain, *Praedo*?" He speaks with cautiousness in his voice as if he's beginning to truly notice the similarities between me and the Queen, but he doesn't shut me out—for which I am grateful.

With a sigh, I descend into the pit of snow below me and allow my fingers to disrupt the pristine sheet of white. I feel Antares beside me replicating my position as he watches me intently.

"Look at Vega." I bring up the story of my mother and the elements that I've pieced together throughout the day. "She was overwhelmed by love at the beginning of her reign. She cared for her daughters and her husband deeply—so much so that the loss of Eris and I nearly drove her to ruin. It provoked her to kill the man who was responsible."

"She did not contain love for the King if she was so quick to kill him," Antares interjects with haste. His words ring an essential truth, but knowing Vega's nature, the explanation is simple to come by.

"Her love is fleeting, temporary—but nonetheless *is* love." My mother's testimony for why she discarded her daughters with such facility floats in my mind. "When she feels it, it is all-consuming and takes hold of her, but once she grows larger than that love and chooses to disobey its control—she can do whatever she pleases. I assume that is what occurred with Mensa Jacque, and it shows how constrained she was as a victim of that connection to him."

Antares begins to counter in disagreement, but I quickly fumble more words from my mouth before he's able to redirect the conversation.

"Vega wasn't at peace then. She was trapped—confined—within the ties she had to her family and she was ruling her kingdom from a vantage point, rather than immersing herself entirely into the magic she held." My gaze has faltered on a melting patch of snow beside my hands and a dream-like stupor inches on my mind, transporting me to not only what I believe Vega's life was like, but what it truly was. Some innate vault in my mind is giving me these words, and they feel so *true*.

I find Antares' gaze upon the realization. "The act that gave her contentment was not my birth, nor was it her acquiring the kingdom. Her love for me, for Eris, for Solaris, is *nothing* compared to the relief she feels as she holds this much power. You can see it in how she carries herself, how little care she seems to have for the things she should be willing to die for."

"We are not all Queen Vega," Antares breathes, reaching for my hand as if he can *love* this mentality out of my head, but it seems to be firmly implanted within me.

"No," I concede. "We are not all her."

Antares certainly is not and neither are most of the others I have met in my life. But I am, Eris is, and the Saints are. What Antares characterized as the fundamental flaw of my mother is not contained to just her—the blood of the Saints carries the trait in varying degrees of potency and has distributed it to me, or the Relasin mind has been tainted with this plague of its own accord.

My attention deviates from Antares as I navigate the depths of my mind, trudging through the sinful tendencies I have collected during my life and embracing the urge for ruination that spreads like vines through me. I know my face is guarded and Antares is kept far from the truth of what my mind holds, but he can infer it all the same—and that comprehension is most likely what makes him rise.

"I've overstayed," Antares says simply, fighting an inflection of uncertainty in his voice. "I should get back to dinner."

I offer him an absentminded nod as he retreats and leaves me as the solitary figure in the wintery room, squeezing clumps of snow as I remain absorbed in my thoughts. I hardly notice the discoloration of my fingertips as I submerge hands that have never been suitable for winter into a languor atmosphere that matches the frigidness of my mind's interior.

It becomes clear now. My recollection of Vega's story and our mutual thought process incited something turbulent from my repressed darkness—and now, with all hindrances torn, that energy diffuses itself.

CHAPTER FIFTEEN

E   R   I   S

---

*C*eres never returned to dinner after Antares escorted her from the table. Even after he returned, both of their absences still felt prevalent as Antares shielded himself from external attention and filled his seat with silence. I knew that my sister was far from the Healer, not when it was far past dusk and her wound seemed to be inconveniencing her very minimally.

I suppose the Healer magic does work.

It's the morning of the procession, and Ceres still hasn't revealed her face—neither did I hear her door opening and falling shut the previous night. It's possible that she never came back to her bedroom at all. I would be concerned for her, knowing that the next few hours consist of the royal procession—which the Queen has allowed us to join her on—but a part of me feels that it would be best if Ceres did not accompany us at all.

My actions during the dinner might've seemed unjustified from an outside perspective, but my motive was stark in my mind. She angers me—and not in the way I was irritated by her in Sun District. I no longer dislike the monstrosity of her powers, nor her ability to assimilate into Vega's presence with such ease—I despise them.

I nurse a hopeless longing to terrorize her mind and rid her of what should have belonged solely to me—those atypical strengths that I now have to share with her and the mother who is beginning to divert her attention from me, not saying I had it to begin with. I should be thankful to be here in Solaris, where my name forms the essence of royalty and my appearance has been shifted into something of ornate value, but I can only think about how I have to live this experience with someone who may be greater than my equal.

I am disheartened that after more than an hour of attempting to connect with my mother's mind and immerse her in mine, I had only earned the respect that comes with blood—not the respect that commands love or esteem. I am ashamed that upon Ceres' arrival to that room where the Queen and I stood, I was discarded like I wasn't the first-born daughter, like I wasn't a daughter at all.

I didn't leave them, however. I collected my delirious thoughts and pressed them deep into my chest, allowing their toxicity to waft about as long as they didn't fall from my mouth. I planted my body against the wall separating me from them and listened to their words for the hours they spoke; I ripped the edges of my fingernails with my teeth, I suffocated trembling hands between my knees, and still, I was not able to suppress my dread.

I never knew the Queen was capable of so many words—so many words that she allowed Ceres to receive without hesitation. She spoke of her history, her family, us, an explanation of her wrongdoings, and through all of it, she saw Ceres as a daughter worth telling her story to.

I am now dressed in a flowing, navy blue gown, the waist painfully cinching into me and pressing fold marks into my skin—all in an effort to replace Ceres' position in our mother's mind. I hold myself how the Queen does, with a strikingly linear posture that hurts more than it helps and tightly clasped hands in front of me. I mimic her aura of elegance that seems more undeniable the longer I fixate on her, and though I still feel like a fraud—perhaps fraudulent behavior can supersede Ceres' unassuming actions.

With a final, comforting glance at my reflection, I reveal my appearance to my mother who stands behind me. I fear her presence in my room is not of her own accord, considering the impatient tapping of her pointer finger against the crook of her opposite elbow and the casting of her gaze everywhere except me.

"I am looking forward to the procession this morning." I test the waters of her mood toward me and the curt nod I receive in return seems to be a signal of the thawing atmosphere between us—at least from what it was yesterday.

Queen Vega is unmoving now that I have spoken, but even the set of her eyes seems to be capable of communicating orders; this one is fueled by her exasperation and her need for me to leave my room and head to the carriages resting outside the palace. She reveals a space between her lips, and for a moment I assume that she'll deliver a verbal acknowledgment of my existence—but her words are much less agreeable.

"I have come to inform you of today's seating arrangements. The messenger is off duty, unfortunately. Your sister, Ceres, will ride in the first carriage alongside me and you will follow us in the second carriage, accompanied by the Council Leaders who commonly direct us in events like these."

Whatever confidence holds my spine upright quickly dissolves, sending me spiraling back to the Sun District model of myself who allowed my emotions to spread their virus and infect my mind shamelessly. It's a relapse motivated by my mother, an indication that, yet again, she prioritizes Ceres' introduction to the people of this kingdom over mine—so much so that she's willing to allow her younger daughter to excel right beside her.

I'm rendered into silence, attempting to find the fabricated voice from my dreams that has been chastising me every chance it has gotten. Whenever it feared I had taken my obsessive tendencies too far, it would feed me repeated reminders of my incompetence and jealousy. It would tell me that it is wrong to channel shallow hostility into anger and escalate it into the urge for destruction whenever my mind traverses this envy-ridden path, but now that voice has vanished. My limits have been swallowed by my propensity for power—and now I've surrendered to the control of my abilities—and the higher power that guides them

"Alright." I swallow, no longer stifling the anger within me, but caressing it instead. "I believe that is best as well."

The Queen senses everything. Her expression is as circumspect as Ceres' is, but she reveals more in her actions—the step backward, the angling of her spine away from me. Ceres may be the mold of her mother, but she sure as hell has perfected the ability of secrecy far more adeptly than the Queen has.

"That is all. Please join us at the front of the palace in the next half-hour so we can begin."

My nod becomes inattentive as Vega's figure recedes from my view and takes with her the aura of familiarity she unintentionally brings. Even with the horrors of her acts being fresh in my mind and battering against the planes of my love for her at every opportunity, she still is my mother and carries with her the inherent quality of family.

And with that thought, Leo flashes in my mind. The image of his death, the jarring sensation of a scream tearing the inside of my throat, and for a moment, I imagine Ceres being in his place. I visualize the dominance of my body over hers, clamping withering wrists as her corporeal pain diffuses through her joints and makes them tremble. In my mind, she is dying and transferring her strength to me—so different from how Leo's death delivered boundless deposits of trauma into my soul.

Alone in my room, in the heart of Solaris, I know only one thing to be true—this one-sided, competitive relationship my mind has conjured between Ceres and me couldn't resolve on its own accord, not without my aid.

———————

By the time my thoughts have reoriented to some semblance of habitual behavior, I proceed out of my room and down the stairs to the area where the procession is forming itself. Upon reaching the arched entrance of the palace that stands at three times my height, I'm blessed with the view of the procession of guests and helpers—dozens of them amongst five majestic caravans.

Past the figures of strangers who compliment my gown or servants who usher me to my designated carriage, I glimpse my first bit of knowledge of what lies beyond the palace of Solaris. Enclosed in my room, I'm offered nothing more than an expansive view of the Lira River and the Astral Mountains, which boast an unparalleled beauty of their own, but have an atmosphere far removed from what Solaris truly is... *this*.

The towns appear to be packed with rapidly moving, bustling villagers who seem nothing other than ordinary at first glance, but when I focus on just one, it's evident that a mystic glee radiates from them. Even from such a distance, I can make out the curvature of smiles as families dance around the streets, awaiting our arrival with such joyous anticipation that I wish to escape the silent battles of the palace to join them. The children seem to carry an energy of their own, clutching vivid flags and tapestries in their small arms and devoting their bodily strength to painting the horizon with their hues. And that sky that they stand under—it's perfectly crafted with the essence of a dulling sunrise mixed with the blue of the morning.

Vega's expression as she watches the patterns of clouds above her displays an unparalleled sort of contentment that proves her involvement in our surroundings—it's all her. Perhaps the idealism she has the faculty to create is her only respite, drawing from the fact that her attention hardly lies with her people; her eyes travel across the collective trance that her towns are under as

149

if she bears no connection to them. I would be frightened of her obliviousness if I was a subject of hers, but they seem to disregard it—or not recognize it at all.

I clear my throat against a servant's hurried gesturing towards my carriage and I resist the desire to move toward my mother, instead conceding to the hand against my back. The servant boosts me to the high platform and I feel the slip of my dress tangle my legs during the sudden movement, causing me to stumble forward onto the plush cushioning of the seats. Eyeing the interior of the carriage, I admire the deep blue velvet coating every tangible surface and surrounding me in an environment of tranquil beauty. My gown nearly blends with the hue and I find that fact amusing as I hold the ruffles of my sleeve up to the fabric of my seat and watch as the magic circulating through the air nearly blends the materials.

I recognize that I've entered the backseat of the carriage and I crane my neck into the space before me to notice Antares and one of his fellow Council leaders speaking in hushed tones with their ducked heads keeping me separated from their conversation. I hardly catch words from their rhythmic speaking, even while I understand the convoluted language their tongues form, and it frustrates me almost as much as the sight of the caravan ahead does.

Over Antares and the other woman's heads, my eyes draw over the silhouettes of Ceres and our mother standing with their shoulders brushing. The Queen's side profile is visible to me while Ceres' remains eclipsed as she faces forward, insinuating that it is my sister who is receiving the undevoted regard of her companion. My vision begins to stray once a distasteful feeling builds in my throat, and I notice a servant, or Healer, standing beside Ceres' carriage, but not quite doing anything. She simply stares at Ceres with an inexplicable emotion written on her face, and I struggle to pinpoint her identity until she and Antares connect eyes and offer each other friendly smiles.

Oh, this is the Healer.

A moment afterward, Antares notices my attendance in the carriage and introduces the Air Council leader to me once more, this time by her first name.

"Alya." Her hand is held out in my direction as a gesture of amity, but I feel too preoccupied with the addictive concerns of my mind to entertain her etiquette.

"Antares, why is Ceres in the carriage ahead?" I respond abruptly, dismissing Alya's handshake with the sort of superiority that I never thought myself capable of conducting. I fix my gaze on Antares with an intent nothing shy of urgency and prevent myself from being deterred by the accusatory glint his eyes send me.

Ceres told him about what occurred during the dinner. Of course, she did.

"Perhaps because she deserves to be. She aims to make a good impression on her people, and you seem too consumed by your misguided agenda to make that a priority," Antares retorts with very little held back from his tongue, his words flowing from the repository of affection he is beginning to curate for Ceres, and it disgusts me. "Have you thought about what you will say to the rest of Solaris?" The immediate shift in the subject of the conversation should unsettle me, but all that stands out is the fact that Ceres' name is gone from his mouth and replaced with mine.

"I'm expected to speak to them?" I question with a small bout of laughter, struggling to comprehend how I'm suited for this with my frail, amateur-like understanding of personability.

Antares' bewildered expression is enough to answer my inquiry and I'm, as a result, overwhelmed with an amusement that makes me feel like I'm not truly in this kingdom, but instead watching it through a filtered lens. Nothing about Solaris feels simple any longer and I definitely do not embody the traits of a competent individual that these people wish to hear from.

"Perhaps you're the villain then." Antares picks up the train of my thoughts with such intuition that for a moment I truly believe that he has taken control of my mind-related abilities—

until I realize that in my half-attentive state, I have allowed concealed elements of my internal being to be spoken aloud.

I gaze at him, partly disoriented and partly appalled by his suggestion that doesn't seem quite as light-hearted any longer. The illness that plagues my brain is expanding and upholding no mercy as it troubles more than my consciousness. The fingers that were trembling during Ceres' first conversation with our mother have begun their seizing yet again and I shift my scrutiny to them, watching their demise with a wry expression.

"Eris, what is happening to you?" Antares is closer to me now, speaking against my ear as he feigns the act of retrieving an item from where I sit. When his body has pulled away, his concern is evident—but constrained by whatever reservations Ceres has instilled into him. "Where did the hesitancy, the kindness, the stability go?"

I listen to him, revisiting the demeanor I exercised in Sun District, and it becomes clear that he is correct. I have lost the formula of everything I used to be—the timid, structured woman who hardly valued her own survival after years of turmoil—and it was my entrance into Solaris that stimulated that shift. I held skepticism for Ceres in Sun District, but it was never at this degree—it never passed childish annoyance.

"What does Solaris truly do to you?" I ask him after a moment of sifting through my experiences, feeling the influence this kingdom has had on my behavior even more strongly now that Antares has pointed it out.

Leaving Alya in the frontmost row attending to the servants at the opening of the carriage, Antares practically leaps toward me with implausible agility and settles in the seat next to mine. He seems... eager to speak to me for the first time since we've met as if there is something he's itching to let out from his system regarding this topic.

"What does Solaris do to you?" I repeat my question when Antares seems to pause in his thoughts while finding words.

"It exerts pressure on you, now more than ever. Solaris has never been one for leaving its people isolated and safe from the reach of corrupted magic—but currently, even entering the kingdom means you're surrendering half of your free will and innate thoughts to an ulterior motive. It's what happens when you're near an entity that holds an insurmountable amount of power—your subconscious can't help but bend to its will. I just haven't been able to find what it is exactly that safeguards that energy." Antares confesses with a gradual release of his words, his voice so contained in his throat that it's hard to discern what he's saying.

Above Alya's knot of white hair, I see the movement of the carriages begin, suspended by nothing but my mother's magic and the air subsequently rushing underneath us as she gestures and guides the carriages along a path. It's alarming but expected, to watch her pause and orient her head in the direction of our carriage—directly at Antares after he concluded his response to me.

Did she hear?

I express a silent inquiry to Antares, clutching the crook of his arm with increasing pressure as Queen Vega revokes her gaze and returns to her task, leaving me descended in confusion. We are too far from her; she should not be able to discern our words.

"She doesn't know what we are saying. It's all muffled sentences in her ears—but she has been able to make out the word 'Solaris' in the past." Antares resolves the doubts in my mind, though the harsh set of his eyebrows still expresses apprehension as he follows the Queen's movements just as closely as I do. The slight turbulence of the carriage's rhythm as we proceed down a hill accompanies our thoughts with a similar level of instability—and it becomes clear.

If my mother can lift and propel these carriages by channeling the influence she has on the gases in this atmosphere, she must also be able to bring all entities and particles suspended in this air closer to her—including the sound waves of Antares' voice. The only inconsistency remains in her reasoning for doing so. Why is she interested in the conversations Antares and I share?

"How do I reverse what Al—this kingdom is doing to me?" I shift the conversation back to my concerns and fight the rising mixture of nausea and adrenaline that comes with my proximity to Ceres. Seeing her through the backside opening of her carriage is becoming more difficult with every moment that passes and every shock of energy that I subject myself to.

"Leave," Antares responds simply, his prolonged pause after the word being enough to tell me that he truly believes that to be true. Perhaps his exposure to a realm outside of this sickening illusion was the stimulant of this mindset that seems to be contained to only him—not being reciprocated by any other Solarian. Their smiles are too wide, chests overwhelmed with too much laughter to feel what Antares and I recognize, but it's difficult to say whether that happiness is faux in itself.

"But you can't leave," Antares continues after keeping me in my thoughts for a moment. "Now that this kingdom rightfully owns you, you have no volition that would enable you to leave— not to mention you would severely aggravate the Queen."

"What do I do?" My voice is pained and wavering on a thread as I regard Antares, for this moment returning to the vulnerable, child-like tendencies I practiced in Sun District. Even Solaris' influence over me isn't intense enough to eclipse these emotions of failure. "I fear I wish to hurt her—deeply."

Antares follows my gaze and for a moment, he believes it lies on Vega and something in his expression is indifferent as if he would willingly subscribe to the death of his Queen. However, after shifting his eyes to where my stare is truly set, he watches Ceres' motions as she weaves strands of her hair in between convulsing fingers, attempting to suppress her abilities for the upcoming event.

"She'd kill you first," is all Antares replies.

———

We have reached the center of the kingdom, our multitude of carriages accompanied by expanding fountains spilling water from stone depictions of the Astral Saints. It's not all water—from some gaping hearts and mouths of the Saints fall enriched liquids of all colors, painting a beautiful, serene environment. I'm half-expecting those godly beings to break out of the stone themselves and lunge forward as if the sculptures are simply a mold over their true forms—most of which are still resting in the palace before their journey back to the Astral Mountains. It's amusing how they overlook their commitment to Sun District so easily, not even comprehending that the festival in their honor is raging amongst the kingdoms and districts separated from us.

Vega exits her carriage, clutching the sides of a billowing cloak in her firm grasp before two servants rush to alleviate her responsibility. They take up their positions behind her, keeping the black fabric off the dusty ground as the hundreds of Solarians I saw earlier begin to gather before us. My eyes slowly travel across the wave of faces of varying ages and structures, all maintaining that characteristic platinum hair that now seems to define the Solarian existence. I self-consciously press the cloak I was given closer to the back of my head, realizing now that the locks I dyed in my longing to blend into the Sun District population are making me an outcast in my true home.

Vega leaves the presence of her servants, nearing the fountains and unrelenting smiles and claps of her people, and she regards her audience with a rise of her hand—one that seems to quiet the rising conversation of the crowd. Amidst her effort to calm the gathering, I swivel my head to find Ceres and Antares gravitating toward each other despite our carriages having been placed far apart, and the sight instigates an off-putting sensation. My eyes find Antares' as Ceres seems to say something to him, keeping their arms close as they communicate, and he shoots a warning glance in my direction. He knows my mind is not at peace with this setting—he knows I wish to appease this urge once and for all.

As if initiated by a cue, whispers begin to circulate amongst the gathered townspeople and their words meet my ears.

"Those are the princesses."

"They're the clear opposite of their mother—no sign of royalty in them."

"You can see the Sun District in their eyes."

I notice the change in the Solarians' attitudes, watching as their faces find Ceres and me. The hundreds of eyes laid on our figures seem to scrutinize every aspect of our appearance, every rise of our shoulders and perk of our eyebrows—and it's unsettling. I never quite considered the possibility before but living in an environment where my own people despise me seems like the beginning of a terrible experience—and I'm holding witness to the first symptoms now.

Vega's voice rings out into the expanse, timed perfectly with the rise of her people's suspicions towards us. She gradually redirects their attention to her—commanding and dominant with such an unwavering permanence to her actions.

"Hello, my people." My mother circles the expanse of the courtyard we've settled in, allowing herself to weave through the hordes of villagers with no concern—and their nonchalance indicates that this is a customary practice. "It has been quite some time since I last saw you, and you last saw me. It is difficult, to say the least, to maintain this state of Solaris without turbulence destroying it. If you have noticed any fissures in the ground, or ordinary objects dissolving into the air, you are seeing firsthand the consequences of living in an entity that is not corporeal. I hope it is true that we will return to our normal state soon—Saints know we need it. Past our current situation, another aspect of my life has been on my mind for quite a while—and it is time for the Solarian people to become exposed to it."

Vega draws back from a young girl gleaming upwards at her with glee. I would have expected her to toss the child an

156

affectionate look, or squeeze her shoulder softly, but none of that occurs. The Queen hardly regards her. This pattern repeats itself on several occasions as I intently observe her movements: the hardly discreet rise of her volume to combat that of a villager with a question, the methodical rhythm of her lips that makes it seem like she is reciting a scripted passage rather than truthful words.

"And so, with all that being said, I welcome the Princesses of Solaris, Eris and Ceres Relasin. The daughters that have been separated from me for nearly two decades but have returned to Solaris indefinitely."

Ceres has stepped closer to my side, seeming to dismiss her earlier reservations regarding me during Queen Vega's speech. Upon hearing the word 'indefinitely' her eyes widen and it takes her a moment to reorient herself, just as I must do. The commitment expressed in our mother's sentence is something neither Ceres nor I were prepared to hear.

During the pandemonium raging in our heads, the eyes that weren't already on us begin to join the general population, their eyes sharp and questioning. I swallow under their surveillance and meet Vega's stare, unsure of what to say and partially terrified to utter a word that these people deem unsatisfactory. It seemed so simple with Vega—her relationship with her people is nothing short of a savior nurturing those below her as she upholds Solaris for them. What is my relation to Solaris, and what can I contribute that will even be accepted?

I can tell that the judgment is weighing on Ceres as well, but she channels it differently than I do. Instead of retreating into herself, she clears her throat and elongates her spine to its full length. She replicates the practices of our mother with an accuracy I could never achieve—everything from the lethargic, yet poised, wave of her hand, the circling of her body through the expanse, and the unreadable smile plastered to her lips.

Considering the stark resemblance she has with our mother in both appearance and voice, it's not difficult to imagine her as Vega, the Queen, instead of a princess. I nearly begin to.

"Hello." Her voice sounds unfamiliar and strange as it rings out into the ears of her people. "I'm Ceres Relasin, a Princess of Solaris."

She falters, not lost for words but rather struggling to find a way to say them. Her blinks appear to quicken midst her rising panic, the only evidence of her overwhelmed state courtesy of her emotional barriers, and she manages to reconstruct her demeanor before the fissure within it becomes noticeable.

Both of our regards land on a young boy not far from us as Ceres allows a natural pause in between her words. He stands with his mother's worn hands placed protectively upon his shoulders and he offers Ceres a supportive smile, urging her to continue while my attendance remains discarded by his mind. The thought infuriates me—having Ceres prevail in the competition for the kingdom's love for the reason of me not being able to step forward first.

"This kingdom, this world—it is all very foreign and disorienting from my perspective, especially since I did not know of its existence until a week ago." I survey Ceres with my jaw held in an involuntary clench and my fingers quivering as they itch to be the instrument of my powers yet again—this time wishing to find Ceres. I tell myself to retract my tendencies—this is not the right time to showcase them. Any point I prove will be overshadowed by the severe consequences that will follow.

"I am not used to this—any of this. Being in a kingdom that I didn't previously know of, being the daughter of the Queen. In fact, I've approached several aspects of this life incorrectly already. Who wouldn't? It's evident that I am not made for this world, not because I lack the human affinity for authority and affluence, but because I don't know how to relate to a kingdom or care for it the way my mother does."

I sense lies beginning to be woven into Ceres' words, as does the Queen as she tilts her head slightly. My mind is coated with envious disbelief when I watch amusement develop on Vega's expression instead of the confusion that I expected—and I wonder if the two of them planned Ceres' speech in their isolated carriage during my absence. I imagine the sight of their heads bent together and Vega releasing sentences and advice into Ceres' reach as she stands there, utterly too young and too undeserving to be the chosen one.

Now, she stands as well, but she doesn't seem to exemplify those characteristics. With the golden shine applied across her skin, the immaculate curvature of her bodice and flaring silk of her gown, and the white curls that tumble below her shoulders and glow under the sunlight, she is lovely. One would not be able to tell that inside her lies a reliance on darkness and destruction, knots of black energy continually clawing their way up the ridges of her ribcage and pounding against her heart—the affliction that curses all of us Relasins.

"But, alas, I am here, and I intend to be nothing short of what this kingdom deserves. I adore Solaris—I feel as though this land, or I suppose the absence of it, is an innate component of my soul and that I'll never truly feel complete unless I am within these borders. With that in mind, I am committed to these duties and you will begin to see that fact soon. You all are not my people, and I believe that is important to say." Ceres' voice falls to a halt with a tone that should resemble hesitance but instead comes across as diluted humility that appeals to the public. "You are Solaris' people. We are all Solaris' people. We are here to preserve Solaris and nurture this magic that surrounds us—after all, it has given us, we owe the kingdom at least this much."

She's fixated on the faces of the Solarians, yearning for a reaction that would allow her shoulders to lower in relief and anxiety to diffuse—and she receives it. Gradually, I see smiles spread across the town, nods circulating through the crowd as the children begin to slap their soft palms together and regard Ceres with the kind of blind elation that the Queen elicits.

Ceres releases a breath signifying her newfound stability, raising her hand once more to offer an elegant wave to those before her, her state contrasting deeply with mine. I tremble with irritation and disappointment, cautiously recognizing that Ceres had done it—she had won approval from both our mother and the Solarian people with minimal exertion involved in the process. She's still the same young girl from a Sun District slum—yet it took her this far—while I have rewritten the entire script of my existence for Solaris, and even so, it rejects me.

Vega, as all others in the town do, takes no notice of my withdrawing figure and heads to Ceres, blanketing her youngest daughter in a climate of satisfaction and support. Her face begins as a blank slate, but her eyes crinkle as she nears Ceres, and then a true smile envelopes her expression—the first I've seen from her.

The two of them stand—mother and daughter—with the vibrating energy of their shared bloodline connecting both of their souls and expressing that relationship with unbelievable intensity. The townspeople appear to notice as well as cheers rise into the air above us, accompanied by the surging of the crowd as they attempt to move closer to the royalty.

I can tell that Antares hardly agrees with much of the words Ceres uttered, neither does she or the Queen, and yet they all celebrate Ceres' success. I believe she expects me to continue the momentum with my own speech when she looks in my direction and gestures toward the people—but another agenda fuels my mind instead.

Upon meeting Ceres in the center of the large courtyard, her hand between my shoulder blades as she urges me to step forward and profess my own words, she speaks to me.

"I don't know what the hell you were thinking last night, but I'll forget it all if we just move forward as sisters, not enemies." Ceres' pressure against my back increases the slightest amount and it's becoming a threat.

I swallow, feeling my body vibrate with a need to turn that touch she has on me into a weapon for my motive, but I find the incentive to hold out just a little longer. The crowds still seem preoccupied—I want to gather the attention of all the Solarians when I do what it is I want to do and have them all as witnesses.

"Do you even understand your privilege?" I ask under my breath, diverting the conversation from Ceres' practicality. "Do you realize that you were the one that was able to live with the trader while I was homeless at 15? You could find something you loved—fighting—while I starved and struggled to find the coins for even water."

Ceres meets my gaze, appalled. She holds out a finger to Antares—who is approaching and most likely coming to notify me that I should begin my speech soon—and shakes her head with fervent disbelief.

"You never loved anyone enough to experience loss. You have lived the most fortunate life one could find in Sun District—*Suns*, you were even able to go to school while I was struggling to prevent my abilities from consuming me whole."

"You couldn't be further from the truth." Ceres' tone bites into my ears with a piercing, honest severity and I believe that if I was any closer to her at this moment, she would find a way to rip my tongue clean. "I have suffered. Living with the trader was traumatic. I was fed lie after lie regarding my relationship with him. I was abused and then discarded. I had episodes that tore me from soul to skin and—"

I raise my voice above hers, not aware that my increase in volume attracts the attention of those around me, including the Queen. "—And you arrived in Solaris, and what? Those visions stopped, correct? That was Solaris' hold on you; I experienced them too. They don't make you special."

Ceres' lips part, disregarding her earlier anger and allowing it to dissolve into confusion. Her hand moves from my back to a reluctant touch against the curve of my shoulder—most likely the closest she's able to get to something resembling familial affection.

"What has gotten into you, Eris? Which facet of you is the authentic version?"

I laugh, feeling the abruptness of the sound scrape against my vocal cords and leave a stinging sensation in its wake. "I don't know anymore—but as long as I'm in Solaris and it continues to curse me… this is my mind. Every time you succeed here, every time you hold Vega's approval, or Antares' sentiment, or this kingdom's allegiance, I will fall apart more." I lean into Ceres' hold slightly, allowing my veins to ease their cinching of the braided energy in me as I coax them out with a gentle touch. "I can't bear to have you be above me here, not when I see you as a threat to my individuality and my power. I've been through so… so much pain that I deserve this, don't you think?"

"You don't deserve anything," Ceres hisses, pushing against my shoulder slightly in an attempt to make me fully face her, but she doesn't realize that the increased force she's applying is only helping me to press our skin together further. "You are jealous, you are cynical, self-important, and unstable. I could use so many words to describe you at this moment, but it would all boil down to the fact that you have entrapped yourself in this vengeful attitude that will only deter Solaris and our mother from further away from you. No one will accept you if you desire to rise without me, instead of with me."

"No one will accept *me*?" I inquire with a twisted sort of mirth coating my voice. "See how well they accept *you* once they witness this."

Ceres widens her mouth to protest but her voice stills in her throat when I launch the energy within me through the channel I've created between my shoulder and her hand. I feel every vein of her touch entangling with mine and the chilling waves of darkness ripping through my insides as they beg to be released, conjuring intense arrivals of pain. I shift my weight against her convulsing body, giving myself more control by clasping my palms over her skull and opening barriers within Ceres that have never felt the fracture of failure before.

Ceres' pain is evident, and it's more emotion than I've ever seen her emit at once. Her eyes follow a slow trajectory as they roll back into her head while she attempts to minimize her shouts into grunts by biting her tongue—so intensely that I see the blood dripping from her gaped jaw. Every bone in me shivers with the magnitude of the dark thoughts I am forcing into Ceres' mind, a reverse tactic that I haven't done since Leo's death and one that I know I will be unable to guide once I cross a certain limit.

And that point is fast approaching, especially considering how I no longer have to coax my abilities, instead having them flow from an uncapped bottleneck, stretching their venomous fingers into Ceres. She begins to collapse, unable to sustain herself on her weakening legs and disintegrating resolve. Upon her fall, Antares reaches the two of us. I feel his hands tear at the grip I have on Ceres, trying to wrench my joints away, but then beginning to share Ceres' sounds of pain when I reallocate a portion of my energy onto him, scalding his mind with my touch.

In my dream-like haze characterized by the flames within me peeling off layers of my skin, I notice how the cheering has silenced and cries of terror are now shouting out for the Queen— who seems to be absent entirely from this interaction and setting. Antares as well seems to be calling for Vega, but I don't sense her bodily presence, and neither do I feel any indication that she's using her powers to pull her daughters away from each other.

As Ceres attempts to choke out agonizing words, I feel tears of relief begin to pool at my waterline, expressing six years of pent-up despair finally being released from the cage of my body. What should be a dreadful act—me bringing my sister to the brink of death in this manner—is enchanting in my mind.

Then, I realize that it may not be the strengthening of my powers that is initiating Ceres' subjugation—it's her. Her efforts to fight against my touch have ceased and now she sits stagnant with no indication of her heartbeat being present. I choke on my breath, lowering to Ceres' level to sense what exactly occurred to her. A certain fear builds in the pit of my stomach—I had not thought of what I would do if this was my consequence if Ceres was truly rendered unconscious, or dead. I believed her to be strong enough to resist me—that was the entire basis of my plan.

I feel myself being launched away from Ceres as Antares catches her body and holds her mouth to his ear as he struggles to find an indication of her breathing. His hands grapple for the hollows of her neck and her wrist, attempting to find a heartbeat, and the lack of hers seems to be reborn in the rapid rhythm of his words to her.

"Ceres, Ceres!" His voice is desperate and thick with emotion as he shakes the shoulders of the woman below him, that violent trepidation keeping away all the bystanders who are gradually retreating. Still, they can't seem to keep their eyes away from the sight of Ceres—crumpled on the cobblestone with vibrant trails of blood leaking from her mind, her nostrils, and the depths of her ears. It's a frightening, gruesome sight that I fear I will never be able to swallow or suppress—not when this memory is attached to it.

Suns, *this was not what was supposed to happen. Why didn't she fight back? I needed her to fight back.*

I'm stumbling backward when Antares suddenly lurches his head, shocked by a jolt of Ceres' arm. His tears are freely roaming the crevices of his face and dripping to his collar, onto Ceres' skin, and he doesn't wipe them away as he lifts Ceres into a sitting position with watchful eyes. The entirety of Solaris has fallen into a silent stupor as we all watch Antares' strange agenda, bewildered by the way he shakes her limp torso and whispers to her.

"You—You just moved. Ceres, you just moved. I know you're there." The feverish repetition of his voice begins to tear at my skull when I gradually turn away from her fallen body, clutching my temples with the same hands that killed Ceres—or at least rendered her to this state. I feel crooked in the head, battling contrasting thoughts as I struggle to even orient myself enough to find a quiet place to collapse, but the crowds of villagers fail to part way for me.

It becomes clear then that they heed me no attention—even when it seems like I just killed the princess of their kingdom. Their attention lies on the collapsed figure of the young woman who cannot even register their concern. That's the state of me in this kingdom—I'm not even important enough to be regarded as a killer.

I feel hands pulling against my shoulders and I release a turbulent sigh that expresses all the pain within me that I'm too suspended in my subconscious to recognize. "Antares, I-I... I'll leave, alright? I'll leave Solaris and not come back—"

Midst my shameful turn to face Antares' presence behind me, I realize that it is not him who has his touch planted on me. It is Ceres.

CHAPTER SIXTEEN

C E R E S

---

*I*t's hard to be fully sure of what it was that brought me back to consciousness—Antares' pleading or the gradual retreat of Eris away from the chaos she created. With Eris' harbored energy so deeply embedded inside my mind, I can't feel or see anything but her. The dark memories that she channeled into my skull meticulously replaced the only bits of comfort I have collected over the past years, and it feels as though my sense of being has been stolen from me and replaced with *her*.

Through my multiplying mental agony and the stifling of my desire to tear a scream from my throat and hurt Eris to an equal degree, I sense Antares over me. I can feel his tears seeping through the fabric of my gown, and I realize that he believes I'm dead. They all believe I'm dead, and they all believe Eris won this twisted battle, holding my dignity in her arms like a child while I waste on this ground.

Vega is somewhere in this expanse as well. The woman seems to be stagnant, from what I can feel of her energy, and I suspect that her stillness is not due to fear or perplexity clouding her mind. She's waiting, watching, to see what I will do—if I will allow my revenge-consumed older sister to steal what is mine.

Any sense of practicality I have instilled in myself fades to naught, along with my intention to maintain a pristine image for these villagers, for Solaris, for Vega. Fighting against Antares' iron-like grip on my upper arms, I grunt as I roll my eyes back to their position against the slick blood coating them. There's blood everywhere, almost dressing me now with its vivid hue and continually spreading state, but that fact fails to deter me as my vision fills with red. Not solely the red of my blood, however. The crimson of my anger, as well.

Reaching Eris is not an easy feat to conduct with my mind convincing me that every joint in my body is deformed, as well as having Antares behind me, clutching onto my arms. After a gradual release of his hold on me, I hobble towards Eris while exercising every notion of agility I have.

As soon as my hands encase her shoulder blades, she begins speaking to me as if I were Antares. Her voice contains an apology, a declaration that she'd retreat from Solaris and return to her mundane Sun District life, but I don't accept that. I refuse to allow words to exit my throat as she begins to regard me with a turn of her body, and I nearly smile when I see that petrified expression envelope her features. In a matter of seconds, Eris becomes exactly who I was moments ago.

My emotions are bitter and convoluted, courtesy of Eris' effort to shred the barriers around my mind, and I struggle to interpret them. A facet of my mind still regards those behind me, the Solarian people who I now commit to serving, and yet, that minor percentage of my thoughts is *nothing* compared to my urge to set fire to Eris' skin, doing to her body triple what she did to my mind. I wish for her to not only go onto her knees like I did but disintegrate into an Aerth where I would no longer have to walk with caution around her, terrified that the slightest action from my end would send her over the edge.

She's my sister, yes, but this setting changed her character. She's unrecognizable to the point where her distraught state before me elicits no concern from my mind—the entity that she sunk her claws into and corrupted beyond repair. Perhaps if I turned around, Antares would tell me to find the forgiveness that exists in an inherent facet of every human's soul. He would remind me that it is my *sister* that I have my hands on and that somewhere along this journey, I must have found a way to love her. But after all, I never was the sort to value love over vengeance.

Her features are twisted in pain and some form of regret, but I can't find the will to register the emotions as anything of value. It becomes clear that the absence of her passion only strengthens mine—and I use it to my advantage. I feel a haze of red and black form around me, my powers showing themselves in corporeal form for the first time, and now I truly unleash the darkness within me.

Throughout the past few days, I have been building boundaries around these abilities as I have struggled to keep them bottled inside me—and now it feels strange to allow them free will. They don't take my leniency for granted, having an immediate reaction to the fallen chokeholds and escaping through every opening in me that they can find. The darkness even makes its fissures in my skin, releasing itself into the air and taking trails of my blood with it.

As the Solarian screams begin to envelop us once more, the muted stinging sensation shredding the inside of my skin reveals itself in the harsh gritting of my teeth and the blood incited from wounds already created by Eris—while she exhibits the effects of uncontrollable agony. The way she looks at me seems to be void of any life or feeling, though the continuous, fractured scream she emits from her gaped mouth calls for a different truth. Her hair seems to be falling out in clumps as the harrowing energy coursing through her body overwhelms the sense of stability she has been gradually building during her stay in Solaris—all her autonomy dissipating in one torturous moment.

I attempt to blink through the blur of my vision and clear my senses enough to reorient myself in the setting, and my persistence to do so seems to yield a sharpening of the screams around me and the gradual thinning of the red haze blocking my sight. Upon registering the true expression of the face below me, I notice certain key details that my mind overlooked easily in its overwhelmed, nauseated form.

The body I am holding is flimsier and lighter than an adult woman's should be, especially when there's malleable skin and minimized bones under my touch. What should be Eris' deep-throated, guttural scream is more high-pitched and childlike. It's not the sound of her. None of this feels like her any longer—perhaps it did in the beginning when I first grasped Eris, but something pivotal has changed since then. The person before me has changed.

My mind, previously occupied to the brim with intrusive thoughts of how much destruction I could leave in my wake, spirals to send commands to my arms, fighting to inform my body that I should stop. This is the wrong victim, this is not Eris, I am killing an innocent person.

My abilities, too far off course from my sense of control to obey any longer, disregard my needs and instead follow a steady rhythm of cycling my energy into the person below me and distributing pain through every joint of theirs. My feet ignore me as well, remaining firmly planted on the Aerth as if the smallest movement would disturb the fabric of Solaris.

I'm not able to turn my head to determine where Eris stands, my powers maintaining too much authority over my position, but I do feel her presence gradually dissipating as she most likely backs away. I feel everyone receding from me with Vega now seeming acres away, the motherly instinct she exhibited in the carriage now erased from existence. It feels like I'm the only person occupying the heart of Solaris at this moment, filling the atmosphere with my violent visions as I enact those fantasies on the Solarian below me that I fear I've mistaken for Eris—and I have no way of ceasing my actions.

The only reprieve I'm granted that begins to cool the burning sensation licking its way up the corners of my mind is the gentle recline of my victim's body from a convulsing state to something resembling slumber. I recognize this shift—it's what I experienced as I lost consciousness just minutes earlier, but this seems slightly different. With a newfound claim over the control my abilities stole from me, my hands aimlessly find her wrists and press my fingers into her veins. I expect to find a faint pulse, but nothing is detectable besides the limp skin that folds under my nails.

Panic besets me as my head struggles to find a way out of this—a method to discern what exactly it is I have done while I fight against the heavy hold my energy still has over my consciousness. Any chance of a path back to reality seems to have been demolished the moment I allowed Eris to redirect my agenda in such a way—an action of hers that seems to have been more calculated than it was impulsive.

Gathering all my morality into one pulsing pit of energy, I channel it into wrenching my hands back into myself and scrambling backward from the body I just delivered to its death. It's mostly colors that register in my mind—the white of a young girl's hair fanned out onto the cobblestone, the brown of her skin tainted with streaks of red blood, the soft green fabric of her shredded dress.

"Oh *no*. No, no, no. *What have I done?*" I whisper to myself in a barely audible murmur, traversing my developing sight to see the horrified expressions of those around me.

The Solarians are suffering in their abhorrence. They have pulled their children behind them and plastered trembling hands over their gaped mouths, struggling to comprehend the image of one of their young ones murdered—with her killer mere feet away. I've streaked a path of blood during my retreat, and it's following me, haunting me, as I force a sense of balance into my feet and continue my cowardly steps backward.

I know this is wrong. I know I deserve to look my people in their face, to look Antares and my mother in the eyes and quiver under the severity of my shame—but one glance in Eris' direction shatters my resolve to do so. She's bloodied and hunched on the ground, having retired to the edge of the courtyard where she's visible to only me, and she's smiling. Her cracked lips have stretched into a haunting declaration of victory, demonstrating to me that her effort to hurt me was nothing more than a prerequisite to what would truly happen—*this*.

My sister tore my sanity out of my skull by reaching for her powers in such a way that provoked me to reciprocate onto her the same pain—only she didn't experience much of her share because she slipped away somewhere between the blackouts in my vision. She allowed a young bystander to assume her place as I must have lunged to find her—all while watching on the sidelines as I tarnished the beautiful esteem I was able to build for myself in that speech.

She truly won, and now I'm too encased in my own guilt, rage, and self-pity to argue otherwise.

———

"Cer! Darling!" A sweet, familiar voice calls out, breaking me out of my sleep. I shift in my bed covers, groaning as I hear the curtains of my window being yanked open, releasing warmth into my skin before it's awake enough to appreciate it. I turn over in the bed that feels too similar to a Sun District cot to be anything but and feel someone sit down beside me, their weight shifting the flat plane. Still doused in the blanket of my slumber, I can't do anything more than crack my eyes open to see who my visitor is— and as soon as my eyes meet hers, my body lurches forward in its surprise.

I open my mouth to utter words of greeting, out of instinct, but those thoughts dissipate quickly as I become enraptured in her appearance, so drastically different from the mother I have memorized in Solaris. I'm staring at her—Queen Vega—except something seems fundamentally wrong.

She's missing the frigid mannerisms that characterize her presence. No regal clothing or striking jewelry is donning her limbs, and no carefully placed white curls caressing her shoulders. Instead, she's just Vega, in her pure form with a soft smile adorning her lips and her platinum locks tumbling out of a messy knot by her neck. My prior impression of her is placated by the `love in her eyes as she reaches a dust-streaked hand up to the curve of my cheek, brushing away a tendril of hair.

"What's wrong, darling?" she asks, the tips of her fingers leaving soft touches on my face as she regards me as a mother would—how I expected her to upon hearing about her for the first time.

I'm at a loss for words, fighting to find the fissures in this persona she's adopted. This woman before me is enveloping me in the motherly care that I was not fortunate enough to receive from her, and the pure eccentricity of it makes me believe that this is not anything that Vega is capable of. There must be some tether back to my reality—this can't be more than a fabrication of my imagination.

"Vega?" I whisper with hesitation as I pull my blanket up to my shoulders. I'm half-expecting that the farther I sink into the mattress, the more likely it will be that I fall back asleep and wake up to Solaris and the true Queen Vega.

"Vega?" she repeats with a small laugh breaking her words. "Suns, Ceres! I knew you were growing up, but I didn't know you were old enough to start calling your mother by her first name."

My thoughts spiral with my understanding of her sentences. Vega using 'Suns' as if she was native to Sun District, in addition to her mentioning her position as my mother, is more than enough to disrupt my fading lucidity even further. Swiping a tired hand over my eyes, I raise myself into a sitting position with reluctance filling my movements and even beginning to show in my features.

Something as disorienting as this is not very feasible for me to prevent from affecting me.

"Well," Vega continues, taking my bewildered silence as a response. "If you insist on calling me something other than 'mother', you may as well call me Levega, Vega seems too... unfamiliar."

Levega. Is that her full first name?

The woman brushes her hands lightly on the dusted fabric of her apron, and the streaks of grime become visible to me, completely uncharacteristic compared to the noble beauty she still upholds. It's unnerving, how even with calloused palms and a simple Sun District dress with dirt embedded into the stitching, her appearance suggests that she is only in disguise and truly belongs in elegant gowns with gloves encasing her arms and jewels woven into her hair.

Upon my mother shifting her attention to a rumpled stack of clothes at the foot of my bed, I take advantage of her distraction and use the moment to observe the simple room enclosing us. It's heartbreakingly familiar, the only furniture is the bed, a small dresser, and an open cabinet, one side holding clothing, and the other side packed with aged books. The setting is not far in looks from how my old Sun District room was—and with that thought in mind, I realize that I wouldn't be very surprised if it was Izar who came in through that door next.

I follow the warm light disrupting my vision, finding that it leads me to the ajar windows, all of which reveal a familiar sight—the Sun District market. The bazaar incites an abrupt pang of nostalgia from within me, considering the days I would spend there simply searching for a place away from Izar.

"Come," Vega refers to me as she places clothes that must be mine into the dresser, taking care to press firm folds into the fabric. I watch her with caution, astounded by her ability to care for my clothing with such ease and willingness—no sane person in Sun District ever offered their clothing respect before dirtying it hours later. "It's nearly time for breakfast. We mustn't miss what Eris is cooking."

My frown deepens when I hear my sister's name, her memory entrapped in my last recollections of her which include the vengeful plot she had enacted to taint my image. Though thoughts of her incite anger from every part of me, I want to see her in this setting I've dreamt up. I want to see what she—what we—would have been if we were not cursed by whatever illness Solaris and our abilities have bestowed upon us.

I take my mother's hand and silently follow her figure as she leads me through a small walkway, leading toward a doorway with delectable scents wafting from its proximity. Upon entering, I'm forced to fixate my attention on my surroundings, stunned by how much the home reminds me of Izar's—and how secure it makes me feel to have romanticized versions of my true family here instead of him.

Escaping Vega's attention for a moment, I rush to where Eris stands with her head bent over a kettle on the stove. Wisps of her now white hair tumble before her eyes as I spin her gently, still carrying a sense of discretion when approaching her.

"What is going on, Eris?" I say hurriedly, not having my voice extend beyond what she and I can hear. "Why are we in Sun District, and why does Vega look like that?"

Eris' wide smile hardly fades as she cocks her head at me and sets down a cup of tea she is meticulously filling to the brim. "What are you on about, Cer? I think you must still be half-asleep!"

She nudges me in a playful motion—as sisters do—and then disregards the message I'm trying to convey to her. She seems more oblivious than she usually is—now harboring a blissfully naive demeanor that aggravates me. It becomes clear that Eris has abandoned the high-strung state of mind that I first encountered her with and replaced the personality with a persona of comfort and warmth, though she is far from it in reality.

Nothing about her seems quite the same, with every particle of her existence having undergone some minor warp—as with Vega.

Seeing her with white, Solarian hair is perplexing, however. If my mind is trapped in Sun District and I have curated a version of Vega that molds into this town, why has Eris surrendered the one physical characteristic that connects her to Sun District—her black hair? Perhaps it's all to make her seem like part of our turbulent family again.

"Mensa, make Ceres some breakfast." Vega interrupts my straying thoughts by announcing the arrival of a new individual into the kitchen—a man. The image of him is blurred and morphing before my eyes as if I'm not truly sure of what he looks like—but his identity is confirmed when Vega presses a tender kiss against his cheek. This is my father, the man who tore Eris and me from our home and forced us into lives that only reaped pain.

He's dead, Vega killed him 16 years ago, but in front of me, he seems as alive as Vega and Eris are, only with a haze of uncertainty covering the true appearance of his face.

I watch, bewildered, as my father affectionately runs a hand over Vega's blonde locks and then turns to regard his daughter, a smile crinkling the corners of his eyes. Eris offers Mensa that same piercing grin that is infectious if you become too consumed in it, but I can't manage more than a half-second upturn of my lips.

He looks so much like Solaris, *is all I can think.*

His white locks are short and scraggly with threads of brown peeking out from his scalp as indicators of old age. He smiles in the same way Solarians do, crooked with a slight dimple forming on his chin, and his tall, looming stature grants him the royal presence that I know he had.

This idealized family of mine now begins to arrange themselves around our circular dining table, exchanging embraces and words of amusement as Mensa begins a monologue of the events of his day. His words and Eris' unrestrained

175

laughter are accompanied by the silent smiles of Vega as she seems content with watching her husband and eldest daughter enjoy themselves. After a moment of my absence, she realizes and beckons me over.

Following the guidance of her hand motions, I rest in a chair beside Vega and observe the conversation between Mensa and Eris with as much focus as she does, but instead of my intentions being fueled by love, I'm overwhelmed with paranoia. It becomes clear to me that this setting and atmosphere I have created—it's not meant to be a replica of Sun District at all. This dramatic shift was not executed with the agenda of immersing myself back into Sun District, but rather with the motive of grasping specific elements of my life and morphing them so they make me content.

Eris isn't supposed to have black hair in my mind, and neither am I supposed to have powers or be in Solaris. I'm not supposed to have a dead father and murderous mother, and now I've created a story in which I don't.

"So, mum?" Eris speaks through the food stuffing her mouth. She apologetically grins at Vega like a misbehaving child when she receives a disapproving tilt of the head. "When is Antares coming?"

My face pales when I register his name, realizing that he too will be a part of this fantasy, and the shock of that fact is enough to slip the ceramic plate in my hands past my fingers. I expect to flinch from an incoming crash as the plate dissolves on the ground below me, but I hear no sound announcing that event. I avert my gaze for a moment so I can see what is below me, and I find the plate to be gone, having been replaced with still air.

This place truly is a utopia, I don't believe I could make an unfortunate occurrence happen here even if I tried.

"Antares is coming?" I repeat Eris' words as I run over in my mind all the possibilities for his arrival. Everyone in my dream is connected to me through the pivotal role that they play in my life, rather than the projection they embody in Solaris—which is why I struggle to deduce Antares'.

176

Eris slowly nods in response to my inquiry, raising her eyebrows. "Why wouldn't he come, Ceres? You two are going to be engaged soon!"

I can't help but laugh upon my sister's declaration; the fact is so absurd that it seems impractical for Eris to even consider it. My amusement begins to fade when Vega grasps my hands and it becomes clear that she shares the same sentiment.

"We're all beyond happy for you, Cer!" Vega entwines her fingers with mine and I feel the radiating comfort of her skin without the indication of magic always being between us. "We know how much you and Antares have been through together. The both of you love each other very much, and we're happy for you."

I'm rendered speechless by Vega's words, watching as they signify that in this world, Antares and I have been together romantically for quite some time and an engagement is nearby. I shake my head softly as I imagine the possibility of being with someone without the caveats of political play, where the person you choose to marry is free from the judgment of your kingdom and you cannot use magic as a weapon toward them. I have that respite here.

Mensa offers his support as well with a stretched hand firmly planted on my shoulder. "It's fine to be nervous, sweetheart. I'm sure he's going to make the proposal perfect."

They all seem to insert more methodological excitement into their bodies with every passing moment, and the sight begins to terrify me. This idyllic setting was perfect in the beginning, replicating everything a child with a broken family dreams about, and yet, I'm starting to welcome the fear that creeps into my mind. The permanent smiles etched on my family's lips are unwavering in their intensity and I nearly want to reach out and relax the muscles that uphold that expression, along with inciting enough chaos in this home to the point where they have no choice but to revert to their customary demeanors.

I would treasure a utopia, but my mind cannot sustain it—not without depriving myself of the pain and ruin that I feed on like sustenance, needing it to propel me forward.

Half-hearted smiles of gratitude are all I'm able to offer as my family continues to shower me with support. My mind remains enraptured in the upcoming events of this dream, but visiting the concept only fills my body with dread and disorder—an unwelcome deviation from the wave of nonchalance that I usually wrap around myself. Eris' eyes crinkle for a heartbeat, a sign that she has something to say, and I quickly move to overpower her voice and begin a new conversation independent of Antares and his suspected proposal. That effort seemingly goes to waste when the man lets himself in using the front door and reveals his presence to me.

Antares is a mirror image of the man I met at the Thieves Gate with scraggly platinum hair licking at the edges of his ears and a clear display of gaiety painting his expression. He looks beautiful and familiar, the only unchanged element of this experience, and I begin to wonder if that fact means anything, if my mind is trying to convey something to me by leaving Antares consistent in my visions and reality.

Thankfully, Antares decides for me and quickly closes the distance between our bodies, enveloping me in a sweeping hug. His scent spreads through the atmosphere around us as I return the vehemence of the gesture, even grinning when Antares gives my torso a final squeeze before setting me back down.

"Hey," he breathes in a rushed sort of manner that indicates that his journey to our cottage was not delayed in the slightest. That evidence fills my core with an inexplicable reassurance, knowing that I am with someone open enough to show me that their care for me isn't eclipsed by distance or external priorities. I fail to reciprocate it, not feeling more than a slight spark of affection as he embraces me, but the sight of his endearment feels like something I want to treasure.

It appears Antares is reaching into his pocket and those behind me nearly pulsate with their pure ecstasy as they shift their positions, on the lookout for the ring they care for so deeply. I, on the other hand, sense that Antares' movements are too slow for him to just be revealing a ring. His expression also falls slightly, being quickly superseded by that stagnant smile, but the shift was noticeable enough for me to draw concern.

I stumble backward, having lost a great deal of my dexterity in this dream-like version of myself, but Antares' hand sharply catches my wrist. It's not a gentle touch. His fingers all but tear into my skin and incite a wave of anger from within me. I struggle against his grip, fighting to alert my family of the strangeness of this encounter, but they fail to move. Upon the rash swerve of my gaze in their direction, I notice their bodies being nearly paralyzed in place with those expressions of joy still imprinted on unmoving features.

They're gone, they've left this dream that is no longer a utopia—and the moment Antares plunges his sword into the flesh of my stomach, I know I have left as well.

CHAPTER SEVENTEEN

C E R E S

*I'*m woken by a terrible gasp leaving my throat, accompanied by my shoulders lurching forward as the dagger is driven into my body—a shallow area of my stomach. My mouth opens in a soundless scream that rakes at the edges of my body, the pain of my wound coursing through my veins and cluttering my mind. My chest arches upward as the sword is pulled from my flesh in a swift motion, blood sputtering from the divide in my skin and soaking through my dress.

I shouldn't have fallen asleep once I arrived back at the palace. I shouldn't have allowed myself to become so indisposed that I left my sense of security at the entrance of my bedroom. I didn't even think to keep *Letalis* sheathed. My vision is blurred, and yet I still look in the direction of my beloved weapon to see her resting within my wardrobe, the ajar door allowing me a glimpse of her glint. I search for the threads of energy buried inside of me that can propel *Letalis* into my palm, but I find myself far too drained to grasp ahold of them and incapable of ripping my limbs from the ropes that are encircling them.

Descending into the fear that accompanies *Letalis'* absence— my torso trembles with withering breaths as I struggle to calm the rhythm of them. It's difficult with the sensation of hands moving across my body, my skin, pulling at me, scratching me.

I'm not offered one momentary encounter with peace before a rough hand grabs my hair and pulls forcefully, along with the sword coated in my blood shifting its focus to the ties around my wrists, waist, and ankles. It slashes the ropes to the ground and offers me the opportunity to stumble out of the bloodstained bed and onto all fours on the hardwood floor.

Upon regaining some semblance of strength and holding my arm out in the direction of the shadowed closet, *Letalis* detects my presence and rappels into my hand with immeasurable ease. The burning at the bottom of my stomach falters with the newfound reassurance of *Letalis*, though my mind reels due to the continued loss of blood that isn't stifled in the slightest by my hand.

In my weakened, but newly capable state, I regard my attackers through hooded eyes and observe the quality of the weapons they wield in their gloved hands. The three of their faces are masked with black material, along with the strictly covered remainder of their bodies, allowing their figures to blend seamlessly into the darkened surroundings of my bedroom.

"Who are you?" I inquire amidst a wince that the movement of my chest stimulates. My words are simply a method to fill time as my eyes flick about their bodies, concocting a plan for my escape—or their departure.

A young woman steps forward before her companions do and peels the mask from her face, revealing her features as she steps into a ray of moonlight. Her eyes are taunting as she lowers her body into a crouch beside my crumbled form. With an unwavering self-assurance, I meet her stare.

"Do I look familiar?" she whispers, harshly pulling my face close to hers through a clutch on my chin. I swallow against the touch she has on me, knowing that having her in this position means I could overtake her in a matter of seconds, but instead I choose to enact my plan with my longer method.

I observe the girl with the intensity that she's asking for, memorizing her silver eyes and olive skin. Her white hair and square-like jawline meet my gaze, both of which incite an inkling from the depths of my thoughts, but don't present an answer to me.

Growing impatient with my attempts, she eventually answers my question for me. "I'm her sister."

I internally wince. That's who she vaguely reminds me of—the girl I mistook for Eris and killed. She's the adjoined victim of my murder, and now she's before me demanding the justice that I'm not able to give her.

I pride myself on my ability to not fall to the addictive appeals of emotion. I'm able to disassociate from my spiraling emotions to the degree where I no longer hold them within me and they do not affect my stability or outward appearance—but *this*. This cements itself in my skin and provokes a single tear from my right eye—one that travels the curve of my cheek and resides at the corner of my lips.

It's an expression of frustration rather than sadness. It's self-pity as I apologize to my body, to my mind, for having to reap the consequences of that unfortunate event. It's anger toward Eris for pushing me to commit such an act without reservations about holding me accountable. It's pure shame for having my first kill be nothing worthwhile, nothing warranted—just pure, vindictive destruction.

"Let me tell you one thing, Princess Ceres," the sister picks up her voice after she left it behind with a tremor. Her fingers unsheathe a single dagger from her belt, this one is pristine and bloodless, though she most likely expects it to be painted red in moments.

The atmosphere the girl sets in the room is what she intended for with the two men behind her standing dark and foreboding and my open wound rendering me just incapable enough to prevent my motion—but the dagger is her weakness. As Antares had described, common Solarians don't receive formal training in sparring. In fact, they hardly have access to any weaponry at all, so though the girl's blades seem legitimate, she isn't comfortable with them.

Her movements reek of inexperience as her grip on the dagger's handle remains too loose and her flashy spins of the weapon between her fingers are stuttered and nearly awkward in their execution. Though her lack of adeptness eases me, I cannot deny the unnerving quality of her words.

"Solaris is cursed to have you as a Princess."

I release a long exhale, the comment puncturing me but raising a new wave of rage at the same time. I perpetrated an ungodly act during the procession, which is not hard to accept, but I will not tolerate blatant animosity from the people that Vega has nurtured this kingdom for, not when it was Eris who sparked the initial flame and influenced me to spread its reach.

With this mentality, I'm able to see the experience from Vega's perspective, mirroring her self-important opinions regarding our pivotal roles within the kingdom. I even enjoy these mannerisms, growing fond of the practice of valuing your own priorities above those of the kingdom but connecting your motives to the benefit of the people in elaborate lies.

"Let *me* tell you one thing," I respond in a muted tone, leaning forward with every word of mine to the point where my forehead and hers are nearly touching. "It's pathetic to think that you could overpower me."

The girl hesitates, and the split second of her doubt is all I require to attack.

My hand flies forward, swiping her dagger from the ineffective grip she has on it. Utilizing a fighting technique I picked up from Antares, I lurch upward with my heel gaining momentum as it connects with the length of her neck, causing a satisfying crack. The image of the girl's head spinning in a frightening direction with her body simultaneously collapsing backward is enough to capture the attention of her hands. She has them leave the proximity of my body as her fingers reach for her fractured neck, clawing at the skin while both her men rush forward with recklessness characterizing their movements.

I meet one with the blade of the dagger I procured from the girl, sliding it effortlessly into the flesh between his ribs, causing him to wheel to the side in shock. The other man reaches for the base of my throat with large fingers, and I respond by wrenching his arm farther behind his back than it should safely go, forcing the bones in his shoulder to splinter.

No movements persist from the three of them, all consumed by their wounds and misplaced joints, which allows me to release the wail of pain that was fracturing my tongue with its weight. Safe from the eyes and ears of those who would think less of me, I'm able to express my hurt in an unrefined way—and it's a relief to do so.

Quivering under the physical and mental exertion of the previous fight, my mind begins to flicker in and out of consciousness, offering me a clear sign that I need to find a haven before my attackers regain lucidity. I find a vague path to the corridor outside of my bedroom where serenity would reside in this late hour of the night, and with a palm cupping the blood exiting my wound, I stumble toward it. The chilled air of the hallway takes me under its arm as I fall through the opening of my ajar door, the impact releasing a jarring sting through my torso as my open flesh grates against the fabric of my dress.

I gasp in agony, eyes yearning to close and relieve myself of this discomfort, if only for a moment. With my procession dress soaked to the seams and the lesion on my side showing no sign of reducing the size of its opening, I find myself crawling past Eris' door, though it is my closest path to assumed safety.

Instead, I proceed to the farthest door down the expanse of the royal quarters—the one behind which my mother sleeps.

———

I had regained consciousness sometime between Vega taking my arms in hers and heaving me into her bedroom and her nudging a spoon of a sweet liquid into my mouth.

By the time my eyes tear themselves open, I'm resting on a plush mattress that eclipses the quality of mine by far and is surrounded by fabrics and comforters that exude wealth. Even the headboard behind me presents its luxury in the reflections of light that it casts onto my skin.

Though there is no way to misinterpret my location—the Solarian palace—elements of this setting remind me of the ideal world I experienced in my earlier dream, where Vega exemplified the characteristics of a mother. Now, with her gingerly perched on the edge of the mattress with a small bowl clutched in her adorned fingers, she seems exactly like the Sun District version of herself—though her body is now clothed in riches and her face still hasn't surrendered its guard.

"You should rest," Vega suggests, her eyes holding a shadowed emotion as she rips her gaze from my wound and averts it to the liquid in her hands. She seems inclined to do that—act like she does not care or is indifferent to my condition, while the clear aid she has offered me begs differently. Most likely having originated from a Healer, Vega had me take a medicinal potion that she weaved her magic into, considering how I feel the stitching of the skin around my wound tighten itself together. She had propped my head up, repositioned *Letalis* in my fist, and refrained from mentioning the earlier events of the procession, all of which reveal a craving within me for *more*.

A strange yearning for her motherly presence fills my body upon registering these facts in their entirety and I sputter out words that would've been discarded with one more second of contemplation. "Do you know what I dreamed about?"

I regret the question as soon as I release it into the air between us. I'm not sure I want to share such an intimate moment of mine with her, especially not when I still interpret my current vulnerability as discomfort.

"I dreamt about you." Against my best judgment, my words take advantage of their free will and escape into the air between my mother and me. All my eyes can do while my tongue empties itself is watch as Vega skips a breath in the rhythm of her consistent breathing, a rare indication of her disarray.

"It was strange. I thought it was real. It seemed so real. The dream took place in Sun District, nearly exactly how I remember it." Vega's eyes sharply flick to me with a fledgling curiosity burning behind the movement. *Even when in her softest state, she still finds a way to seem vicious,* I think as I retreat further into the events of my vision.

"I woke up, and you were next to me. Except you didn't look like you. You were wearing peasant clothes, your hair was swept in a knot, and your hands were streaked with dust." I continue, my voice quiet, but deafening in the silence. A furrow develops between Vega's eyebrows as she considers the possibility of my description being her appearance, and some form of intrigue enters her composure.

"You were so youthful and—and *loving*. You never stopped smiling; it was like you cared about the people around you so much that the emotion was too expansive to hold within yourself." Now it's me who breaks eye contact, feeling my tone wavering under the focus of my mother's stare. It's terrifying to bare my thoughts to her in this manner, not knowing the reactions she has in her mind. Perhaps this is angering her, perhaps she believes that I'm tainting her royal image by perceiving her in this light—but I continue my monologue anyway. "You weren't the only one there, however. I saw Eris and…"

I falter, my voice dying in my throat as I stop myself from uttering the name that Vega had torn out of her life. I assume she refers to him with little hesitation, but something prevents me from doing so—as if it is only her who has the right to refer to my father, having experienced the most pain from his actions.

"Mensa," Vega speaks for the first time since I began my retelling, her voice taut and cloaked with the tension of having this all between us. "You saw us together as a family for once. It must have felt nice."

I'm silent for a moment, attempting to sift through the thoughts cluttering my mind to deduce my true opinion of what I experienced. It's difficult, considering that the state of mind I was swept in came with both intense comfort and prevalent paranoia. As much as I wish my circumstances were as simple as I dreamt them to be, I feel as though an inherent part of my soul craves the darkness that accompanies *this* life. This life is a tragedy characterized by its tendency to value devastation over one's sanity, but the adrenaline I receive from it is too indispensable for me to overshadow with practicality.

I thrive off of the thrill of ruination, as does the rest of my blood, and that quality is impossible to neglect.

"It was nice," I finally respond, words slowly leaving my mouth as I struggle to pick the correct ones to proceed forward. "It was nearly perfect, and I think that terrified me. It frightened me to not have the sensation of my abilities prickling at the back of my skull. It was unsettling to be experiencing a flawless relationship with you and Eris as if the three of us aren't proponents of mutually assured destruction. I felt like I wanted to leave at a certain moment when I was crumbling under the love that was directed toward me."

"You've faced wildly different circumstances for so long that it's impossible to revert to a quixotic reality like that one," Vega grasps the final threads of my reasoning with her inference and I nod, affirming that she's correct.

"Everyone called me 'Cer'," I say suddenly, remembering the name that seemed so customary at the moment, but now is foreign against my tongue. "I've never been called by that nickname."

"I used to call you that." Vega fills the void in my mind where that inquiry lays, the disclosure rushing from her mouth. "It became my name for you when you were only a few days old. It felt sinful to use your true name, though it symbolized both an Olden Ages goddess and a celestial entity we revere. My reluctance was because your father called you Ceres, but he said it with an overwhelming distaste. He said it like the name was a swear, useful only to spit out ruthlessly."

The hurt is apparent on her face and it inches onto mine as well. I had never yearned to learn about my father before, what he was like, and his opinion of me. Maybe it was because I was so invested in my mother's story that the thought of Mensa Jacque never crossed my mind, and now that I register what this man thought of me in its most truthful form, I feel grateful that my thoughts never allowed space for his presence.

"I swore to myself that I would never use that name. It carried too much disgust—the emotion that later fueled Mensa's dismissal of you and Eris. So, I chose the alternative, the half of your name. Cer." A troubled exhale falls in between Vega's sentences, an indication of how buried these memories were before this intimate exchange coaxed them out of her. "I still think of you in that name, only verbally calling you 'Ceres'. I suppose it is my way of holding onto the version of me and you that existed 16 years ago when we weren't plagued with such animosity and affliction."

I consider what my mother says, repeating her final words in my mind almost as a chant. *Animosity and affliction.*

"Do you truly see it as a plague?" I finally inquired, referring to the congenital trait of mine that I have been assuming all in my family share, but never receiving confirmation of that theory. "Do you think the pain we inflict on ourselves and others is not something to be cherished?"

Vega's breath hitches, as if this is the first time she's considering the possibility that my words hold truth. After I notice the resolute fixture of her stare on her fisted hands, however, I realize that this is not the case, and her speech affirms that understanding.

"Maybe the more I call it a plague, a curse, a misfortune—all the words I use to describe our situation—the more I'll believe it. Perhaps I'll wake up one morning and condemn all my past actions and the dark entity I've woven a once sunbathed Solaris into. I could gradually rewire my mind into something ethical, kind, and *good*—"

"—But you don't want to."

"I don't want to—I thrive off of this energy. Sometimes I believe it's the only thing that keeps me living now that I've lost every sense of love and affinity that I've had." Vega pauses as she reinstates our steady beam of eye contact that existed for most of our conversation. "It's why we're in this state. I've been lying to you—to the entirety of Solaris. We are not fueled by light and the magic of the red ruby that brought you here. This kingdom is not suspended in our minds because the shift of power was too drastic for the Aerth to handle; we're here because we lost the magic that allowed us to be existent.

"If you've noticed, my abilities concern the life and natural matter that exist in Solaris, and though I was able to commit treacherous acts with my powers, the potency of what I could do reduced significantly when I unknowingly transferred Solaris' magic to my daughters. When you two were born, I believe the moral and sinful elements of my abilities were split—severed along a line between you and Eris."

I consider how Eris' abilities began with the act of selflessness, where she sacrificed her well-being to relieve the pain of others—and only due to the misuse of her abilities was she able to shift her magic into something of corruption. Eris didn't receive the portion of Vega's magic that supposedly fuels Solaris—the darkness that is rooted in this kingdom and had allowed it to exist with power and influence through centuries.

Vega releases a slow, labored breath as she considers how to execute her next few declarations. Her hand is trembling with a certain fear as she lays it on top of mine, matching the motion with the words that initiate the end of my sanity within Solaris.

"That dark fuel is within you—within your magic that has no potential for good. During you and your sister's 16-year absence, Solaris was no longer able to maintain its roots in the land that held it. The dark magic that connected the kingdom to its territory became one-sided, and in fear of rendering Solaris nonexistent, I channeled the Aerthen energy I possess to transfer this kingdom to the most two-dimensional of existences—our minds. Solaris began to adjust to the equilibrium of light and dark. It was strange and mundane, but the Solarians relished in the absence of the overwhelming darkness—you. I assume they had spent too long in contact with the potency of that energy, feeling its magnitude even while the Astral Saints had measured it to balance out its corresponding lightness. The witches, in particular, being in tune with the Solarian Aerth in a manner that I could not even begin to explore, sensed your absence with the most glee and attempted to speak out. They wished to inform the public that it was *you* who tore the peace from our kingdom and plagued our people with misfortune—and I had no choice in my mind but to kill them. I killed every last one of those witches and warlocks, Antares Arinel's parents included, all in the hope that your safety and secrecy in Sun District were insured."

The conclusion of my mother's sentence was said so casually but carries a weight that feels scandalous to witness, like I should not have been in the room when she referenced Antares' parents.

The first emotion that parades through me is utter confusion—*they were witches? They were a part of the group that was plotting against me and tainting my name?* My mind falls down the familiar path of disorientation, realizing that this inconvenience of Vega's was enough in her perception to kill a young boy's parents—a boy who she knew would face the Order of the Grim, a boy who she engineered to join her army, a boy who became her Sun District correspondent and her Fire Council leader. It all feels so ludicrous when I reiterate Antares and Vega's interactions in my thoughts and recognize that my mother's intentions with Antares have never been honorable.

Perhaps this has all been a ploy to make Antares her lap dog; perhaps she's done this to several unassuming children of witches and finds some toxic security in it every time. I understand that it seems beyond hypocritical for me to criticize her ethics when my moral collapse is beginning to tick backward, but Vega aggravates me with her twisted decisions. Maybe because I don't see myself doing anything differently, yet again.

"It is true that I fear I cannot protect you any longer. Look at what is happening to Solaris, to you! I stepped away from the scene during the procession because the Astral Saints prevented me from touching you. They truly feared for what would occur to my life if I went under your influence the same way Eris and the Solarian girl did. Look at your attackers that were let into the palace by servants who align with their cause. The movement and unrest in this kingdom are growing—and you, my dear, are at the heart of it." My mother shakes her head with a bitter sort of finality and gestures around her, compressing the entirety of my attention within one sweep of her arm.

Though her hand follows the expanse of her bedroom, I can tell that it's not what she's referring to. She's pointing toward the dramatic shift in Eris' behavior, to the death of the young girl this morning, to the attackers that tore blood from me—all terrible indications of the misfortune that previously never showed itself in Solaris and now exists in unison with my presence.

There's a warning in Vega's tone as she utters words that circle through my head before I'm able to understand the gravity of them. "The witches and warlocks have seen that your plague has returned, and they're relentless. I fear there is one in your proximity, one that threatens you... but I cannot place them with a name. I only feel their energy—their anger."

"Could you tell me more?" I ask my mother once my lucidity has reeled back into my mind and the churning of my stomach has eased. Her words are revelations in my mind as elements of my life begin to slide into place and what made little sense before is now explicit in its significance. All I want is to hear more, to finish the last pieces of the puzzle in my head and understand what exactly it is that I must do to save myself from this fate that Vega fears is imminent.

"During the procession," my mother says as she reinstates her position as the guide to this tale, having experienced its early plotlines and having a clear understanding of its concurrent effects. "It became confirmed for many townsfolk—the fact that you were exhibiting such a large and potent amount of dark energy, a gift that no one should hold in such a way. I assume many began connecting the misfortunes in their own lives to the sight that they witnessed from you—courtesy of the witches from decades ago who cemented this rumor in the first place."

"Those witches included Antares' parents." My tone should be rooted in anger and disbelief as I recall Vega's words from earlier, but with the state of my mind being precariously uncertain, I feel as though I am unable to allow passionate emotions to overtake me. Rather, I feel an aura of indifference settle over me.

"Correct," Vega responds with a shameful shake of her head.

Though the guilt is apparent on her features for a moment, especially with the image of Antares rappelling through both of our consciousnesses and bringing with it the tragedy of his murdered parents, she quickly wipes it away. It's an indication that what she stated earlier is correct. Her regret regarding what occurred to Antares' parents only goes so far; she values the gratification of enacting harm with a far larger intensity than anything her moral compass can reorient.

"Dozens upon dozens of families were separated following the beginning of my persecution, but I did not cease until every proponent had ceased to exist. I knew that wherever in Aerth you lived, no matter how developed your abilities had grown to be, you would be put in immense danger upon the public release of your importance."

"I'm struggling to understand what that importance entails." With unabashed ease, I begin to put forth the multitude of inquiries that I have, no longer restricted by the boundaries Vega and I previously had between us.

Vega shifts her position on the mattress so that her torso is facing me, crossing her legs underneath her in a youthful sort of motion. She doesn't realize it, but her newfound openness is what keeps this conversation moving forward in my mind—not necessarily the contents of it.

"As the newly appointed Queen of Solaris with an abundance of magic granted to me by the Astral Saints," Vega begins, circling her tale and beginning far earlier than I expected her to go. "I contained the same balance of chivalry and sin that all the previous Queens were given, except I chose to have children, whilst none of my other predecessors chose that fate. I was still young and my mind and love were unblemished—it was the wrong decision but at the time it felt nothing but right. I thought, *'what is the purpose of having just a vast land if I lack people to share it with me?'* "

A few weeks earlier, I would have felt offended by Vega's statement that my birth was the wrong decision—but considering her circumstances at the time compared to now, I find the interpretation understandable, to say the least.

"As I said earlier, the facets of my magic were split between my children, meaning that the inherent dark energy that allows our kingdom to thrive was dependent on you, and only you. I still held the capability to commit acts of evil, but it was no longer my purpose to do so. The Saints interpreted the division of my power instead as a shift, so they chose not to interfere, a decision they would soon come to regret."

"But here they are," I recall, vividly placing myself back in the setting of that first dinner where the Astral Saints settled into Solaris like this was their home instead of the mountains. "They're in Solaris, treating us like friends instead of subjects while they disregard the kingdoms and districts that require their promised aid."

Vega emits a bitter laugh, shaking her head as she considers her Saints. "The Saints are an enigma in themselves. They created a world in which they are revered, which was the original intention I assume, but they believe themselves to bear no responsibility for the fallout of their poor decisions. They almost live in an isolated realm containing only them and Solaris, solely due to the power it possesses that attracts them so consistently. I suppose they became my allies after realizing that the power I have nurtured is much too potent for them to still consider inferior, but you and Eris are a different story."

"It felt like they were almost threatened by us." I allow the conversation to be led even further astray as I place all my lingering questions in a position where they're answered. Vega doesn't seem to mind. In fact, she seems to engage in every conversation of ours just as ardently as the last. "It was as if they were just waiting for Eris and me to become involved in whatever political power surrounds Solaris."

"Yes, they're wary of you two—not because of anything you have done but because your existence should not have been allowed in the first place. You should not be princesses; Solaris has never had princesses before. The Saints believe that if you exist, then you must be Queen, but they respect me far too much to abdicate me." Vega sighs faintly, directing her gaze towards the expansive window opening the adjacent wall to the beauty of Solaris. The view allows us a glimpse of the faded peaks of the Astral Mountains and her sight holds a wistful note as if the Saints currently exist in those cliffs instead of her guest quarters. "I will tell you that they were surprised to see you back, as was the remainder of Solaris who had grown fond of your absence. Perhaps that is why they greeted you with such doubt before you gave your speech.

"The witches were vocal, to say the least, in expressing their beliefs. They saw your darkness as a plague and believed themselves to be restoring the balance of nature and magic, but I was only concerned with the tarnishing of your image. For the first 15 years of their campaign, I did subscribe to the fact that Solaris thrived with its good fortune. I began to somewhat believe that your absence was the greatest gift Solaris could have received, despite my longing for the energy that I so sorely missed. Solaris, being physically tied to the magic you hold within yourself, could no longer function as an Aerthen kingdom, so I even went as far as to spin a web of lies to the public to fabricate a reason for shifting the kingdom to our minds. I grew so weary in the absence of the magic that is so integral to Solaris' existence—to *my* existence—despite the distaste the people have for it." I now begin to sense the plot holes and white lies in the stories I had heard from Antares and Vega respectively, Antares' being in the tent during the Astral Festival and Vega's during our first encounter. Fogged bits of my mind begin to clear with the realizations of this modified tale.

"So, you changed your mind?" I ask, knowing the statement to be true but still holding too much disbelief to accept the answer without confirmation. It seems strange to me for Vega's mind to have been swayed on so many occasions, first with the love that she had for Eris and me before our departure, then the gradual acceptance of our leave, and then the growing discontent with her earlier actions and the need for a prompt reversal, no matter the cost to her people.

"I feel as though I need to make this clear," Vega continues after a nod of her chin. "It was not you and your sister I was yearning for. It was your power, which is a shameful thing to admit, but true."

"I know." I have always known. "It's understandable. I say this in my mind frequently, but I think that you deserve to hear it in your ears to comprehend the forgiveness I'm offering to you, whether you are prepared to accept it or not. I would have done nothing differently if I was in your circumstances, we are the same after all. I have learned to not blame you for actions driven by your subconscious, which yearns for iniquity as much as I do."

I utilize the same endearment that Sidra expressed in her similar speech, reminding me that our abilities are nothing to cower from. My mother seems to appreciate the sentiment and she offers me a tight smile before concluding her thoughts.

"I called for you and Eris to be brought back to Solaris, damn the consequences the people experience, but now I'm beginning to see the dilemma. I'm beginning to worry about the pivotal change in character Eris is experiencing. I am far into my worry for your conscience when considering the girl you killed and the countless number of deaths that will fill your tally."

I falter, my eyebrows displaying my pique in interest as I grapple with Vega's last words. "You believe I will kill more?"

Her firm stare planted on me is more than enough to confirm my thoughts, and the words she dispels only add to the weight now pressing against my chest and confining my breaths to shorter spurts. "I believe you will kill every day for the remainder of your life in Solaris, whether intentionally or unintentionally. Your powers are far too calibrated for me to think otherwise."

My heartbeat travels to my skull and resumes its incessant, rapidly climbing rhythm as my mind experiences a jolt of realization. What I thought was a one-time occurrence, just a fluke in the unraveling of my life instigated by my sister, was now going to become a customary element of my life. My body assumes all the indications of my mind spiraling: the paling of my cheeks, the tendency to press my hands underneath me as the pressure of my thighs suffocates the life from them, the capture of my lower lip by my teeth, and the repetitive gnawing that follows.

I could hardly handle today, neither the moral fallout of what I've done nor the task of reorienting my sanity—how must this become a lifestyle for me?

Vega notices my discomfort with the keen observance only a mother can exercise, and she offers a solution that I find that I trust more than anything else that has come to my mind.

"If I could put this magic into you, there must be a way to remove it from you. There's a possibility we could discard of it or entrap it in an entity far from Solarian soil—all in the favor of alleviating this land of its troubles." Vega's tone carries a hesitancy that could be visible from paces away, along with twinges of distaste that suggest that this is not what she wishes for.

My mother savors the results of my return, having faced no direct consequences and being a willing worshipper of this chaos. As much as I want to adhere to her best interests, I value my own much higher, so I take her offer with a nod and minimal consideration of her reservations.

"We would be robbing you of the majority of your influence and ability to cause pain and depositing us all in a Solaris free of adversity—a dramatic shift but one that I see you will tolerate."

"Anything to keep this murder from occurring again." I register the incline of Vega's head as she misinterprets my sentence as sympathy for the victims, and I quickly add to my statement for her benefit. "It's not the lost lives that concern me, however. It's the effect that they have on me; I feel lost, betrayed, and shameful. It also isn't very enjoyable to tolerate the familial discourse of killing a person." I refer to the now bandaged portion of my stomach where a blade sliced clean through the skin. Despite the amount of medication offered, the event of three people against an indisposed girl still left its mark.

"We can make that sensation leave you with a visit to the Healers." Vega's statement is so resolute that I'm baffled. How can the Healers, whose magic is centered around rejuvenation, take hold of a curse so ancient and deeply rooted?

I express my inquiry to my mother as she helps me to my feet, securing her forearms under mine as I ease forward and we begin to proceed towards her doors. My feet move in short, sporadic steps that aggravate me with their lethargic nature, but Vega doesn't seem to mind the pace we are moving at. I see no indication that she wishes to move any faster—which possibly draws from her qualms regarding doing this to begin with.

"Can we go to Sidra?" I ask after a brief hesitation. My mind still doesn't feel comfortable with baring the depths of my mind to someone that has not been previously exposed to it, especially after the majority of the kingdom witnessed the procession.

Vega responds with nothing more than a curt nod, evidently more consumed in following every movement of mine with hers. From the slight tilting of my body to the stumbling of my feet, she's there to catch it all with a dedication that she has never expressed before. Something shifted in the connection we hold between us—and I'm beginning to savor it far more than I resent myself for allowing it to build.

By the time we reach Sidra's door, the Sun has risen into the pale blue sky, bathing the hallways and interior of the palace in golden light. The hue of warmth that settles over us contrasts deeply with the incessant churning within my body, every pulse of my heart almost acting like a declining timer for what is to come. As much as I condemn myself for doing so, I allow my fearless tendencies to be superseded by paranoia—which is why it is me who knocks twice on Sidra's door, not Vega.

I hear an instantaneous shuffling from the other side of the door as if Sidra had already been right there upon my arrival. After a moment, the door is wrenched open and the familiar Healer hesitantly reveals herself, still harboring a bedhead within the fine threads of her hair. She regards me with immediate panic, the emotion consuming her entire frame, and confusion quickly follows when she views the wound I'm attempting to hide with my fingers. "Again? Ceres, you were only just here—"

I appreciate her concern to an extent, for the emotion exists so plainly that I have to convince myself that it is not fabricated, but I have little time to entertain the conversation that will inevitably follow. With a tight smile presenting itself on my lips, I ease my hold on Vega and shift my weight to the doorframe, feeling Vega's body retreat slightly once I'm no longer in need of her. She seems to ignore much of everything around her, including Sidra's astonishment at seeing the Queen in such a casual setting, and takes the silence as an opportunity to bid me a farewell.

"Ceres, it will be alright. I must go now." Vega is already turning her frame away from me when I halt her motions with an abrupt declaration of confusion.

"You're not going to be here with me?"

Though my mother does not reveal to me her face at this moment, I know exactly what sentiments she has traveling across the dips and valleys of her features. She's apprehensive to enter the room with me and experience the destruction of the magic that she so deeply adores, and also carries a sense of tolerance regarding her interactions with me. She doesn't want to return to the attachment that she nurtured before her husband sent Eris and me away.

My mother is so simple to predict once one memorizes the patterns of her mind.

Vega closes the door during her departure, incentivizing Sidra to finally express her building questions. "What happened to you? Why did the Queen bring you here? Are you alright?"

I reach out my weary hand in the middle of her words, gesturing for Sidra to do the same once her voice falters in her throat. Upon the newfound skin-to-skin contact I've established with the woman, I allow the smallest pinch of my energy to swerve through an internal barrier and explode into Sidra's palm. I shock her with the intensity of such a small percentage of my power, and I watch expectantly as she emits a hiss of pain, squeezing her eyes shut and tearing her touch away before I can unleash more agony onto her.

Sidra is filled to the brim with immediate disgust upon registering my abilities, and though she rapidly recovers her composure and releases a feeble "What was that?" into the air between us, her initial reaction still elicits suspicion. Her eyes are wide and wild as she observes the skin I manipulated, and I'm partially terrified that she too believes the theories of those witches and warlocks.

"Sidra." I swallow back the thoughts that convince me of Sidra's skepticism, the ones that rattle into my mind that upon hearing the story Vega recited to me, Sidra would leave my side. It's not very often that the harbinger of evil walks unscathed, of course. "I hold the power that allows Solaris to survive, I'm sure you've detected it by now.

"Yes," she breathes, sitting me down on the cot that still holds rumples from her night's rest. "It's also bitter and violent when I sense it like it's just waiting to lunge out of you."

"It's something that I've grown fond of, something that is inherent to my being and essential for Solaris' vitality—but it is bringing forth consequences that need to cease." As much as I want Sidra to have an idea spark her mind as to how to rid me of this curse, a part of me hopes that she remains as dumbfounded as I am. I half-expect to see her shake her head in dismay, telling me in one motion that she cannot draw out such an intense form of magic—but instead, she does the opposite.

While Sidra's face contains a mixture of emotions that are too intertwined to analyze, her actions are definite in their purpose as she brushes a hand against the top of my head in what I assume is an affectionate gesture before orienting my body so I'm lying on her mattress. She unclips my cloak and slides it from my shoulders, revealing the core where that dark energy pulsates and thrives. All that separates Sidra from it is the velvet of my procession gown, and the bob of her throat suggests that she recognizes this fact.

"We can attempt to draw it out of you, first by subduing your body and almost placing you in a coma, and then coaxing out that dark energy with a gentle tug." Sidra's mind is suspended in a place of deep thought as she stares at the blankness of her ceiling. Her fingers twitch as if she is already casting spells on me, but from the way her joints are angled toward the door, I can tell that it is not me she has her focus on. She is demanding the attention of others, ones that she is calling to her room with the all-reaching abilities of her magic.

"I want to utilize another resource." Sidra turns to me with a contemplative expression. "I want your sister to do what she did yesterday during the procession, except instead of inserting dark energy into your mind, I want her to wrench it out of you."

The thought of my sister being the essential element of this plan stirs unrest within me, but I take the offer with all the unwanted allies and tumultuous uncertainty that comes with it. I need Eris for this, and I suppose I cannot continue blaming her for the behavior that my magic causes.

PART THREE

WHY DID YOU COME HOME?

THE KINGDOM OF SOLARIS

Mors mihi lucrum.

~~(death is my reward.)~~

CHAPTER EIGHTEEN

S I D R A

"*Open your mind to me, Sidra," she says, pressing her palms gently against my face as I kneel before her. I'm trembling as sweat cascades down my cheeks and mixes itself flawlessly with my tears. My lip quivers as I exhale heavily—the consequence of a fragile mind attempting to fight forces infinitely larger than it.*

Those very forces are courtesy of my mother's polished witchcraft, the sheer vigor of which allows her to sift through the contents of my being as if I'm an unlocked vault in her grasp.

"I-I don't want to." I tremble, shaking my head vigorously as my small frame experiences that casual plethora of fear that invites itself into my body every few seconds—an emotion that my mother believes herself too great to succumb to. Hindrances don't seem to play a factor in her decisions, her actions being driven by a desperate, ravaging consumption that is oblivious to the prospect of danger.

"Please, my girl," she whispers hurriedly, wiping the tears from my face with a rashness that burns my skin. "I need you to do this. Your father needs you to do this—"

"—For your benefit," I sputter, looking away from my mother's unrelenting stare as the bitterness growing amidst my

apprehension becomes prevalent. I want to appease her, she's my mother, after all, but her convoluted agenda is heading in a direction that implicates more than just me. She's placing the entirety of Solaris under her fingertips, while I exist too young, too oblivious of the world, to understand her mind.

My mother sighs and loosens her grip on the sides of my face. She runs a weathered palm over the peaks of my scraggly hair in a comforting gesture, before bringing a knuckle to my chin and making herself the subject of my attention. Her expression is steadfast in expressing its silent plea, holding in its shadows every emotion other than regret. She feels no guilt, no remorse for allowing her situation to escalate to the circumstance where her hopes and prayers rest on the delicate shoulders of her daughter.

"This is not only for our benefit. It is for yours. It is for the good of Aerth and all living on it."

"H-How?" I question in disbelief, running my weakening mind through the piles of information my mother had deposited into me during her years by my side. I know the concept well enough, having heard the same conversation reiterated countless times between my parents, but the magic surrounding the phenomenon has always held a certain mystique that my knowledge still has not comprehended. The Jewel of Darkness has a quality in its description that characterizes it as a myth, a legend, nothing more than a story my mother would tell me to rock my body to sleep.

But here she is a year later, telling me that our kingdom's stability is at risk because of a rumored abundance of dark magic and that it is our responsibility to eradicate this energy before our inevitable destruction.

"The Jewel is powerful and demonic, so much so that it is impossible—simply impractical—for one kingdom to hold all her power. The reason Solaris has been robbed of its peaceful existence is because of this jewel. She makes us weak and susceptible to interference. She upsets the balance of magic in

nature altogether, robbing Solaris of its good fortune in the favor of unconditional power."

These declarations of hers are what I have already memorized in her voice, but the tremble of desperation that accompanies her syllables is foreign to me. A child mirrors the pain of their mother—as much as they wish to rid themselves of that connection.

"It is my duty to rid Aerth of the imbalance—the human *that has assumed control of that magic upon her birth. You as a witch born into the Solarian Kingdom share that responsibility." My chin bobs in agitation as her hand continues to caress the curves of my face as if the loving gestures of her touch are enough to eclipse the gravity of her words. "That is why you need to do this for me. You need to open your mind to me and I will weave you a destiny—a purpose. I will train you and place you at the forefront of change, my girl, and you will thank me for it."*

"Why must I be involved?" I attempt to drown the rising fascination in my head with a downpour of skepticism. I mustn't relinquish my guard, my mother can bend me too easily otherwise.

"Because there is a possibility that your father and I have not been as discreet as we should have. There is a chance that the Queen knows of our involvement in the public rallies and printing of pamphlets." My mother releases a wary breath, sweeping her head in a rapid motion as she confirms that her surroundings are not filled with any foreign ears. "Do you remember what happened to your friend Antares' parents? That fate is not far from your father and me, but you, my dear, have a lifetime in front of you to fulfill our goal."

Something like desire strengthens in me alongside my escalating paranoia—channeling the deserted elements of witchcraft that lie somewhere in my body. Though I was born with the same fundamental connection to the Aerth as my parents, I have lacked the complexity that ties me to my powers—at least, until now. What my mother speaks to me in this monologue feels dramatically different; it tells me that I can follow our family's culture of witchcraft, for once, instead of descending the path of an understudy in a magical, power-starved world.

"Kill Ceres Relasin, my child. Kill the Jewel of Darkness. Permit me to cement a destiny in your mind so I can be sure that you will fulfill our task if I fail." Her eyes are glistening with tears as familiar knuckles tighten their grip on my shoulders—turning the loving gesture into something like a warning.

I realize in a moment that my mother's request is nothing of the sort—it's a demand, a requirement. It becomes increasingly clear to me that even if I do not voluntarily surrender myself, her crafted destiny will traverse its way into my mind and implant its curse in the facets of my consciousness for an eternity.

Watching and silently waiting for Ceres Relasin's return became my fate after that single interaction between my mother and me. In the 15 years that followed what occurred in the dilapidated cottage of my childhood home, my father was executed by our Queen for his organization of a riot against the palace. My mother was rendered mute by a swipe of the Queen's sword through her tongue and now resides along the outskirts of Solaris. I haven't seen her in years, which makes me believe that her disappearance is yet another fabrication by the Queen. I wouldn't be surprised if it was both my parents who died under her sword's touch instead of one.

Thankfully, Ceres' arrival was an earthquake in my soul—something so disruptive that it would've been impossible to dismiss. I always had an inkling that she couldn't stay far from here for long, especially not when the Queen sent Antares and his obliviousness to find her, but I should have met that suspicion with strength. I shouldn't have watched as Solaris unraveled; I shouldn't have allowed my brain to be warped by the effect of Ceres' proximity.

I shouldn't be *here*, crumbled against my door, instead of in Ceres' bedroom with a knife in my grasp and my destiny pulsing in my thoughts, finally coming true.

My spine was resting against the plane of my room's door, aching from the amount of pressure I was applying on its joints. The apex of my head, the length of my shoulder blades, the sharp bones of my elbows—they were all pressed against the wood behind me because I had no choice but to keep them there.

I felt like I sensed her. It felt as though she was right there on the other side of my door, pressing her back against the wood just as passionately as I was, and my intuition turned out to be beyond correct when that knock sounded. It was all bad timing—I was a mess. My hair was in disarray after hours of restless turning in my cot, my mind full of thoughts of Ceres, and my limbs aching to have an excuse to proceed to the royal quarters.

It had all been so simple when Ceres Relasin was not present in Solaris. I had felt nothing out of the ordinary concerning my magic and was able to rest in an unbothered state without any visions or abrupt indications of important truths. My only responsibilities were to mend fractured bodies throughout my day and return to my sanity in the silent evenings, molding my life into a comfortable routine free of any suspicions of dark magic drifting about Solaris. For 16 years, I was not burdened by any affliction of Solaris' or my own, and it was a welcomed transition from the illnesses that preceded Ceres' departure.

My good fortune was fleeting in its stay, however. Once the Queen began persecuting the witches and warlocks who stepped forward and spread to the public the true reason for our mutual turmoil through the past, I knew I needed to turn my agenda into something of secrecy if I wished to keep my life intact.

As a witch by blood, having the intrinsic ability to sense shifts in the foundation of our Aerth, it was more than clear to me what the dark energy of Solaris resided in—or rather *who*—and I itched to join the forces of my kind. They paraded through the streets for months and ransacked the royal palace with a fervent initiative, all to incite a large enough public uproar where their influence would exceed that of the Queen, Saints, or the Grim, but the upper hand was eventually won by Queen Vega. Our beloved keeper of darkness and tragedy exercised the philosophy she knows best—silence through murder. The murder of countless families, the erasure of my mother, the death of Antares' parents—all her doing and all occurrences that have been held far from the Solarian public's notice, disguised as disappearances and the consequences of epidemics.

With my community terrified into silence, we began to assimilate into the improved Solarian environment, carrying the hope that our suspected princess would never return with the wave of affliction inherent to her soul.

And for 16 years—she didn't. The princesses remained lost with the true significance of their magic being hidden from the public, and we found that it became the Queen who failed to recognize the beauty in our refined world. She always held an affinity for dark energy and grief for its sudden absence, along with the loss of her husband and daughters descending her into a realm of distress. We shouldn't have expected our Queen to be content leaving her daughters in a world other than her own; we should have prepared for the reentry of Ceres Relasin into this kingdom.

From the moment Ceres stumbled into Solaris and uprooted the monotonous fabric of our lives, I have felt a burning desire within me—not one of love or lust, but instead resembling obsession. I managed to keep the feeling at bay the moment I first laid eyes on her, indisposed, wounded, and hardly capable of defending herself against my touch—only because it was a soldier carrying her to me, him being a stark reminder of the consequences I would face if I acted of my own volition. Along with Vega, Antares was vividly present in my mind, watching me, holding me accountable for my actions, and keeping my morals grounded, even if that resistance ended up fading fast.

It then became clear to me in an unsatisfactory realization that before I could act on any of my impulses, my motives needed to be mellowed by secrecy and trust—a feat that would take me weeks to accomplish.

It's almost as if every time I see the princess, I'm compelled to resort to the most violent tendencies in my mind and finish the two-decade-long mission of those witches. When I witness the deafening results of Ceres' connection to the kingdom, like the shifts in the behavior of my closest companions and the death of the Solarian girl the previous day, I know that it's my natural duty to Aerth to extinguish this plague, despite the supposed benefits of her existence.

I find it hardly relevant that Ceres being in Solaris allows the kingdom to return to its corporeal state, that tangible quality of ours only succeeding in exposing us to the surrounding kingdoms and simultaneously forcing the Astral Saints to rise from their decades of hiding. The fundamental truth of it all is that Ceres' arrival disrupted the thin fabric of Solaris' delicate peace, and with every hour that strengthens the bond between Ceres and her abilities, I can sense the stitching of our kingdom losing its grip and tumbling down in threads.

As sleep-deprived and lethargic as I was when Ceres and the Queen came to my room and announced their need for my aid, I was intrigued. It was the first proximity I was able to procure from Ceres since my potions had healed her first dagger wound in a matter of hours, and I had an idea of what to do with this opportunity. When Ceres showed me her abilities, as if I did not already know of them, I did experience a fall in my composure, but the gift I was presented with next redeemed my chances drastically.

She told me she needed to draw her connection to Solaris out from the depths of her being; she told me that she needed my help to accomplish that feat, but what she didn't realize is that her goal is nearly impossible. It would be unfeasible to transfer such a potent, deeply rooted form of magic when the host of it is so young and ideal for the energy to live in. Ceres would never succeed in ridding herself of the dark magic within her, but my involvement in her attempt to do so places me in the most convenient position to elicit one more death from her—one that would render her fragmented and torn along her seams.

A broken Ceres must be the easiest to break further, after all.

CHAPTER NINETEEN

A N T A R E S

*A*fter Ceres had fled the procession with the blood of her victim dripping from her dress, the entirety of Solaris seemed to halt to a standstill.

I didn't even turn once Ceres had awakened from her stupor and focused her sights on Eris. Instead, I kneeled in that same position with my eyes fixed on where Ceres had once lain dead, though now she was visibly full of life, her entire being consumed in trying to exercise her abilities to their maximum. I could hear the screams rising behind me and all around me within the Solarian public, but I did not dare to bear witness to Ceres' true wrath—not when realizations were developing in my mind and a scream too shrill to be either Eris' or Ceres' overtook my ears.

The moment I understood that the Solarian girl had died under Ceres' touch was the moment I began to believe the whispers that had been circulating. It had been going on since Ceres' arrival—the witches and their endless chatter and discourse about the misfortune they deemed would soon descend upon Solaris. I trusted her to contain her powers enough to prove them wrong. I even connected Eris' strangeness to the kingdom, not Ceres. But I was dreadfully wrong on both accounts.

I am still reliving the procession as I attempt to drown it from my mind through the pounding of my fists against the training mats of the soldier's complex. There stands an invisible opponent between me and the wall that I'm pummeling into the cement, but the uneasiness I feel is unshakeable no matter how hard I try. It expresses itself in every aspect of my appearance and I fear that if someone approaches me at this moment, I will bring them to the floor in my storm.

That's why I find it beyond inconvenient when I feel I have company next to me, someone who brings with her that air of Solarian royalty that I have to grudgingly acknowledge with respect.

Eris comes to my side, leaning on the training wall as she surveys me—not in a sense of superiority, but out of pure caution instead. The self-assured demeanor that she had gradually adopted during her stay at Solaris is beginning to erode—and I can only associate that fact with the error she committed the previous morning.

"It's not me you should be apologizing to," I say to her, breathlessly hitting the wall with trembling fists. The tighter I wind my hands, the more cinched my windpipe becomes until I'm forced to loosen the passion on my own.

Eris, clearly flustered by my words, reluctantly lays a hand on my forearm, ceasing the motion a moment before my knuckles collide with the cement. We stay in that position, my chest heaving with exertion and hers still with the apprehensive hold she has on her breath. I finally break the daze we have both landed ourselves in by tearing my body away from her and reaching for the towel draped across the floor, lethargically swiping it over the beads of sweat on my forehead. I try my hardest to put Eris' existence behind me, setting a new agenda in my mind to visit Ceres and sift through my conflicting feelings about her.

I wish to send her away from Solaris, back to Sun District where I know she will not endanger any more lives than she already has, but I simultaneously want to shelter her in my arms so she is out of harm's way. She's a convoluted human and one who I believe I'll forever have mixed feelings regarding.

The woman standing behind me, however—my interpretation of her is clear, but she doesn't seem to accept it. Her dogged persistence appears in the furrow of her eyebrows as she shifts to a new position before me and counters my complaint with her own words.

"I think something is wrong," she murmurs in a rushed tone, keeping her voice down though there's no one around us.

"Saints, of course, there's something wrong." I shake my head with disbelief, attempting to move past Eris' small frame, but her shoulder pressing against mine stops my motion again. The frustration compounding in my mind stimulates more words, which I'm more than happy to release from my tongue. "You compelled Ceres into murdering an innocent girl, you're hellbent on destroying her and capturing the attention of the Queen, witches are rallying up against Ceres—"

"And Solaris is no longer in our minds," Eris interrupts with a harsher tone than mine, and then I realize that her determination to get me to hear her words has nothing to do with an apology. She's warning me.

"What do you mean?" I falter upon meeting her eyes and notice unshed tears collecting above her waterline.

Eris brings her fingertips to her mouth as if she regrets speaking that loudly. Her unsettled composure rights itself after she completes an abrupt survey of the space behind her and then refocuses her attention on me. "I tried to go back to Sun District. I tried to leave this land. But I couldn't."

My breath catches in my throat upon her confession and the multitude of worries that previously consumed my thoughts immediately shift their priorities to Eris. She attempted to leave the kingdom—she was desperate enough to do that. It suddenly dawns on me that her words to Ceres before she exerted her full capacity on her sister were true after all.

"Eris, what?" My eyes are wide as I take her shoulders, shocking her and myself with the vigor I place in the action. "Are you serious? Doing that with no guide, no supervision, no one to help you if—"

"I'm here, aren't I?" she counters in a spiteful retort, wrenching her torso from my grip and retreating far enough back to where my hands can't shake more sense into her body. "I attempted to use the shard of the ruby that got me here to begin with, and—well, it presented me with darkness. The path that was so clear to me on the earlier journey is now nonexistent, replaced by an endless void of uncertainty. As I searched for Sun District, it became very clear where I was."

"You weren't traversing an alternate plane..." My voice picks up where hers left off with an unnerving sort of surety. The sensation is further amplified when Eris transfers the ruby into my palm and reveals to my eyes the dilemma she's referring to. The moment I feel the jagged edge of the piece, I know she is circling the truth.

The jewel no longer exudes a wealth of power; it doesn't pulsate with the lives of the Solarian population held within it. Its remaining fragment lays in my palm as a shattered stone—and that's all it is.

"No," Eris nods her head when she recognizes that I've caught onto the train of her thoughts. "I'm in the same plane as Sun District. We are all on the same plane. What is it you said regarding the circumstance that caused Solaris to be shifted into our minds?"

"The shift of power was too great for the royalty and the land to consume equally. Solaris was fading on the Aerthen surface, and the Queen sought a solution."

Eris snaps her fingers, her thoughts caught in a realization that shakes her core with excitement. "Unbalance of power. That is the key, is it not? An equal allocation of power between the land and the royalty."

Before I can complete a nod that affirms her statement, Eris already finds her way to the exit of the soldier's complex with a plan of action cementing itself in her fragile consciousness. Her fingers hover over the doorknob that would expose her to the world outside the confinements of this building, where so far she and I have existed separate from the horrors unfolding in Solaris. I don't wish for her to open that door, but she does.

"Antares, what's changed between now and then? Royalty has arrived in Solaris once more, specifically Ceres who holds more of that sadistic, Solarian power than any of us."

"You're saying Solaris' equilibrium has been met? That Ceres' arrival grounds us back to the Solarian land?"

"It's a newfound balance, and I say we've reached it. The witches may be consumed in the fact that Ceres brings calamity in her wake, but she returns us to our land all the same."

———————

We chose to proceed toward Sidra first; my mind trusts her more deeply with these new findings than I could with Vega or Ceres. After all, being the first to come across this theory, we needed it sanctioned before exposing it to the attention of royalty who evidently had greater issues enveloping them.

Or at least that's what I tell myself. In truth, it feels as though I'm being guided to Sidra, Eris steadfast on my heel with inquiries brewing on her tongue. I can sense the warmth of Healer magic everywhere, courtesy of the numerous scars littering my skin, and I know this is it. We're not moving towards Sidra due to our own volition—she's compelling us to.

Her reasoning becomes clear the moment we've entered her quarters, and we view Ceres in her subdued state atop the Healer's mattress. With her platinum locks strewn about and blood crusting along the crevices of her wrists and hands, she's a sight that evokes all the memories of the procession. She is also a sight of singular tragic beauty.

Eris can't keep her eyes fixed on Ceres for much longer than I can, the guilt evident in the lowering of her eyelids and the posture she shrinks into under Sidra's scrutinization. The regret seems to be for naught, however, considering the impatience the Healer displays towards our stalling and our attempts to convey our epiphanies.

She presents us with her own instead—the reason for Ceres' sudden descent into a slumber and the need for Eris to put an end to the spell that Sidra had begun to weave within these walls.

"I-I don't understand," Eris stammers, rushing her gaze between Ceres and Sidra with a frantic confusion that tears at the resolve she's been able to build. That's something I'm beginning to notice about her, her confidence is often fleeting and always accompanied by the rise of self-doubt, as evidenced now.

"It's fairly simple," Sidra clarifies with a reassuring note inserted into her words. Her confidence is unnerving to me. "The Queen came to me with a request—to remove the dark magic afflicting Solaris from Ceres, its host. I have only done so much. During your absence, I cast an incantation that has rendered Ceres unconscious, at least for the time being."

"And it will allow Eris to exercise the true form of her abilities with no fear of Ceres awakening and lashing out at her in return," I finish for Sidra, understanding the importance of this new task beyond what Eris had piqued my interest in just moments earlier. Yes, our notion that Solaris was now truly existent holds gravity, but nothing compared to the safety of Solaris that Eris is now entrusted with.

Bearing the weight of this role with a refined mind, Eris only allows a brief hesitation before letting Sidra murmur instructions, words of comfort, and incantations in her ear. I watch as the older sister of the two kneels on the carpeting. I watch as the violence within her starts to fade behind hidden doors, progressively replaced by an overwhelming sort of promise as she regards Ceres' unmoving features. The light grasp Eris now has on Ceres' palm is just another indication of the resurgence of her morality; she no longer has anger in her heart.

That procession may have altered the Solarians and lost a young life, but it also presented a purpose in Eris: redemption.

Recognizing that my presence is beginning to be more of a bother than an asset, I retreat into the shadowed portion of the small room and enclose myself within it. My eyes remained fixed on the exchange before me, entranced in Eris' ability to resume her powers so easily, already placing her palms against Ceres' scalp. Her touch starts gentle, her mind easing into it and building on it in an act of assiduity that only experience can bring.

She releases a shuddering breath from the impact of the magic blossoming inside of her as she coaxes it out of her more and more. For something so potent as magic flowing through her veins and across the channel she creates to Ceres, little shows on the outside beyond a twitching of Eris' eyebrows and the quickening of Ceres' previously shallow breaths.

Eris keeps her eyes trained on her sister, even as fatigue starts to set in on her expressions, and her unwavering focus is proven correct when Ceres' abdomen lurches forcibly. I feel a desperate urge to reach out and grasp onto Eris' hands because the evident pain she's putting Ceres under when she's incapable of defending herself is a situation so similar to what occurred the previous morning. Sidra's silent warning keeps me in place, however, which is further backed by just the upward flick of Eris' fingers.

Not a moment after Eris harnesses that portion of Ceres' power, a scream erupts from her limp frame, rattling her body with a turbulent ferocity. The spine that previously lay still and lifeless now arches upwards as an intolerable agony burst through her figure, the pain destructive enough to break through the barrier of Sidra's subjugation.

I intend to rush forward and emphatically urge Sidra to deepen the spell Ceres is under, to heighten the coma so that she won't feel the pain of the extraction anymore. I'm nearly close to the three of them when a deeply rooted growl from Eris' throat shocks me in its intensity and builds a certain fear in me.

"I'm sorry for this, Ceres," she says, the regret blatant in her trembling tone. Eris is overwhelmed—it's obvious from the way her face contorts into an expression that mirrors Ceres'—but still she continues her practice.

Just then another scream erupts from Ceres' gaping mouth, this one hoarser and louder. She begins to lose sight of the unconsciousness that protects Eris. Her body begins flailing on the cot, twisting and turning and painfully pushing her closer toward reality. With every passing moment, Ceres grows closer to opening her eyes and repeating the events of the procession— except now in the confinements of a room filled with the people who would understand.

I'm just about to exclaim that that's enough, not being able to witness any more of Ceres' painstakingly slow awakening, when I see the slight tendrils of darkness escape her. The dark energy in her core stirs before my eyes, traveling from the opening of her mouth, the slits of her half-opened eyes, and the heart in her chest. Her silence indicates that this is what she wanted—she wished for this energy to leave her—but something feels amiss.

Ceres' face twists and her cries escape through gritted teeth as her torture continues. Her body becomes consumed in the flames of her abilities, enveloping her flesh in the wake of its growth. The majority stays within the guard of her ribcage, festering like cancer as Eris' abilities wrench deeper into Ceres' body and attempt to draw out more dark energy than she's already asked for.

I don't realize it quite as quickly as I should, but somewhere between Eris' tears streaking her skin and Sidra's stoicism settling in, Ceres pulls her eyes fully open and lands them on her sister. Even from my vantage point, I can see the silent threat in the stare and the severity of the thoughts circling Ceres' mind.

It's destruction just waiting to happen, and Eris with her eyes screwed eyes, nearly tearing herself at the seams with exertion, doesn't realize it yet. She doesn't notice the deliberate shifting of Ceres' abdomen; she doesn't hear the mumbled words escaping Ceres' lips. Most of all, she doesn't feel the reabsorption of the darkness floating above Ceres and the rechanneling of that energy with the single hand she places on Eris.

"Ceres…" I whisper into the silence that persists despite the sporadic whimpers that Eris emits. I look at her pleadingly, half-expecting that will obstruct her imminent actions, but Ceres' eyes move past me to land on Eris, her jaw hardening when she registers how involved her sister is in the extraction.

In one rapid series of events, I watch Ceres narrow her eyes slightly, followed by a hardly audible grunt rising in her throat as her anger continues to multiply and multiply. She attempts to lurch forward, pure vengeance being her driving force as she flails within my sudden grip. I begin to call out for Sidra, meaning to ask her for aid with the task of restraining Ceres, but I notice that she appears to be folding herself into the shadows of her room, retreating from the scene.

I internally curse at her as Ceres scalds my skin repeatedly, needing another set of hands to diffuse the amount of exposure I have with her. Even the slightest brush of her skin is enough to send a jarring jolt of heat through my body. With a prayer to my pain tolerance, I lift Ceres completely into my arms and grind my teeth together against the predictable agony that follows—expanding from the heart of my chest through the lengths of my limbs and collecting in every portion of my body that can register pain.

"Antares, let go of me." Ceres' voice leaves her raw and cold, her tone resembling that of a stifled scream, and the heaviness of her words shocks me. "I can't control it. Antares, please. I'm going to hurt you!" Ceres continues, pressing words off her tongue as she thrashes against my grip and allows me to experience even further contact with her skin. I let out a guttural yell from my throat.

Screams circulate the small expanse now, Eris' originating from her frustration and exhaustion, Ceres' driven by desperation and burning anger, and mine just from unbridled physical torment. Even though we all feel mutual pain of varying intensities, none of us cease our actions. We've come too far to even contemplate stopping.

I can feel Ceres' power rising against our attempt to tear the dark energy from her. The rapid heaving of her chest, the veins protruding from her skin, and her eyes—once brown and full of light and now dark and brooding—are all signs of our losing battle, but Eris remains the most resilient of all of us. She stays rooted in her starting position with her eyes crinkled so tightly shut that I fear she'll never open them after this. The woman propels the entirety of her potential in this one act, though she is quickly losing control as she persists.

Ceres shakes her head furiously—which remains the last sign of her restraint. As burning tears begin to form in the shadows of her eyes, she mouths her final apology, a tragic declaration of complete resignation to the darkness overwhelming her. She's sent sprawling back into the cot against her own will, stretching her limbs out in her sister's direction with an animalistic sort of tendency.

Despite my attempt to claw at her torso, Ceres' position cannot be influenced as she shudders into the fabric of the mattress, gripping the sheets with her clenched hands as yet another grating sound escapes her hoarse throat. Her eyes seize for a moment and then roll back into her skull, replicating the scene from the last morning with terrifying accuracy. It's the moment I realize that choosing to conduct this extraction was a poor decision—this day would not end in satisfaction. One of us would die under the wrath of Ceres' unrestrained powers.

I turn to Sidra after sensing her presence retreating, my features coated with apprehension, and I find her on her knees and bent over her spell book, stumbling on a spell under her breath. The little hope that I'm able to garner from this sight doesn't remain unblemished for long, however, for Sidra's efforts seem to accomplish nothing despite allowing Ceres to inch closer to Eris with the absence of a pair of hands holding her back.

Ceres releases a ragged yell as Eris grasps another thread of the dark energy that she manages to meticulously capture. As her chest heaves and a sheen of sweat breaks out across Ceres' forehead, it's evident that the part of her subconscious that was once holding her body in check is withering away with every tendril of her power released to Eris—and she despises it.

The dark gleam in her eyes flickers incessantly as she brings her hands to her head and buries her trembling fingers in her tangled locks, grinding her teeth together as she struggles to find lucidity during the pain, and I find myself thankful that she experiences distractions such as these. They provide delays before the inevitable occurs, and as childish as it feels—I savor that limited time.

Ceres brushes my touch off her impatiently as if my years of garnering strength mean nothing to her elevated state of dominance. Her palms find the sides of Eris' head and the effect of her touch is immediate and frightening in its passion. Her abilities find and latch onto Eris in unprecedented power, as if she was withholding the true peak of her strength from Sidra and me, conserving it for her true victim

Eris releases her first true cry of pain, Ceres' physical torment driving them both to the opposite wall. Even though Eris is flailing, Ceres exercises her grip with determination and begins to insert a high enough degree of pain into her sister that she resorts to a pattern of frantic seizing. I can almost see the energy radiating off of them both in my paralyzed state, the hazy glow surrounding the sisters haunting my thoughts and distorting my vision to the point where I can no longer make out where Ceres' body ends and Eris' begins.

Ceres' screams join Eris' as she gains the clear upper hand and begins drowning the life, the *blood,* of her sister that she shares. Ceres' back arches as she gasps through the action, the pain somehow providing her with an exhilarating rush of adrenaline and only deepens her grasp. Eris' consciousness becomes lost within her mind, the sudden surrender causing her writhing limbs to fall limp against her body.

It's a terrible sight that I can't approach, Ceres' magic creating almost a shield around both of their bodies that extends her powers beyond just her frame. Now, even nearing her proximity burns my skin and sends me lurching back to safety— but I still maintain a vivid view of the events before me.

I watch through a pained silence as Ceres descends onto her sister, eliminating every last indication that the woman below her still maintains a semblance of life. She wrenches out Eris' heartbeat, her sight, her touch, her breathing, her movement—a new loss occurring with every ragged sigh from Ceres. After a moment it becomes clear that Eris' state is beyond salvageable; her body is far too mangled to witness without turning away, there's far too much blood collecting underneath her than to consider normal, and the silent scream in her mouth is suspended in is too unmoving to have any life within it.

Ceres continues exerting her power until Eris is far past dead, until her vitality has been shattered so deeply that there's no way of even showing homage to it. She cries atop her sister's body, she screams into Eris' skull with bitter words of resentment and pain, she unsheathes *Letalis* for the first time today and plunges the dagger into Eris with repeated, frantic, demented motions.

Almost stilling the scene with her words, Sidra tilts her head in my direction and speaks. "Now do you see how she is a danger? Do you understand the cause that your parents died for?"

Sidra's words don't register in my mind. Nothing registers in my mind except for the horrifying image of Ceres' anger. She attacks every inch of her sister's body, tearing an individual of her own blood into mere flesh, and then lurches backward to witness the results of her unhinged masterpiece.

And we watch it with her.

CHAPTER TWENTY

C   E   R   E   S

I had retreated from the hub of the city early today, stumbling back into the palace and clutching the polished walls with tired hands as I made my way into my bedroom. My mind failed to waste a moment before harshly slamming my door shut behind me, isolating my withering mind with the destructive thoughts pounding within it.

Antares and Sidra still have not notified the Queen of Eris' death, making me wonder if they're expecting me to do so. The thought terrifies me—I'm in no condition to address the Queen, not when my body is frail from withholding food from myself and my conscience has dissolved into a state of disrepair. Somewhere over the past week, I've lost my ability to guard my exterior and now I've descended into pure, uncontrolled vulnerability where my emotions present themselves clearly within my demeanor.

Even *Letalis* is seemingly unable to recognize me, or perhaps she lost more respect for me with every slice I made her commit into Eris' lifeless body.

That's the only part of her death that I can even recall—the aftermath where I broke out of the trance my powers had entrapped me in and completed all my following actions within the bounds of my own free will. A clawing, ravenous frustration stimulated the tears that I spilled over Eris' wounds, and a contrasting turbulent fury drove the swinging of *Letalis* that concluded my time in that room.

I had walked out with a bloodied *Letalis* clutched in my hand and a feverish sensation fogging my mind, leaving Antares and Sidra to clean my mess, to witness the monstrosity of the death I caused, and I hardly even felt shame. I hurt Antares, I hurt Sidra with the potency of my powers that I so mercilessly directed towards them. I put them in a position where they were forced to watch Eris' life and heartbeat fade to naught—and I don't feel regret for any of it.

The thought makes me nauseous and threatens to tear up the internal contents of my body with the sickness that begins to envelop me. I want to feel something; I want to despise myself and condemn my actions, but no viable reprimand comes to my mind. Time has passed since Eris' death—I should be showing some signs of healing or acceptance, but all I can manage to do is recite the events of that day in an incessant loop in my mind. Replaying it over, and over, is how I choose to cope, attempting to find some hint that suggests that what occurred did not make me at fault.

Without tangible evidence, I am at fault—no matter how much my mind protests the fact. I may think Eris deserved her fate because of what she did to me previously, nearly driving me to the same state. Perhaps I partially blame Antares, Sidra, and Eris in the first place for allowing their experiment to grow into such destruction. Maybe it's Vega's fault for putting me in this position, both in terms of giving me this abundance of dark energy and suggesting that I tear it out of myself.

As I went through my past few days, I've somehow avoided the presence of them all—Antares, Sidra, and Vega. My new customary routine has been shifted from the palace to the town, where I trudge past passersby and avoid eye contact with anyone I come across in fear of them recognizing my face. Though the general public does not know of Eris' death, nor what I did to her, they never quite forgave me for what happened to that young village girl, which makes the village just as precarious of a haven as the palace.

For a princess who spent three days in extraordinary luxury and experienced a sudden shift in circumstances, I suppose the degree to which I am coping is respectable, even when the faces and crooked smiles of my victims flash through my mind several times a day. At first, I believed the occurrences were amusing, like a gift from the Saints reminding me of my sins, but now I lack the tolerance to see them as anything more than twisted threats.

They're the same threats that haunt me even now as I sit on my bedroom floor, collapsing in on myself and lowering my forehead to my knees as my body seizes with silent sobs. This is what I've learned to do—let out my hurt now, in the confinements of my bedroom where expectations and formalities fail to exist while simultaneously disappearing from society. After all, if I render myself nonexistent, perhaps my crimes will fade just as deeply.

My knuckles turn stark white as I dig my fingernails into my skin with passionate severity, not caring for the slight tearing of my skin and the blood beginning to coat my fingertips. Not caring for the way I'm crumpled on my carpet in the clothes from two days earlier and what bits of Eris' blood are still hidden on my body. Not caring for the tears cascading down my cheeks and soaking into my dress, the feeling of the wet fabric reminded me of how shamelessly I cried during my sister's death.

After a moment, I draw in a long, shuddering breath and begin to nurture a terrifying idea that bursts into my mind, the one that revisits my mind with every shutter of my eyelids, every moment I allow myself to get consumed in my thoughts. I slowly raise myself off of the ground, resting on my knees as I flutter my eyes closed, contemplating whether or not I should do what every cell in my body yearns for me to do.

If I hurt myself just as much as I hurt Eris, perhaps I could gain some semblance of peace.

The thought frightens me. Hurting myself to that extent—to the point where I could relinquish my control over my abilities and push myself far enough on the brink of insanity that I would be left in the same state as Eris—it's appealing. Even though fear courses through me as a result of contemplating this idea, my mind tells me that I need to experience something even close to the pain she felt to feel the regret and shame I deserve. I need to feel penance for the wickedness of my acts that generally go unanswered in punishments, and this could be the first of my attempts—even if my motive is more fueled by self-preservation than it is by morality.

In a moment's time, my mind has settled upon the decision to continue and I begin to sink into myself—replicating the position of my victim, because today, I am my victim.

I surround my torso in a cage of my touch by wrapping my arms around myself, all for the sake of giving myself more contact with my skin. It takes several lasting shudders of my body to orient myself in the position, ready to exert an unimaginable pain that has already been delivered in full force to two other individuals—and soon, me as well. With my stomach churning with a mixture of anticipation and developing agitation, I press my eyes tightly shut as I search for that inkling of darkness within me that has been present on so many other occasions.

I traverse my mind, my heart, the space encased by my ribcage where my powers are nurtured and the moment my consciousness brushes over the first tendril of energy, goosebumps erupt across my skin. I manage a grim smile once I wind the magic around my being and lift it from the crevices in which it lays, diffusing it across my skin with a gentle cautiousness that I never exercised with anyone else. Perhaps this newfound control can aid me—perhaps I can learn a way to maintain a hold on my humanity during this process.

Perhaps Vega's foretelling holds faults in its candor—Solaris doesn't have to be cursed by the presence of my magic if I do not allow it to be.

CHAPTER TWENTY-ONE

A N T A R E S

*A*s I stand stationary at the palace entrance, I contemplate whether or not I should go towards Ceres' door, it being possibly the hundredth time the thought has crossed my mind since Eris' death. My fingers absentmindedly trace patterns on the marble wall beside me as my head ducks lower, hiding the furrow between my eyebrows from the servants that bustle past my stagnant body.

I swallow hard, knowing that I should be with my soldiers, either offering some encouraging words or training with them, pushing them to the limits of their strength and simultaneously driving myself to my breaking point. I should be at Sidra's door instead, questioning her about the words she uttered to me as Eris' death was unfolding, the abrupt declaration of the reason behind my parents' deaths. I should be diverting my energy to a number of tasks—but my mind remains otherwise occupied.

I haven't spoken to Ceres in days, my only interaction with her being when I hesitantly walked up to her one night, offering a small smile. As I expected from her frigid persona, I only received a nod of her head in reply before she brushed past me like I was the stranger she met in Sun District instead of the man that witnessed the murder of her sister. As much as I would like to continue condemning Ceres' actions and make her gaze at herself in the mirror, recognizing what she has done to a woman connected to her by blood, I can't bring myself to.

Instead, my mind circles around the fact that Ceres isn't herself when she's consumed by her powers—it's what I've told myself countless times as I've attempted to justify her actions, or at least find a motive for them. Reluctant to truly criticize her amidst my growing affection, this is the compromise I've reached—as flawed as it is.

My feet begin to move on their own accord as I choose to proceed forward towards Ceres, tracing the path I have followed so many other times to deliver correspondence to the Queen. I keep my eyes trained forward as I make my way through the palace, up the staircase, and past the people who attempt to stop and speak with me but falter when they see the disinterest in my expression.

There is only one person I yearn to see and question to ease the inquiries in my mind, and I believe that if I wait any longer than the year that has already passed, I'll never find the will to step forward.

I harshly bite the inside of my cheek, leaning forward slightly to feel the polished texture of her door against my forehead as I flutter my eyes closed. My breaths are slow and labored, as I hold my fist a mere inch away from the door, struggling to do even the simple motion of a knock. I'm so close to her, *so close*, and yet I can't find the words to say to her that would rebuild the shared intimacy we were beginning to generate, or the actions to take to alleviate the obvious turmoil she is facing after what she did to Eris.

My hand falls abruptly when I hear the slightest noise from the other side of the door, a muffled sob. My lips part in surprise as I hesitantly hold my ear to the wood, unsure if I heard it correctly, but my notion is confirmed as the sounds of anguish continue, ones that seem painful and abrupt in the way they leave her body.

An inexplicable emotion stirs in my chest and I abandon all attempts of knocking on her door. Instead, I allow my fingers to surround the marble of her locked door handle and wrench it open in a not well-known technique I learned as a palace soldier. I recognize my blatant disregard for her privacy almost immediately, but the sight of Ceres causes it to fade quickly, being replaced with a fervent concern for the girl I've never seen shatter.

She sits curled into herself, her forehead resting on her knees and her arms wrapped around her frail body. Her fists are clenched with the blood dripping from her fingertips, originating from the punctures her nails have placed in the skin of her palm of their own volition. Her hair hangs limply like a veil, shielding her face from view and draping over her pale skin like a curtain of white sand. I want nothing more than to pull those tangled locks away from her eyes myself, but I force myself to show patience as I lessen the pace of my approach.

After a moment of silence between us, I lower to my knees before her, reaching over to touch her hand in a comforting gesture. When my skin is a hair's breadth away from hers, Ceres flinches, tensing her body with a newfound awareness of my presence and showing her distaste for it.

"Ceres," I mumble in a tone just audible enough for her ears to catch. My voice is hoarse and cautious, weighed down by the thought of causing her to retract even further from me, but thankfully she does the opposite. Ceres lifts the apex of her head slightly, and for the first time since I entered her room, I can see her face.

"Don't," she hisses with a pained edge to her voice. I nearly reel backward in shock when I register the pained edge to her voice that displays her current state—terrified and gradually losing her sense of sanity. I fight the urge to look away when I register the dark circles below her bloodshot eyes, indicating days without sleep and hours of shameless turmoil flooding through her body.

Though Ceres is torn and fragmented at this moment in time, something in me relishes this glimpse of her because it's the most vulnerable she has ever allowed herself to be. Even though it's painful to see her like this, I only want to see more, so I complete the hesitant reach of my fingers to rest below her chin. In slow motion, I lift her face fully to my view and silently sigh with relief when she delivers no movement of anger.

"Please leave," she says after an extended silence between us. Even in the tranquility of our surroundings, Ceres manages to make her voice barely detectable and instead eclipsed by the gravity of the silence between us. Her discontent becomes further apparent when she shivers slightly and nudges her head backward to shake away my touch which still rests on her.

Channeling the blossoming urge within me, I lift the thumb I have under her chin and brush it across her cheek lightly. The action feels improper, defamatory, even, but I can't help but do it in the hope that Ceres feels the inkling as strongly as I do and she would allow the distraction to invade her mind. I have to believe that this is all that this is—an ill-fated distraction that only has a temporary place in my mind

"I'm not leaving." And that's why I speak, my words losing their touch of doubt as they penetrate her skull and their glint becomes apparent in her eyes. Even stronger than the pull between us, however, is her ignorance of it. Ceres frowns against my voice, her eyes flicking across the room as if she is trying to look at anything around her other than me.

It's a gradual process of her returning to her previous state of withdrawal and silence, and one that I comprehend much too late. It is only when a sharp pain shoots through my fingers, sprouting directly from where my fingers are holding Ceres' chin, that I realize the true occurrence before me.

The eyes that I lost myself in only seconds earlier have shadowed themselves with Ceres' eyelids and are accompanied by a vicious gleam that darkens further with every subsequent heave of her chest. Ceres tilts her head back to rest on the wall behind her, conducting the action lethargically which should indicate her serenity but instead expresses her unraveling condition.

Overwhelmed with a selfish instinct, I shift backward and remove the grasp I have on her. As much as I attempt to suppress the thought, I am only reminded of the scene of days ago, where Ceres exerted what I just felt, only magnified, on her sister and robbed the woman of her blossoming life as royalty. The difficult task of maintaining my sympathy for Ceres becomes more impossible with every revival of that jarring pain that my mind generates, making it a miracle that I'm able to dispel it from my thoughts.

"What are you—" I begin, watching with an unnerving intensity as Ceres' skin fades to a pale brown, the shift in hue only able to be conducted with the aid of magic. The drops of blood exiting the crevices her fingernails have built in her skin become even more apparent against their unsaturated background and the sight is concerning. Somehow forgetting the severity of the pain that Ceres' touch has caused, I stretch my fingertips to Ceres' face to ease the rapid movements of her eyelids, to pull her eyes back to a forward position instead of having them roll back into her skull.

She's too fast for me. Her body dodges my touch with a harsh slamming of her shoulder blades into the wall behind her, but her facial expression doesn't even seem to acknowledge that pain— it's too consumed in the magnification of what she is doing to herself. What's before me is not simply an emotional breakdown as a result of the incident. In fact, I'm struggling to believe that guilt or shame has anything to do with Ceres' sunken state. Instead, I'm inclined to think that Ceres has adopted a separate agenda—unleashing her destructive power on herself to experience her notorious touch.

"Ceres, stop!" My hands are quick in their attempt to cover hers, trying to wrench her touch away from herself, but I only succeed in stimulating the release of sharp stings up my arms, rooting from the point of contact of hers and my skin. "Why are you trying to hurt yourself?" I seethe, partially overcome with frustration as I fight to understand her current mentality and internally chastise her for resorting to such a desperate measure.

Ceres trembles as her hands shift to grip the exposed skin of her arms, ridding the air between her joints and allowing her body to feel the immensity of her power. Enveloping herself in an eternal shudder, she begins to curl into herself—a simple, lethargic action that expresses all that her mouth doesn't have the strength to say in words. Her hands, still dripping with blood, fade the skin below them to a stark white, and I can't help but wonder if she even notices.

Can you notice the pain as shallow as that when you're forcing the most violent form of energy through your body?

"You—" Ceres chokes out in a ragged tone that seems painful to emit. "You have to leave. I could hurt you."

Her declaration shifts a facet of my mind, revealing a plethora of previously obscured thoughts that now pour into my skull. I recognize the inkling of care that she exhibits in those words—as vague as they might be—and I find a dangerous sort of hope in it. I begin to ignore the consequences of her skin touching mine and instead bring my touch closer to her once more, repeating the same ill-fated process that I know will only result in my pain.

However, when she finally raises her face, all those reservations dissipate and I'm left solely focused on her voice.

"Did you feel that?"

I expected her to voice another complaint regarding my presence, but instead her vision shifts directly past me and instead travels towards her ajar window. In that fraction of space, where the contents of this room mix with the Solarian air, Ceres remains transfixed and stagnant in thought.

I shake her shoulder softly, realizing moments afterward that the previously piercing sting that her powers induced has now faded to a dull ache that I barely notice. The furrow between

Ceres' eyebrows that seconds ago demonstrated the mental turmoil she was under has now deepened with a different emotion—fear.

"You must be able to feel that," Ceres whispers, completely disregarding her previous state when she stumbles to her feet and nearly falls towards her window. She clutches the panes with her red-stained fingers and brushes her gaze across the Solarian landscape at a precarious pace. There are sensations at the tip of her tongue that she's yearning to spit out, but she doesn't know how to express them.

"Feel *what*, Ceres?" My curiosity morphs into concern with every gradual blink of Ceres' eyes, each one more delayed than the last as if she is fighting an incessant urge to collapse.

"Something just… shifted," she says in the most hesitant tone I have heard from her yet. Ceres turns her chin towards me and her eyes follow the motion, resting on me with an air of uncertainty that I can't even begin to dissect. "Somewhere between you entering this room and now—something changed in Solaris. I know it."

"Describe it to me." That's all I can manage to put forth, especially when Ceres appears to be swaying slightly atop the balls of her feet and I draw my body closer to her in the instance that her knees give out.

Ceres' hands twitch as she half-heartedly raises them, evidently under the assumption that she could display her thoughts in gestures, but she quickly discards that idea. Instead, she allows a convoluted string of words to tumble out of her with enough truth that I'm pulled back to her eyes without a second thought.

"I've always felt some form of… discomfort here. In *this* Solaris—where we're kept far from the remainder of the world. At the beginning of my visit, it always felt as though I was balancing between two worlds, not fully in one while trying to get to the other—and it hurt. Some innate part of me ached with that state of being and wished to tip the beam so I could be somewhere

237

that felt like home." Ceres' voice falters in a way that sounds like she's attempting to recollect her thoughts, but I know that she just fears voicing them. "And then I learned that my suspicions were correct—we are in between two worlds. Vega placed us here as a result of the kingdom lacking the dark magic that grounded it to its land."

"And you are that dark magic... an anchor to the Solarian Aerth," I finish for her, beginning to connect the same threads in my mind, drawing from Eris' revelation nights earlier—a thought that she never had the chance to voice herself, not when we got caught up in Sidra's rushed request.

"And I'm here, finally." Ceres breathes. "I've been demonstrating that energy, nurturing it, feeding it with my skills—and now it's thriving within Solaris. The corporeal Solaris."

I revisit the final deduction of my last conversation with Eris and I shiver with its newfound candor. Ceres' words make it all true; her presence did bring us back to our land, and everything she feels in this moment most certainly confirms it.

"Is that what you feel? Is that what you were struggling to say?" I ask, nudging Ceres along her thought process as I coax more words from the lips that are already beginning to purse closed.

She shakes her head, narrowing her eyes at the Solarian plain as she flicks her gaze across the landscape. I initially thought her stare was nothing more than a daydreaming reverie, but upon noticing the scrutinization in her expression, I can tell that she is not watching—she is searching.

"No... That's not it." Ceres draws closer to the window, pressing her stomach against the rim as she leans further into the outside air, almost drawing her abdomen into the expanse before her. "It's that I don't feel safe here anymore—and I don't believe that it's because we're on Aerth. I think something far worse has occurred."

I raise myself onto my feet, mimicking Ceres' aura of seriousness without even realizing that the intense concern I previously harbored has faded. "Could it be because of the witches and warlocks? They're conspiring, I know it. My soldiers are even saying that your attackers that night—the ones that Vega sent to the Grim—are a witch and two warlocks in disguise. They're saying that the assault was not only driven by an agenda of vengeance, but also by magical inclinations."

"That is true," Ceres murmurs, evidently replaying the initial events of that tragic night in her mind. I notice the slightest shift of her torso's position, right where her waist remains bandaged, and even that signal notifies me that this wound is something that will stay with Ceres, an eternal reminder of her moment of weakness. "If they had abilities and a connection to the Aerth, they would be able to override the defenses of the palace and reach my bedroom. It would explain their agility and access to weapons."

Ceres' current revelation seems separated from what was stirring in her mind preceding it, so I allow her to guide her speech back to her initial thoughts.

"But, it's not that I detect. It's a sense of vulnerability." Ceres squints her eyes at the land before her, as if she is attempting to focus on an entity that doesn't exist. "It feels as though the land has been opened—revealed. The energy that I hold is now being tampered with and intruded upon."

My breath stills in my chest as I recognize the gravity of her words. "Are you saying Solaris has intruders?"

"I'm saying Solaris is not as secluded as we would hope for it to be—not when we've resumed our stay on the Aerth without any of the protections that we had previously. Foreign souls are approaching—hundreds arriving since Solaris left our minds days ago."

"How can you be so sure?" I join Ceres, following her gaze to the horizon where faded shadows seem to rise from the Aerth and pulse under the daylight. Upon first glance, the figures seem like a mere trick of the eye, but as I begin to stare as feverishly as Ceres, I begin to see what she sees.

It's soldiers—hundreds of them. Just as Ceres said.

Their frames inch closer, though they still walk miles away, and I can sense their militant posture and movements of them. I can sense the faint outline of flags above their heads, as well as the evergrowing immensity of their crowd as they become visible over the horizon. I half expect the Solarian townspeople below us to share in mine and Ceres' curiosity, but their focus remains planted on their daily duties, not paying any mind to the imminent danger crossing the barren landscape that leads up to Solaris.

"How.... How can they be here? How could they find us— we didn't even know we were back." My mind pulses with desperate inquiries that I'm not sure Ceres has the knowledge to answer, but I release them anyway. My sight burns with the vision of the approaching kingdoms, only an hour's journey from our susceptible land and borders without sufficient defenses. It's a catastrophe in the making.

My body itches to notify the councils, to deploy them for the first threat they've witnessed since Solaris was shifted to our minds, but Ceres' words hold me in place.

"If Solaris contains the magic that enables me to sense their presence, the neighboring kingdoms must boast a similar trait. They must have detected intruders just as I did, except theirs was magnified by the mystery surrounding Solaris' decades of absence." Ceres rests the tips of her fingers against her lips, an indication of the confusion spiraling through her mind. She does not know what to do any more than I do. "And they had days to mobilize themselves during our ignorance. They had days to procure their best witches to map out Solaris' emitted energy and find our location. They had the safety of the Saints being preoccupied within Solaris and our Councils being unaware that there was any threat at all.

"We must inform the Queen," I say hurriedly, attempting to tear my presence from the room before my soul bonds itself with

Ceres any further, but my movements are halted by a firm hand on my wrist.

As quickly as she put it there, Ceres rips her touch away from me as if the entire action was nothing more than an accident, leaving me stagnant in my bewilderment. Upon stepping towards her again and observing her facial expression, still fixated on the approaching figures, I begin to understand what is going through her mind. It is what occurred during the procession, it was what I saw in Sidra's room just before Eris' death, it is what I see now, and its meaning is loud in my ears.

"I feel the darkness—it's rising." Ceres grits her teeth together to hold in a pained scream, and I almost believe that she's successful until a stifled grunt meets my ears. "Why is it rising?"

It makes perfect sense in my mind, my eyes having witnessed all of her silent progressions towards losing control. "You're angry. You feel violated by these intruders."

I begin to understand now that in Ceres' presence, I lose my understanding of rationality. In my haste, I don't comprehend that touching her will send repeated waves of agony through my bones, so I do it anyway, cradling her turned-away shoulders in my palms. And of course, I feel the spurts of fire shoot up my arms, emanating from my hold on her, and yet I still pull Ceres into my chest.

There are very few words in my mind that can sufficiently describe my reasoning for why I'm willing to hold her this close even while she hurts me, but the logic fails to bear any consequence in my mind. Not when Solaris is trembling and Ceres coughs up the energy that fuels its descent—leaving me as the mediator of such a turbulent exchange.

"Antares, let me go. I'm hurting you," Ceres sobs into the crook of her elbow, attempting to resist my grip, but I'm unrelenting. Even as her entire torso falls onto me and I feel her violent threads of power multiply and ricochet through my bones, I do nothing but join Ceres in her rising screams.

I lack a view of her facial expression but I can tell that it's constricted and dripping with agony as she repeatedly tries to swallow back the energy that she knows is out of her control—all in an effort of preventing one more kill. From the way her hands fumble at my hold on her and wrench her fingers in between mine, it's apparent that her desperation is climbing with a rapid speed. She doesn't want to do to me what she did to two others, or perhaps she is only concerned about her moral fallout.

Nevertheless, that state of mind she is currently harboring is my imagined ticket to her peace—having her learn how to control her abilities and let humanity overpower her thirst for destruction. Restraint has never been a characterizing trait of Ceres', but tendrils of it begin to show themselves when she gasps for air, and in the process, retracts her energy into herself for a moment.

The occurrence floods my body with more hope than I should carry, and the overindulgence presents itself in the newfound capture of my arms within Ceres—allowing even more of my skin to bear exposure to her touch. She seems to lose her concern for the fact that I'm the recipient of her energy, instead of the approaching soldiers that are the stimulus of it, and holds my arms with an unnerving intensity. The fear I have been attempting to quell now rises in my throat like a surge of liquid, pooling at my vocal cords which are raw from the yells they have been emitting.

Through the blurring of my senses caused by the cosmic amount of pain I have allowed myself to be placed under, I hardly recognize that the additional hands pulling at my body are those of palace servants and soldiers. In the previous minutes, dozens of them have been alerted by the jarring screams emanating from Ceres and me, and they have haphazardly gathered around the two of us, Sidra's presence is the most apparent to me as I hear the soft hum of her voice against my ears.

I want to tell Sidra that I understand what she said to me about my parents. I want to thank her for being the first one that has been truthful to me about their deaths, but my voice seems so far away from my grasp, diminished by my fear.

For the first time since knowing Ceres, since being in her constant proximity and witnessing the horrors of what she can do, I am afraid. I am afraid that neither I nor the servants will be able to tear her touch from me, and I will suffer the same fate as the village girl and Eris before me. I am afraid that I am wrong—that whatever connection Ceres and I have is eclipsed by her longing for ruin and that all my weeks of hope have been for naught.

All notions of optimism I clutch onto continue to fade when I see threads of black appear atop Ceres' skin, appearing like winding veins throughout her body and pulsing with a rigorous rhythm. I comprehend the sight easily—it's what I saw before Eris passed the boundary of no return, it's quite possibly the last thing I will see from Ceres.

I find in myself to endure the pain of yet another touch, my faith already dissipated and falling at my feet as threads of my consciousness unwind from my fingers. With little accuracy in my movements, I manage to tilt Ceres' chin towards me, revealing dark voids of energy and blackness where her eyes once were. She can see me, I can sense it in the way her nails dig under the skin of my wrist upon her gaze finding mine—and that instant of contact is enough for me to feel her abilities multiply tenfold.

The screams we both emit grow stronger in their intensity, wider in their reach, and they barrage my ears with trails of blood falling from my eardrums in their wake. I feel all the pain that I thought myself too grown, too resilient, to feel, all the way from the splitting skin of my forearms to the boiling blood within my body. I can't find it in myself to protest her actions—all I can do is tremble as I find myself descending onto the Solarian ground with Ceres' weight settling atop me. Her palms press into my chest; her forearms plant themselves on new patches of exposed skin; her eyes drip crimson blood onto my cheeks and mix with my blood from reopened wounds that she caused.

Even with the physical and mental turmoil coursing through me, somewhere in the depths of my thoughts I find repeated forgiveness. My subconscious doesn't consider Ceres to be acting of her own volition, and I don't believe I would consider any terrible act she did to be completely her own choice. My mind has been warped and misguided in that sense—I'm too overwhelmed by my fascination with the woman before me to accept her faults.

When Ceres' weight lifts from my body, I immediately attribute Ceres for the action, believing against my better judgment that she latched onto that inkling of humanity and allowed it to steer her back into reality. It's immensely relieving—having my chest released from her agonizing hold, though I'm plagued with a fit of coughing as I attempt to get blood out of my windpipe. Coughs rappel out of my body, and with each tremor of my torso, my injuries burn with the aftermath of Ceres' dark magic.

My eyes are not yet open, still plastered shut to prevent myself from looking at the severity of my wounds, when I hear a heartbreaking wail that sends a frigid shiver through my spine. Ceres.

The Queen's muffled tone finds my ears, reprimanding and desperate in its entirety, while I feel her slender fingers ripping the remainders of Ceres' touch off of me. It was her who ceased the agonizing interaction between the two of us—no one else would have the strength to control Ceres in such a manner, nor would they have the courage to intervene in such a precarious situation.

Though Vega consumes herself in questioning me, almost adopting an accusatory tone in her speech as if she's inclined to blame me for her daughter's downward spiral, my hearing is filled with the sounds of Ceres' painful sobs. She screams of self-destruction and guilt—a harsh divergence from her previously indifferent stance regarding the people she hurts, and I find myself relishing in the thought. Even though I lay here, half-conscious, with an eternal ache implanting itself in my skin, there's some sort of joy in me blossoming from my success in getting her to understand the gravity of her actions. As twisted as it may seem, this was what I wanted all along—for something to terrify Ceres to a degree where her mind experiences a fundamental change.

By the time I raise my eyes and witness the sight of Ceres, the servants are long gone and Vega seems to have newly departed, clearly recognizing the threat to her kingdom through Ceres' window. I let my mind linger on that fact for only a moment, quickly dismissing it in favor of drawing closer to Ceres—who is now curled into herself and leaning into the edge of her bed frame as she cries violently, reprimanding herself repeatedly.

This is the moment where she looks more human than I've ever seen her, with eyes that are no longer black voids but now exhibit a red, teary sheen and skin that has been wiped away of black veins and is now flushed and stained with blood. There is true emotion on her face, expressions of relief, hatred, and frustration. In this instant of time, Ceres exists in an altered universe in which she can release her internal chaos with reservations, and I fear that moment she realizes where she is, for that is when I lose this version of her forever.

Her lurch back into reality comes sooner than I could have imagined, accompanied by a jarring pain through the core of my chest. Ceres lunges forward with unimaginable speed the moment her eyes register the situation, attempting to pull my torso towards her and pull my body away from further danger, but her actions aren't quick or precise enough. Instead, they only manage to divert the aim of the sword from my heart to my ribcage, allowing the blade to implant itself in the crevice between two of my ribs.

I didn't hear a swipe of air that would have signaled the sword's presence, an intuition that I spent years developing. I didn't feel the trajectory of the weapon as it rushed at me—my only knowledge of it began the moment it punctured my skin and reopened wounds that were just beginning to heal from Ceres' inflictions.

"Antares…. Antares, no, no!" Ceres stammers with her words blurring in my mind as I struggle to register the amount of pain the sword wound has inflicted upon me. This is the pain of magic, the sensation of every inch of my body being in flames and knife blades cutting through the most sensitive of my insides. This is equivalent, if not greater than the torment Ceres delivered, and the jarring bolts of pain that ricochet through my torso with its every involuntary rise contribute to that even more.

Ceres has abandoned her initial position beside her bed and now rests on her knees in front of me as she grapples at the wound in my side. Her trembling fingers search for the puncture, recognizing that there are two on either side of my waist, accompanied by the sword blade being plunged clean through me. That realization spurs a horrified gasp from her lips.

I find the coordination to place my hand on Ceres' waist, needing to calm her heaving shoulders, her breathless sobs, and pulsating heart, so my mind could have some semblance of orientation, but her panic only rises in its intensity. She's screaming for a moment, allowing her already raw throat to tear itself apart even further, and somewhere in her words, she's calling for a Healer, for the Queen.

She's crying into a closed door, she's crying to the approaching soldiers who would tear Solaris apart with more vigor than what was just exerted upon me, she's crying to the other woman by my side who stands idle with her hand empty and open. I can only sense the other woman's presence as she reaches for the hilt of her weapon and unravels it from the hold my body exerted, releasing waves of blood and stifled yells from my lips. The pain that I didn't previously believe could magnify any further eclipses my expectations and reveals the magic woven into its metal—for Aerthen magic is the only fuel of such a wound.

Ceres beside me still collects words in her mouth and pushes them out just as fast, but I wish I could tell her that she's wrong— that no Healer or the Queen would be able to aid me in this stage.

A part of me wonders where the true origin of her fear stems from, whether it's my impending death or her disgust knowing she's on the frontier of her third kill. And judging from her nearing guests—she'd better grow comfortable with death now, for there's many coming.

CHAPTER TWENTY-TWO

C   E   R   E   S

---

*M*y first scream escapes through the barrier of my bloodied teeth, gritted together so tightly that the pressure is felt throughout my body. My vision seems to have darkened at its edges, focused solely on the sight of a sword planted in the flesh of Antares' chest, forced so far in that the glint of its tip is visible on the opposite side of his ribcage. The situation itself is enough to make bile rise in my throat, and this time, I welcome the sensation of self-hatred.

Antares was incapacitated as a result of the pain I inflicted on him. The reason he was caught off guard to begin with and allowed that weapon to reach him, is because I forced him to be. I rendered him incapable; I facilitated his demise and that fact pulses in the back of my skull incessantly, growing in its vicious intensity as I stare at him for long.

I can't explain the reason for my sudden inability to act or think or speak. I'm unable to find a reason for why tears pool at my waterline and the corners of my eyes prick with more rising. I don't know why I look at Antares and envelope myself in an all-reaching sadness that stretches to my soul and cinches it painfully. I didn't feel this way about anyone else I've hurt; I never allowed morality to situate itself in my mind—so why is it here now?

Why am I able to draw out genuine care for Antares, especially when I should thrive off of experiences like these? I should see his blood and associate it with my power; I should know that his death means my rise—and yet, none of that holds a place in my thoughts.

"Antares? Antares!" I speak with a wavering tone as I freeze on my knees beside his trembling body. His eyes can hardly remain open, flickering across the room as if he's trying to look for something—find the source of some sound—and the moment I see Antares' body lurch upward, I know where his curiosity lies.

Sidra, small yet foreboding in her entirety, stands on the other side of Antares' figure with a sword glinting in her right fist—the same weapon that only seconds ago was plunged into Antares' body. It glistens with the violent hue of red, almost taunting me with the glints of light it sends in my direction.

"Sidra… Why did you—" My voice leaves me in hesitant sputters, rendered incompetent by the growing disorder in my mind and the emotions that are threatening to burst past my carefully maintained composure. Vengeance seems to be the furthest thing from my mind, a condition completely out of character for me, but I can't fathom it at this moment—not when I lack the cognitive strength to string a sentence together.

"I should probably explain myself," Sidra confesses with a sigh distorting her words.

She takes her position beside my bed, leaning on the frame with her sword positioned before her and streaking red onto the pristine fabric. My eyes follow her figure with my spiraling consciousness struggling to maintain focus, and I know Antares is enraptured as well, even in his deteriorating state.

"I'm a Healer, but I'm also a witch." Sidra's words ricochet shock through me so passionately that I feel the indications of nausea rising in my stomach. "It's a convoluted story, so I'll make it simple for you. My parents were part of the rebellion 16 years ago. My father died only months after Antares' parents were killed, all three of them executed under the orders of our lovely

Queen. My mother has changed—she certainly has no life left in her after the trauma that your darkness inflicted upon her."

My hands are trembling as they move to clutch the damp fabric of Antares' shirt and mold it in between my fingers. Sidra's confessions rampage my mind while they still exist in their highly vulnerable, splintered state and begin to widen every fissure even further with the glaring truth behind her sentences. Her betrayal is starkly apparent, and she makes no effort to shield it from my view or romanticize its presence, which only deepens the hit of her criticisms and forces me to duck my chin into my chest. I yearn to crumble right here before I witness the remainder of Sidra's explanation and the inevitable occurrence of Antares' death, but I know my soul will keep me here, chained to this kingdom until my penance has been served.

"I picked up their goals where they left off. I assumed control of their agenda to eradicate Solaris of its illness and restore our peace, and my plans started the moment you stumbled into my room. You were wounded and unconscious with your dagger severing your skin, and I fed you lies to gain control of your trust. I'm not a kind, morally righteous Healer, I'm far from it." Sidra allows a soft laugh to tumble from her lips as she watches my mouth open, then close, and then hover in a state of incapability as I fight to release words as easily as she does.

"He's going to die," Sidra says simply, running the blade along the side of my dresser to wipe the blood off of the silver. Her movements carry a notion of ease as if hurting Antares bears little consequence to her—which I suppose is the mentality I carried for longer than I can admit. "He's going to die, and you, Ceres… You have a similar fate coming."

Sidra takes her time to lower to a kneeling position, looking at me over Antares' stagnant body as if she expects me to pay attention to her instead of the life receding below me. I find the possibility outrageous for a moment, but after a prolonged period of allowing tears to fall from my eyes, I realize I'm tired of caring.

Exhaustion plagues me and it becomes easier to look past Antares rather than try to speak words to him that are untrue. Whatever my emotions are exhibiting—the tears, the screams— all feel foreign and painful against my tongue. My expressions act against my mind's volition, and I begin to chastise myself for subscribing to wild feelings of pain when they make me vulnerable to this extent—but I'm not able to reorient myself. I don't believe I ever can.

"What?" I finally say to Sidra as she waits for my response in silence. I begin to adopt a facade of ignorance towards Antares, pushing his muffled grunts past my ears and disregarding the hand that moved from my waist to my knee. I tell myself that this is all inconsequential, that Antares will die, whether it be from what I exerted onto him or the sword wound that lasts in his chest. No amount of sympathy from me would fill that void in his vitality. I tell myself it all—and it stretches the sensation of defeat in my mind tenfold.

"My sword is crafted by the witches, my ancestors. *Tenebris*, I call her," Sidra murmurs as she runs her gaze across the red-streaked metal and follows the beams of light it reflects with her fingertips. "Any wound inflicted by her is tinged with Aerthen poison and makes death certain. If you didn't already begin Antares' death, I just did."

"Why did you do it?" There's no resentment in my voice; there's no burning hatred. I only exhibit lethargic indifference as I fight to rise above the surrender my body is committing, the final ode to Solaris as I witness the wreckage I've caused and realize that none of this power fulfills me.

"I need you like this." Sidra tilts her head at me as she runs her fingers across my cheek, leaving trails of Antares' blood in their trails. "I need you disoriented and depleted. I need for you to look at yourself and see no human or soul deserving of holding power. That's why I engineered Eris' death and put you in the exact position where you would have no choice but to add another kill to your list, your body and soul becoming weaker with each one. You came into my room that day yearning for my aid, and instead, I got yours. You facilitated your own demise by killing. You didn't understand that before, but I assume that now you do."

I turn Sidra's words over in my mind, treating them with an unnerving delicacy that proves their candor. The terrible truth of her speech rings clear in my ears. I *am* as shattered as she described me to be. My soul has never felt anguish of this intensity, nor have I ever prepared myself to feel something so potent. I have trained myself, my body, to be invulnerable for longer than I can remember, so *why* am I in pieces? Why did I allow such a wretched care the ability to overpower my sanity?

Variations of these thoughts barrel through my mind, knotting with my already rising desperation to leave this all behind me—to run from this room, this palace, this kingdom, and return to Sun District as nothing more than I was when I left.

I could blame Antares' death on the portion of my powers that I cannot control. I could blame his death on Sidra—but the truth remains imprinted in my mind. If I never attacked him, he wouldn't have been on the ground, to begin with. He wouldn't be weakened and oblivious of the sword rappelling towards him. Antares shouldn't have been in that state, he could have saved himself if he wasn't previously enervated—and I denied him of that opportunity.

My slick fingers slide across the carpet below me, struggling to keep my body upright as the urge to collapse and close my eyes over Antares' body becomes almost too large to ignore. I imagine I'm creating a pitiful sight in Sidra's eyes, especially when I've smeared the white interior of my surroundings with tears and blood and my hair hangs in a knotted curtain in front of my eyes.

Sidra can't see it, but my skin and heart are stained with a bitter agony that I never knew I would have to feel. And I don't just feel it, it envelops me. At this moment, all I am is my pain; all I can see is the people I've hurt dying, over, and over, and over—like a colorless memory reel. My temple stings mercilessly, some kind of internal remark shaming me for leaving

Antares stranded below me. For allowing his blood to pool, I feel guilty.

Sidra attempts to divert my attention back to her face when Antares murmurs a word with his final breaths, but I find myself leaning into Antares anyway. My ear finds his lips and I allow Antares to heave his chest for the last time as he speaks the sentences that I would find to be imprinted in my mind for every second afterward.

"You are *Letalis*." A cough rattles his throat and sprays blood onto the side of my face, but I wipe it away with my thumb, waiting for the remainder of his breath. "You are not Ceres, you are not a princess of this kingdom—you are a weapon in yourself. One that cannot be…. cannot be wielded, or controlled, or learned. *Lethal*."

I release a sob at his last word, recognizing the simultaneous love and betrayal that was contained within it. My hand finds Antares' chest, searching for the heartbeat that I never allowed myself to learn. I lift my head when I realize that I'm met with a flat, motionless plane that no longer shakes with labored breathing. My gaze travels to his jaw, his lips, and the slits of his eyes, and I subconsciously trick myself into believing he's smiling at me. I smile back, teeth dotted with the blood I wrenched from my lower lip, and I imagine the sight of us at this moment—destructed in our entirety with my only hope of peace being with what I predict Sidra's proposal to be.

"The kingdoms are on their way to Solaris." Sidra begins again, tucking a curl of my hair behind my ear as she speaks. "When they see you, when the townspeople tell them of all you have done—they will kill you."

She's speaking too soon. She's speaking and rushing words into my head before I can process them, still reeling and internally deteriorating from the abruptness of Antares' fall, of his death. It's difficult for me to interpret this scene in these few moments that I have, my mind severed between the part of me that loves him for offering me something other than Sun District and the other part that feels indifferent to his existence and is attempting to not care about his death either.

"Isn't that what you want?" I ask in a muted tone, still reeling in my head and struggling to put words together. "To kill me?"

"You are the Solarian jewel." Sidra traces the puddles of Antares' blood with the blade of *Tenebris*, her sword, as she speaks. "You are the Solarian curse. You are a plague to the Solarian people. According to my line of witches and warlocks, you and the magic you carry are not dead until you have been killed by a Solarian and removed from this land."

"Eris was killed by a Solarian," I whisper into the air between us, still not fully meeting Sidra's eyes and instead shivering from the chill of Antares' body that is still underneath me. Not breathing, not blinking, simply haunting me with his memory. "What did that mean for Solaris?"

"Her body remains here. The Queen has procured it, and she has buried it. The moral power of your sister will remain in this land and she continues to bless us to the same degree she did before her death." Sidra *tsks* and shakes her head slightly. "She's never been enough to overpower your influence, however. You leaving the land for 16 years only allowed you to come back. We can't have any of that. We mustn't."

"You wish to kill me," I breathe, lurching my eyes upward to find Sidra's gaze. She's resolute in the way she looks at me, with no fluctuations in her stare, and it's frightening to the version of myself that I've lowered into.

"I wish to kill you. I couldn't do it before because I've learned one very important piece of information after observing you these weeks—Ceres Relasin cannot be killed until she wishes to be." Sidra breaks her frigid expression with an abrupt laugh that shocks me with its intensity. "So here we are. You yearn to leave Solaris, to run from your shame and the misfortunes you have descended upon your people. I yearn to rid the Solarian people of that very same misfortune and simultaneously restore the balance of magic to the Solarian land. I wish to return to the haven of our minds, where no other kingdoms can threaten us—and we can do that with your death."

"With my death," I hesitantly turn my gaze to the window above me, beyond which are dozens of troops heading for a direct collision with Solaris—and the people of it, "Solaris is shielded from a war. The people live."

"And you're free from your powers," Sidra says in a soft susurration that contains more ulterior motives than chivalry, I know, but her words are compelling in themselves. They burn into the insides of my mind and I start to worship them. I begin to smile at the future they create, where I lay far from the monstrosity that these abilities have turned me into and leave good fortune for the Solarian people in my wake. It could be a form of redemption I can procure for myself, the one form of redemption.

Against my better judgment, I reach under my gown to find the sheath in which *Letalis* rests. With quivering fingers, I bring the dagger into my open palms and reveal it to the light of the Solarian Sun, watching as the crafted metal work reflects beams of light onto my surroundings. It's a reminder of my life in Sun District, where my problems consisted of a fraction of what I feel in this moment; it's a tribute to Antares' death where he united her and me as one entity; it's a final goodbye to Solaris as the weapon that got me to this land bids me farewell from it.

"Are you convincing yourself that you're regaining your morality?" Sidra whispers, meticulously removing *Letalis* from my touch and shifting it to her fist almost tauntingly. "Are you fooling yourself into thinking that you're not a coward?"

My breath catches in my throat and I fight for the retort that would have surfaced if this interaction occurred only hours prior, when Antares was not dead and I didn't feel the magnitude of my losses and ruination. Now, however, I only find myself listening and agreeing.

"My dear Ceres, princess of Solaris." Sidra leans forward over Antares' body, allowing blood to rise up her dress as she feverishly addresses me. "The events that have led up to this moment have made you a coward already. Leaving the mess you created is the least you can do for this kingdom. I wish I could say that we will miss you, but we will not. We will thrive in the absence of your sinful powers that killed one of our people only days ago."

I allow newly formed tears to empty the cavern of my eyes, tasting their salty prints as they distribute heat across my skin. My chest reverberates with stifled sobs that encompass me in my entirety, representing the 17 years of pain I have experienced before this instant but I have believed myself too impenetrable to feel or accept. Now, I have relinquished those boundaries in favor of escaping this false reality, and I find Sidra to be correct. I have surrendered to being a coward.

"My mother—"

"The Queen will hear of your death in due time. Your mother will return to the woman she was before she had children, where she is no longer blinded by the love of a royal family. Family is not what rulers are meant to have, and soon she will have none."

Sidra positions *Letalis* above my heart, pressing the blade deeper into the cavity of my chest to the rhythm of my breathing. Acting on an urge, I raise my hands to match hers, covering the handle of my dagger with my touch and applying pressure along with her. My tears fall onto our conjoined hands, but the two of us only continue to break the barrier of my skin.

The pain blossoms almost like a flower, following the pathways of veins across my body and rupturing flesh to the soft beating of my heart. My mouth falls ajar with the agony that threatens to raise bile in my throat; my skin pulses under the warm blanket of blood that spreads its touch across my chest; my lungs shiver with the pressure of forcing repeated breaths through my windpipe.

I begin to wonder if this is how my mother killed her King.

"Tell me I am *Letalis*." Perhaps that is my dying wish—to know that no matter how many lives I've torn and disintegrated too early, I became what I've always yearned to embody. A weapon of skill and violence that paints beauty in others' demise.

Sidra's response comes in a soft laugh tinted with disbelief. "You are *Letalis*."

She completes a prompt shift of her frame, redistributing her weight to plunge the dagger into my already fragmented heart. My fingers fall from the cohesiveness we created atop my blade and a smile dies on my lips.

Letalis.

Izar,

I apologize for the absence of communication. Solaris has changed, and I have changed with it—tremendously. It's strange to live in such a land again after the reprieve Ceres granted us, but as I told you, her presence is no longer with this kingdom.

I suppose you don't know how you feel, I can imagine. It's difficult to comprehend that the woman you grew up with—the one you raised—committed such acts and cursed the Solarian people in such a way, though I interpret it all as a blessing to this land. Nonetheless, it's nearly impossible to understand that she is dead, along with Eris and Antares' absences being left in her wake. I hope your inner turmoil ceases in due time.

I have a trader bringing Ceres' ashes to the portion of the Hosh Forest that borders your cottage. We cannot bury her here, the Solarians forbid it—especially the witches and warlocks—so I ask you to do this service for my sake.

I feel it would be a lie to say that Ceres appreciated you in your entirety, but I can assure you that I do. Perhaps if Mensa never placed the burden of your younger sisters on you 16 years ago, you would be living a more content life.

Now that Ceres' energy has exited Solarian land, we are continuing our eternal abstract existence in our minds. Join our dream, why don't you?

Vega

Acknowledgments

Einstein's theory of general relativity was revolutionary. It described the beginnings of space-time, specifically how the continuum originates from the big bang singularity and ends in the singularity of a star or the entire universe.

I feel thankful that during my existence within space-time, I was able to create the character of Ceres Relasin and her Kingdom of Solaris, but my mind was never alone during the process. Some consider the human desire for reliance to be a fundamental flaw of our existence, but reliance is what created Letalis.

Thank you to my sister for slaving over these pages with me at terrible hours of the night, even if your all-nighters never ended up working for you. As annoyed as I may have seemed at the time, I appreciate all your nit-picky criticisms and endless support. I'm sorry I changed the name of the Kingdom.

Thank you to my parents for believing in this story from the beginning and supporting me during the final days of editing it, even when I threw a few tantrums and said everything with an irritable tone. Mom and Dad, thank you for always thinking of me in my best light and propelling my aspirations.

To my father, your dedication to this novel is astounding. I adore how much energy you place toward me and motivating my dreams, so thank you for everything.

Thank you Sia for dealing with all my cover art drama and producing a product that I can never stop staring at. There's a reason why everyone who looks at Letalis tells me they're obsessed with the cover—it's because your art is incredible. You're my favorite business partner.

Books Go Social, thank you for tolerating my endless video calls and steering me on the right path with this novel. Katlyn, thank you for being one of the first to read this manuscript and giving me the reviews that motivated my continuance. My extended family and friends, thank you for the abundance of kind words, even when this book was nothing more than a collection of words. I appreciate all of you so much.

Thank you to my favorite books for instilling this love for literature in me. You all may be pretentious in your writing, but are beautiful in your influence.

About the Author

Rishika Porandla is a rising junior in Dallas, TX with a passion for literature and everything concerning the interstellar world. She is a proponent of the fusion between the scientific and literary worlds, and she displays that love by reading theory and completing her own astronomical research. Rishika loves nothing more than to delve into the works of her favorite psychological thriller authors, or the classics of Agatha Christie and Edgar Allan Poe, and can spend hours at a time lost in other worlds. Get to know this budding author at rishikaporandla.com.

Made in the USA
Coppell, TX
17 August 2022